POLARIS
Bear Wind of the North

BLUE
Whale Wind of the South

MAGNIFICATS
RETURN OF THE DEMON WIND

BY

Gwyn Dolyn

Plowshare Media
LA JOLLA, CALIFORNIA

Library of Congress Control Number: 2016946470
Dolyn, Gwyn
Magnificats: Return of the Demon Wind

ISBN: 978-0-9860428-7-4 (trade paperback edition)

Cover art and illustrations by the author, except for *Alphabet Images* (p. ix) and *The Ogham Tree Grove* (p. x) © Yuri Leitch, Glastonbury, United Kingdom, http://www.yurileitch.co.uk

Published by:
Plowshare Media
P.O. Box 278
La Jolla, CA 92038

To Tak, for teaching me the magic in coincidence.

Clouder Regions of the World

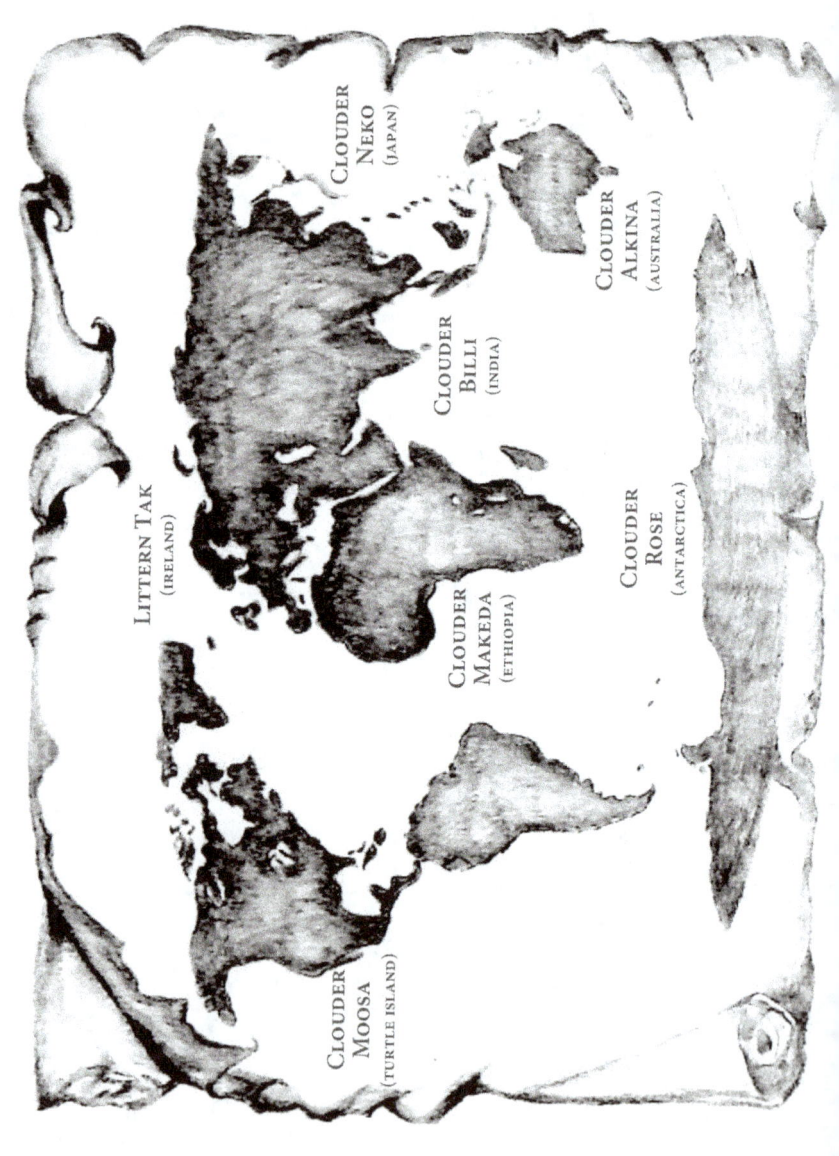

Clouder Neko
(Japan)

Clouder Alkina
(Australia)

Clouder Billi
(India)

Littern Tak
(Ireland)

Clouder Makeda
(Ethiopia)

Clouder Rose
(Antarctica)

Clouder Moosa
(Turtle Island)

CONTENTS

PROLOGUE .... *xi*

1   AN IRISH SHEEGEE 1

2   LIFE WITH ARCHERS 7

3   AOIFE O'HEGARTY STANDISH 14

4   RASTA'S PRINCESS 22

5   DEMON WINDS 32

6   CAT DREAMS AND SCIENTIFIC PROOF 40

7   SIR THOMAS O'FERAL 47

8   EMPRESS MING FANG 52

9   FETCHING CLOUDER MOOSA 63

10 KRYSTAL KAY KENNER 67

11 THE REMAINING CLOUDERS 80

12 ORPHAN WINDS 95

13 DRAGONS IN THE CLOUDS 113

14 A MAGNIFICAT CEREMONY 122

15   FERAL ABDUCTION 134

16   DISSOLVING HOODIE 141

17   KITTENS, LAMBS, AND SPIDERS 151

18   SWEET GRASS OF AFRICA 157

19   ALCHEMIST DEER AND STICKY WEBS 162

20   AFRICAN CAT WOMAN 167

21   CRESCENT WINDS 171

22   STEPMONSTER REVEALED 177

23   SACRIFICIAL LAMB 184

24   NO HOME, NO MORE 189

25   WIND AGREEMENTS 195

26   TRADE WINDS 199

27   WORLD WIDE WEB 206

28   TIC TOC TAK 212

29   NO GREATER LOVE 224

30   'TIS ALWAYS MAGIC 231

     GLOSSARY 241

     ABOUT THE AUTHOR 247

ALPHABET IMAGES

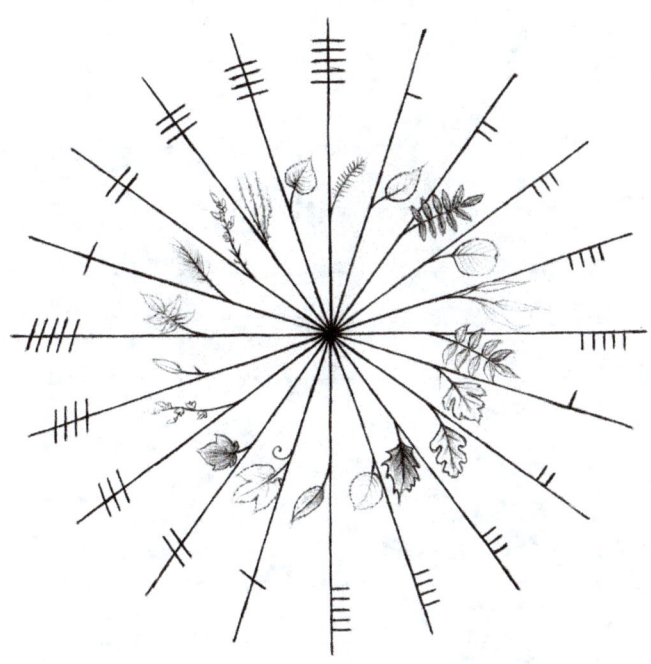

THE OGHAM TREE GROVE

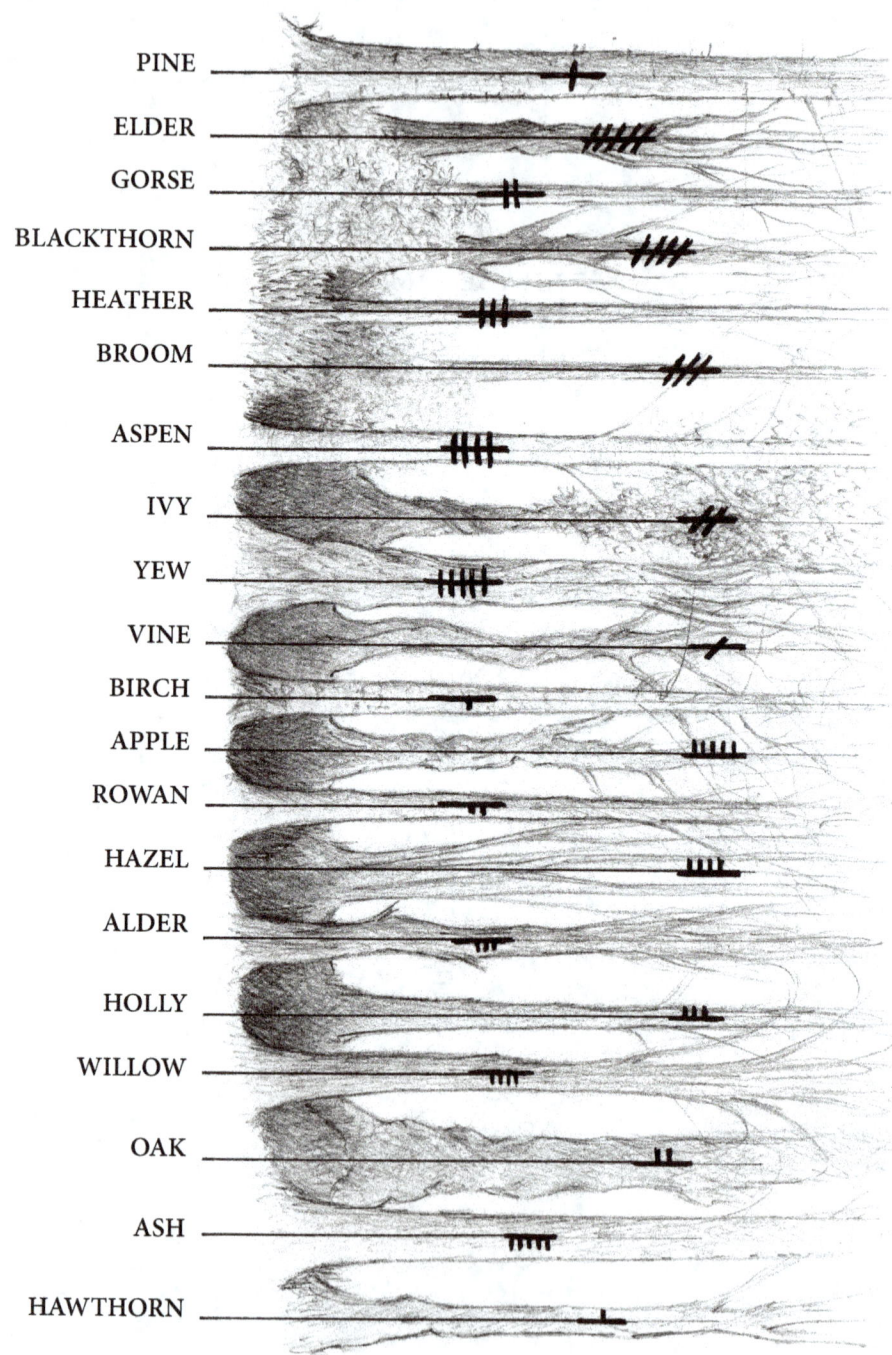

PINE
ELDER
GORSE
BLACKTHORN
HEATHER
BROOM
ASPEN
IVY
YEW
VINE
BIRCH
APPLE
ROWAN
HAZEL
ALDER
HOLLY
WILLOW
OAK
ASH
HAWTHORN

Prologue

Long, long ago,
past three river falls at middle bend,
in a beautiful garden
all kingdoms were friends,
the tree kingdom, wind kingdom, and creature kingdom.

Chief Tree stood at the Garden's center,
giving food, air, and shelter to all who entered.
The only thing she asked from the others
was to treat her wee fruit as sisters and brothers.
Do not pick them.
Allow them to grow in my care,
'til their life naturally ends,
and they drop through the air.

One fateful day, while Chief Tree was at rest,
the creature kingdom betrayed her simple request.
One stole her fruit that looked so delicious.
Soon all creatures joined in on the act so vicious.
The screech owl cawed, inciting the deed,
stirring the wind and spreading her seed.

The faithful watchcats arrived too late
to save the poor fruit from their ghastly fate.

For stealing her children straight from the branches,
Chief Tree denied any second chances.
The act brought wrath from a distant star,
all kingdoms were banished
(as their shared language vanished)
and today they still are.

CHAPTER 1

An Irish Sheegee

Dance there upon the shore...
What need have you to dread
The monstrous crying of wind?

—William Butler Yeats, "To A Child Dancing In The Wind,"
Responsibilities and Other Poems, 1916, Dublin, Ireland

"...And don't be callin' me Apple Stand, ye bleedin' maggots!" thirteen-year-old, flaming-haired Apple snapped back at her classmates, just before a whirlwind, an Irish sheegee it was, blew her skirt up to reveal two very freckled knees.

"Hey, Red Apple Stand, those be some fetchin' legs yar flashin'," teased the teenage hooligans, rolling in the shamrocks, laughing. Her easy-to-mock name, Apple Standish, made her a mark for taunting around the tree-filled Dublin school campus. Her curly red hair, set free by the wind, only fueled the shenanigans. As if in defense of Apple, the wind sent a smattering of stinging leaves to pummel them into silence as she marched by with her nose up and a smirk on her face.

Meanwhile, just down the street and past the cheese shop where her brother worked, Tak, the lanky old cat who lived under the ancient parish church on Apple's route to school, sensed something awry in the autumn air. This sheegee was a concern.

Sniffing, he tickled the air with his whiskers, then remarked, "Hmm, interesting autumn wind; deliberate, with a stench of malice."

While Tak was indeed a cat, he was not your everyday, meowing, rodent-chasing, scratching-up-the-furniture sort of cat. He was the leader (to be exact, Littern) of a clandestine order of numinous nine-life cats, known far and wide in creature kingdoms as Magnificats—keepers of sacred knowledge and masters of the winds.

Tak had just shimmied out from his lair, as he did every afternoon at precisely three o'clock, for a spot of tea. Shaking off the shiny spider webs clinging to his gold-ticked fur, he leapt to his favorite spot on the craggy wall surrounding the parish courtyard to bask in the sunshine. From his comfortable perch, Tak had open sight of the sidewalk from the stony ancient ruins next-door all the way up to Apple's school. Even the big-hearted reach of Francis, the faerie tree in the center of the yard, did not obscure his view of stiff, two-legged Archers (commonly known as humans) like Apple crisscrossing here and there, always in a rush. "Perhaps I would be in a hurry too, if I had only one life," he mused, taking a puff off his pipe to veil himself behind its mystical smoke.

As part of Tak's afternoon routine, Thomas O'Feral, his orange tabby roommate, scurried out toting a copper pot gripped in his fangs and a dappled blue cup looped over his crooked tail. The steaming vessel swung to spilling as he jumped onto the wall. "Ooch," he howled, dropping the pot and springing back through the flap of the lair. Tak snickered. Thom's theatrics provided a much needed laugh for the old Magnificat. Although Thom was not a Magnificat himself, but merely a common cat, he was Tak's cherished friend.

Apple tugged down her tartan-print skirt as the swirling sheegee snatched her father's letter right out of her hand. She was not sorry to see it go. It had brought bad news. Apple had to spend her first teenage vacation with her dad and stepmonster in 'bleedin' Egypt,' of all places. She had been there before, on digs with her father. It was miserable, hot, and the constant blowing sand stuck to everything like glue.

"I can't believe he can jest be snappin' his fingers and Mum agrees," she whined, kicking a whirling leaf with a Finn-McCool-stomp (coined for the Irish giant who created the Causeway in the north).

As Tak sipped his tea, he was gobsmacked to see the spinning sheegee wind morphing into a lofty grey funnel as high as the church steeple, resembling a child-stealing goblin in her ash-colored dress—a gwyllion. The wind caused the rarely-used bell above his head to knell. Tak began to chew the end of his pipe apprehensively. "Not a good sign," he hissed charily.

Unwilling to allow any wind to disrupt his teatime, he was just about to pull out his wand and blast the gwyllion to smithereens when he glimpsed a splatter of red dancing smack-dab in the middle of it. "Well I'll be!" he gulped, honing in on Apple, "That's a ginger-haired Archer child!" With flailing arms and flying hair, the young Archer was barreling directly towards his parish, as if trapped in a shaken snow globe rolling down the city sidewalk. No matter how fast she walked, the wind kept pace. Whenever she stopped, the mini-cyclone stopped and frenzied around her. "In all my nine lives..." Tak seethed, shaking his head at the bizarre sight.

While Apple crudely spat out a bit of leaf that had made its way into her mouth, Tak could hear her gripe, "As if I should be jumping for joy at Dan's li'l muzzy." This was in response to the part of her father's letter where it was announced that he and Amanda had a new 'brat,' or in his actual words, she had a new baby brother. "I'll be swelterin' in the middle of that bleedin' desert and expected to babbysit, to boot. Good Lord an' all," she continued, waving her arms.

The irony of this announcement was that her parents had divorced because Mum refused Dan's globetrotting lifestyle once Apple and her brother were both in school. He blamed the children for strapping her to the land.

Tears of anger almost leaked out, but she held them back, recalling she had sworn right in the middle of Mass on her twelfth birthday that there would be no more cryin' for her—ever!

Tak had known many winds. In fact, the old Magnificat had stirred up some legendary storms of his own. This wind, however, caught everyone off guard. His brow wrinkled in concern as birds and squirrels dashed from their shelters, all at once and in all directions. They had not seen it coming either.

The strange sight of a girl caught in a whirlwind caused car screeching, men's caubeens flying, and children diving for cover under their mums' waving skirts.

Apple was quite unaware that the sheegee encircled only her. "Whatcha' gawkin' at?" she snapped at anyone who pointed or stared at her, as bits of sand blurred her vision and stung her eyes. "Cursed wind!" she shouted, loud enough for even Thom to hear inside the lair.

"What's goin' on out 'ere Tak?" Thom popped out and asked, just as a mighty gust rocked the grand whitethorn—a tree old-timers say was there before the Druids or the Vikings, even before Ireland's forests mysteriously vanished. One and all knew not to bother a Chief Tree. Tak had learned the hard way that bad things happen when faerie trees were disturbed.

While it was common for a wind to exact Tak's attention by clamoring, or even becoming dangerously demanding, it was unheard of for a wind to disrespect sacred grounds. "What sheegee dares upset my peaceful parish?" he hissed. "What coward uses a child as a shield?" He watched in horror as the funnel even stole Celtic dust from the ruins next door. "A feral wind living off of the work of others," he accused, still gnawing the tip of his pipe.

"Aye Tak, 'tis a thief," affirmed Thom, just as the outlying winds of the gwyllion spat flotsam and jetsam in their direction. If not for Francis, the charitable faerie tree, buffering the attack, they might have been seriously injured! Thom nudged up alongside the frail Magnificat leader to stabilize him, doing it in a way that made it appear it was he who needed the support. Thom often did things like that to help his aging friend.

Motionless, save a wary puff on his gilded pipe, with his tall ears perked, Tak read the swelling atmospheric tempo as the tree swaying intensified into bough-bending gusts, and twigs stampeded like clicking snares. Thom, who could take no more, dove in through the spit flap for safety, causing it to swing back and forth to the high-pitched tone of a piccolo.

Tak's ire flared. "Unacceptable!" he growled as he saw one poor faerie sucked away, right along with HIS magical smoke! The gwyllion inhaled it like a vacuum, exposing Tak's fawn-colored fur for any Archer to see. No wind had ever had the audacity to take away his invisibility in all of his nine lives—and right over hallowed Viking burial chambers, to top it all!

Tak knew that he could not assault the wind directly without putting the Archer girl at risk, so he strategized: "If I draw a round of fire, this sheegee will have to reload to muster another pelting round, and that will give me time to mount a defense."

Sure enough, as he tactically raised his oversized ears, he drew the expected influx. Blinking but unflinching, the old Magnificat sunk his long, razor-sharp claws deep into crevices in the wall, like tent stakes. He squinted into the heart of Apple's gwyllion, as his diamond-shaped pupils blazed with cobalt-tinged fire. Then he dematerialized into a wraithlike cat figure, the clarity of amber honey.

Taking a long deliberate draw off his pipe, Tak popped his powerful jaw to exhale a series of cerulean smoke rings, one after another, to stand as a barrier against the prevailing wind. They expanded and rose up to link together in an impenetrable, yet still billowy, sapphire wall that pressed towards the perimeter of his parish, like soldiers locking their shields for battle; click, one, two...click, one, two...click. This chainmail-like armor forced the incoming wind back towards the ruins. Through this shield, the wind could not pass.

At that instant, Apple reached the hedge dividing the ruins

from Tak's parish, and, without so much as a cough, emerged out of the cyclone and right through Tak's smoky wall, unaware that she had ever been held captive by a gwyllion, or that she had broken through an arcane Magnificat curtain.

Apple stopped her single-minded march unconsciously in front of the parish to offer a routine 'sign of the cross' over her face and chest, and a quick curtsey. Sandwiched right between where she dipped one knee and looked up at the crucifix, Apple spotted a translucent gold cat atop the courtyard wall. Her glance rested on a sparkling cross that dangled from his jeweled collar. It was an Egyptian ankh, reflecting brightly in the afternoon sun. Apple and Tak locked eyes and a chill ran through both of them, from head to toe. "Why on earth would a transparent cat be wearin' a key o' life?" Apple wondered under her breath.

Tak gave a concluding fangy hiss at his smoke-ring wall. The blue haze dragged any remaining wind down to the ground with it. Taking another puff, Tak's blue smoke covered him once again. Apple quickly dismissed the smoking cat with an ankh around his neck as a figment of her imagination, prompted by all the 'going-to-Egypt' business. She continued her stride to the library—her sanctuary.

Outside the parish, a small rumble followed, like a mild earthquake. Stunned onlookers began to move about normally. Tak nonchalantly tapped his pipe empty and started towards his lair to work on his centennial speech. Thom peeked out cautiously, "Ere you okay, Tak?"

"Aye, Thom," he answered.

"Oi'll be t'ankin' Spitface for her swinging-flap invention for a month o' Sundies," Thom gloried.

Before Tak slipped back into his lair, he noticed a large leaf pinned under a rock. Knowing very well that "nothing is happenstance," and "coincidence is always magic," Tak pricked the tip of the leaf with his sharp claw to carry it inside. He did not notice the odd inscription on it.

CHAPTER 2

LIFE WITH ARCHERS

Go to the people.
Learn from them.
Live with them.

—Lao Tzu, *Tao Te Ching*, 4th century, B.C.E.

This was Tak's ninth and final life. He had perfected his magic, traveled the globe, held the highest office in the Magnificat kingdom, and he had known true love. He was content, but Apple's sheegee had been a distraction he did not need. Now, with that arrant wind subdued, he had just gotten back to work when the stained glass medallion above Thom's hammock up in the rafters whistled. "Blast," he declared, looking in Thom's direction, "I thought I put an end to that wind?" Then he slammed his paw on the desk in frustration, leaning back in his creaking chair with a sigh, holding his other paw dramatically against his forehead.

That desk had been fashioned from a fallen friend, Terence the Oak. A foolish Archer wanted to put a wagon road right where he stood. In honor of his years of service, Terence's remains became the official Littern desk. Since that time, there had never been a single battle plan formed, or edict issued, where Terence was not involved.

"Are you awake?" Tak shouted up to Thom in his bed in the rafters.

"Aye, Tak. Are you beatin' on poor Terence again?" Thom chuckled, recalling how frustrated Tak got over anything out of the ordinary. "Remember when you first arrived here, Tak, when the tree folk were quare and the wee folk sent you arseways?" Thom was referring to Tak's early days as Littern, when Ireland's faeries and leprechauns sent him spinning. They were entirely different from Egypt's giants: pyramids, sphinxes, and fire-disguised Jinn. Tak was a cat after all, and he did find the flitting wee folk almost irresistible. Faeries were especially tempting. Their fast moving twinkles captivated him. Being nocturnal like Tak, there could have been huge conflicts over airspace had he had wings. For once in all of his lives, Tak was thankful he did not fly.

"It took you sittin' on your paws to not gulp the little critters," Thom meowed, still laughing.

Even now, Tak struggled with the wee folk, especially their many fey rules. "Don't scratch on a tree before dawn," or "Never climb any tree on Nadir, the night the thin walls between worlds collapse, leaving the potential for anyone to fall into Faerie Land, never to return." Oh, and, "Never say 'thank you' for a gift from a faerie," and for goodness sake, "Do not stop by uninvited!"

Leprechauns were easier for Tak to avoid, since they slept at night. He had only seen a few of the chipper fellows during his afternoon tea, when he was too relaxed for a chase. Gnomes and pixies were a different story altogether.

His heritage could have made for a difficult transition as well, until he learned that the first Irish Archers came from Egypt, as he did. They had named the land for their son, Ire, who had some anger issues. Tak was happy to learn that his ancestors taught wand skills to Ire's grandfather, a great Egyptian pharaoh. Tak's mother, Miw, made sure that this magical skill passed to her son.

Tak was born on the great continent of Africa, not in Egypt, but Ethiopia. He would often joke, "I am Abyssinian by breed, and Ethiopian by birth, depending on what Archers called it at the time." Ethiopia had been dubbed Ethiopia more than once. It was during a great famine that Miw took her young family north so they would not become dinner for starving Archers.

She named Tak after the six-winged Ethiopian saint, Takle Haymanot, not China's Taklimakan Desert, as was often speculated. His well-traveled nine lives made that assumption logical. Miw secretly hoped that the name might bring him wings, as his littermates sported. It did not. Yet a wingless Magnificat earning Littern status was a testament to Tak's prowess.

The wind whistling through the stained glass also reminded him of his days at his kittenhood home in Egypt, eventually becoming a lullaby. It caused his writing paw to fall to one side and his heavy head to nod.

His mother Miw's image infiltrated his desktop dreams like burning ma'assil smoke billowing under a locked door. Flexing his claws with a toothy yawn, Tak surrendered to sleep when he saw Miw's sable-colored coat, so like his own. Sadly, the details of her face were shrouded in the dust of time. "Oh, how I miss her, still," he mumbled, dropping into a deep sleep.

The sweetness of this memory of his mother suddenly reshaped itself into cryptic, raw images of the blasts that destroyed his kittenhood. It was the last day of a bloody war when a gigantic Archer hand reached into the rubble of what had been his home and snatched him away. Panicked, Miw hissed helplessly. Tak screeched in terror, "Mama, Mama," clawing at anything he could latch onto. Miw could do no more than shield her other kittens.

Tucked into the pocket of a bloodstained jacket, little Tak's screams were muffled as the soldier walked away with him, as if he had only picked a fresh flower, oblivious to the horror he caused the little feline family.

He could barely remember the next week as he was carried back to England, spending most of the time in a dark container being jostled around. He was exhausted by the trip and was asleep when he arrived. A shrill voice woke him—not a high-pitched cat's meow, nor a vibrating Archer bellow; it was melodic, like an angel.

"Oh, Father!" the sweet voice sang in anticipation, "What did you bring me?" Little Tak covered his oversized ears with his paws, shuddering as the tone went from mild to screeching. Huddled in the small box, with tiny punctures to allow in fresh air and pinpoint streams of light, Tak trembled from both fear and cold. His sparse kitten fur barely kept him warm. Not at all like Egypt's dusty dryness, a brisk, damp breeze swept into Tak's dark package. His newly-opened amber eyes stung from the abrupt daylight as the box top lifted away.

"Well now, Celeste," the soldier's baritone voice teased. "How do you know this present is for you?" he asked as he held up the kitten for her to see, then smiled and handed it to her.

Squished against lacy pink fabric, with ribbons whipping his face, Tak flinched as Celeste hugged him. The small Archer was soft and warm, and even though the stiff material of her dress poked his tender belly, he purred. It had been a long trip. He was dazed, hungry, and tired. Tak had meowed so long and so loud, his voice was only a scratchy whisper.

As the little Archer hugged and kissed her new pet, her father carefully pushed her wooden wheelchair back into the house. A hint of sulfur trailed off his British uniform as Celeste plopped the stolen kitten over her shoulder like a baby. While Tak peered back through her raised toile collar, he instinctively feared that once the wind slammed the huge manor door shut, he would never again smell his mother, no matter how mightily he tried.

Tak was awakened briefly by the noise of the swinging spit as Thom hopped out for his evening jaunt, the squeaking back and forth of the flap merged with the whistling wind, sounding like an owl—a harbinger. Tak shivered before drifting back into his past.

Tak's Abyssinian relations would have rolled over in their

sarcophagi to learn he was living as a housecat. He had been born with a pride in lineage and an important destiny. Yet here he was, decked in pink ribbons for all to see. "I have a new ribbon for you today," Celeste would say as she dressed him up like one of her dolls for an afternoon tea party. At every tea party, just as she put her pinky finger up to take a sip from her rose-print teacup, she whispered, "I love you to the moon, Tak." Perhaps this was the beginning of his predilection for tea.

"Oh, the humiliation, the shame of it!" he would have whined, had he not so enjoyed the soft furniture filling every room in the palatial manor. There was no lack of things to do, either. Celeste played with him outside whenever she felt up to it. Her father, a highly decorated officer, had books that Tak enjoyed reading while lying over his broad shoulders in front of a cozy fire. Abyssinian cats like Tak do not like sitting in laps. They prefer a superior position.

With Tak's aptitude, he quickly mastered the Archer household. It took him no time at all to learn to open cupboards and unlock drawers. There were always servants around to get him anything he could not get for himself. "Come here kitty," the chef would call, presenting him special cuts of meat.

"Aw, tiny Tak, here is a fresh linen for your bed today," the upstairs maid would sing. This early pampering provided Tak with a standard of comfort he would insist on maintaining for all of his ninth life (which became one of several criticisms made by Magnificats who had opposed his election as Littern, especially Moosa, Clouder to the Americas).

Over time, Tak's homesickness gave way to fondness for the raven-haired Celeste and her Archer parents. She and Tak adored each other and played in her room every day, once she became too fragile for the outside. As much as he grew in strength, Celeste grew in frailty. He found relics and spoils of war that the colonel had brought back from Egypt. These items awakened Tak's knowledge from previous lives, especially his gift of healing. His ancestral memory poured into him like cool sweet milk on a summer day. All he had to do was rub against any book and it was a part of him. Young Tak could naturally decode any language, and soon he learned to write.

Not fathoming how ill little Celeste was, Tak believed he could save her with Magnificat medicine. That is when he first used his Egyptian healing knowledge, dribbling sycamore fig, the celestial drink of mysteries, on her blistered lips, and laying healing rods, fashioned to sacred geometrical proportions, on either side of her as she slept. He formed old twigs and wires he gathered from behind the carriage house into a pyramid, charged it in the light of the blue moon, and secretly placed it under her bed. Daily, he opened the bedroom windows, letting the sheer yellow curtains blow to dispel the dank air, only to have it return the next day. "Who keeps opening these windows?" the house-keepers would complain as they closed them, while he snickered from under the bed.

It was a dark and stormy day, the darkest day Tak had ever seen, when the manor filled with strangers. Dim beams of light, littered with dust particles, filtered into Celeste's room. An un-seasonable gale-force wind raged outside as doctors feverishly rushed in and out with various concoctions. The colonel and Celeste's mother sat pensively, while friends prayed for a miracle. In the end, their prayers and even Magnificat medicine could not sustain the child. "She was born too soft for this world," Tak heard a doctor say as he shook his head in helplessness.

Tak remembered thinking, "If only I knew more medicine secrets, perhaps I could have saved her." That moment defined his current work as Littern to compile all Magnificat medicine scrolls for entry into the *Book of Secrets*.

SLAM!—Celeste's bedroom shutters rattled, then blew open, as if to let her fly away. The wind and rain poured in. Then everything became ominously still. Tak watched as a translucent Celeste rose from her bed and floated to the window. She looked back at him with a tear on her cheek and blew a soft kiss, "I love you to the moon," she whispered, as a gentle breeze carried her away.

Tak leapt to the windowsill. She was gone. "If only I could fly," he whispered as he hung his head, sad she left him behind.

He puzzled over the melancholy that filled the Archer home. Certainly, the colonel had seen death before, yet he became gray with anguish and refused to let in light or laughter. Quiet company and warm whiskey was all Celeste's father could tolerate. Night after night, the grand officer stared out the window at cloud shadows skipping over the landscape. Tak lay nearby but was careful not to touch him—uninvited touch now brought immense pain to this male Archer, he had learned.

The females in the house were different. He spent the daylight hours curled over Celeste's mother's shoulders like a cape while she read in her child's sun-dusted room. He even perched beside the cook while she cried. She offered no special cuts of meat. No fresh linen filled his bed. No one in the house spoke for a long time. Tak was dismayed that Archers suffered more than Magnificats over death. He too missed Celeste, but was simply perplexed that no one in the entire manor seemed to be preparing a joyous party for her return to her new life—very soon.

It is not hard to imagine Tak's heartache when he learned that Archers had only one life. Celeste was gone forever. A fear struck: "Might he never see Miw again, either?" Curling in the lap of Celeste's mother, making an exception in this case, he was hoping for the escape of sleep.

Tak would forever mark this instance as his first true understanding of Archers and the cruelest of all their winds, the death of a loved one. Their lives were so short and limited compared to those of Magnificats. He hoped he would never have to use this knowledge against them. "Yes," he tearfully muttered, "knowing how to be quiet company is most important when dealing with Archers."

CHAPTER 3

AOIFE O'HEGARTY STANDISH

They say there's a secret charm which lies
In some wild flow'rets bell,
That grows in a vale where the west wind sighs,
And where secrets best might dwell.

—Samuel Lover, "The Charm," 1800's, Dublin, Ireland

Apple knew all about ankhs. Her father, Professor Daniel Standish, was a noted Egyptologist, so she was well versed on Egyptian relics and culture before she was six years old. Her family had spent much of their time on distant digs and teaching assignments, but after the divorce, Dan left Ireland permanently, moved back to the 'States,' and remarried.

Aoife [Eefa] O'Hegarty Standish was Apple's given name. Gaelic for "Eve," Aoife was the name her mum chose for her red-haired baby after a difficult delivery thirteen years before. "'Twas a woman's curse for lying in Eden," her mum would say. To Apple's horror, the detailed account of her birth came up during every family gathering up north in Donegal. To further her embarrassment, Apple's 'yank' father decided her given name was neither phonetic nor American enough, and so the nickname 'Apple' unfortunately stuck, just like the leaves that had lodged in her curly hair from the whirlwind.

Dan used to make fun of her feisty nature. "Apple's temper can scald like a fire-breathing dragon," he often teased, "like bog peat—poof, she is ready for a fight." It was true, Apple had no impulse control when she was mad. Dan would barb that she was like her mum's side of the family, "a bunch of fire-bombers," poking fun at rumors about mum's rebel relations. That sort of jovial sparring left Ireland with her dad.

To prove her dad was wrong about her temperament, Apple learned how to choke down her anger like her grandmother's dreaded castor oil. Lately, she was having trouble keeping that anger down. School had been dreadful. Her teacher seemed to have it in for her, while classmates made her life grueling. Now, when she could be free of such conflict during her school break, instead, she had to go to Egypt.

"Mum should be stickin' up for me," she murmured, as she packed for her trip, tossing her clothes into her wheeled backpack in an over-the-shoulder slam dunk. "Mum should speak out, 'No Dan! She cannot go to Egypt. You are the one who left, so come see her here in Ireland!'" Apple knew her mum would never say those things, though. She never wanted to 'stir up ill winds,' as she would put it.

Since Mum's two jobs kept her away from home, she was pleased Apple would have something to do for the summer other than sitting in the library or watching old American shows on the tele. Not old enough for a job like her brother Karn, and not athletic or artsy, to come right down to it, Apple had no excuse for not going to Egypt. Frustrated, she yelled, "Jaysus!" as she kicked the edge of her bed, hurting her toe and causing her backpack to fall right onto her other foot. "Ouch!" she hollered.

"You okay, love?" called Mum. "We need to get movin'."

Apple whined under her breath, "If Makree were here, she would be stickin' up for me." Abandonment by her father was nothing compared to the loss of her grandmother, her 'mother of the heart.' Apple still swore she heard the Banshee faerie sing the night before Makree's passing. Makree came from the O'Neil clan, so it could be possible.

Her grandmother's magical stories had been a refuge for Apple in the years that followed Dan's departure. Makree would whisper while looking cautiously from side to side, "When I was a wee girl, sunshine faeries would slide down rainbows into me mum's mistletoe gardens." She always insisted that mistletoe, the most holy herb of the Druids, must only be said in a whisper.

"Aoife, a'chroi," (she always called Apple, 'her heart'), "don't you be knowin' the best way to see faeries is out the corner of your eye?" She suddenly recalled the strange cat she had seen for a moment sitting on the rocky old wall of the church. Apple had not thought of magic for quite awhile, and wondered why it was coming to mind now. "You and I are of the Fey," Makree always told Apple, who was never sure exactly what that meant, other than something to do with faeries.

Makree also gave Apple her love of reading. The two would read and drink hot seaclaid and make fun of Dan when he corrected them to say "hot choc-o-lot." That was the only time anyone used her grandmother's Beleek cups. That pair would one day belong to Apple. They waited for her in Mum's china cabinet, passed down from great-someone-or-other, who saved the pair from the Erne River heap, where they dumped all imperfect pottery from the 200-year-old factory. "Beleek," Makree would say, "is made from magical sand, found only in one spot, and only in Ireland."

Apple lost Makree, her father, her home, friends, and even her cat, all in two excruciating years. The only way she could keep from crying was to stay angry and shoot a spicy "NO!" to anything and everything new that came her way. It was easier, she decided, to tromp straight through life with teeth clenched and chin tucked. She did not want or need friends. Her early, deep losses caused Apple to declare, "Not one more thing will be taken from me!"

By the time Apple and her mum reached the Dublin airport, it was jam-packed with bustling, luggage-laden travelers.

They were all quite astonished when Apple passed through the body scanner and her red hair suddenly shot out in all directions, as if she had stuck her finger into an electrical outlet. At the same time, a blitz of wind swept through the airport and right out the sliding glass entry doors, bringing confusion and delays as maintenance workers scurried to check the equipment for faulty functioning. "What the...?" Apple said in astonishment.

Red-faced and rigid from holding back tears, Apple took a last look at Mum, who was behind the black stanchioned dividers. She hoped for a last minute reprieve to let her stay home. Mum was tempted, but instead, "Remember the babby gift, Apple," were her final words, across the grim-faced hoards.

Apple waved goodbye and mouthed "*Gráim thú*" ["I love you" in Gaelic] across the crowd, as she headed off towards her gate like she was 'walking the plank' in one of her Jack of the Baltic stories. She crumpled up the joyce her mum got at the airport exchange so she could have spending money for the layover in London, since the Brits did not accept the Euro. Apple shoved it into the pocket of her jeans, right next to Makree's rosary that her mother said would keep her safe.

The eight hours from Dublin to Cairo included a stopover at Heathrow, where Apple purchased a package of her favorite treat, Hobnobs, which she enjoyed on her flight out of London. It had been rough from the start, but alarming jerks and sudden drops in altitude began an hour outside of Cairo, when the captain assured everyone over the intercom it was all merely turbulence, "which often occurs over Egypt this time of year, what with the high winds and all."

Apple was good at reading people, and studying the flight attendants' facial expressions, their telling glances indicated the captain was being less than forthcoming. "Jaysus, Mary, and Joseph," she prayed with a sense of foreboding. She grabbed Makree's rosary out of her pocket to kiss it, and pulled out a leaf that was stuck to it at the same time. "How did that get there?" she wondered aloud. The leaf was remarkably soft and pliable.

Looking closer, she saw images of small leaves imprinted on it. In school, she had been studying Ogham, the ancient Irish tree language. Southern Ireland was trying to get back to its prehistoric roots, and as a result, the schools were teaching Gaelic and Ogham. If she remembered right, the two leaf imprints meant "Warning!" She tightened her fingers around the rosary and dropped the leaf as the plane continued to rock and jolt.

Darkness had fallen when her plane landed roughly amid a commotion of flashing lights, disaster crews, and fire trucks surrounding it. The plane's interior lights went dark. Oxygen masks dropped and emergency doors sprung open. Yellow evacuation chutes inflated and jutted out as worried passengers slid down, pushed by perfectly manicured, but conspicuously sweat-drenched flight attendants. Not a word came across the intercom from the captain. Once outside the plane, escorts herded the apprehensive travelers, without explanation, towards a terminal entrance beneath large bay windows overlooking the tarmac.

Packed tightly in a crowd of taller adults, Apple saw nothing. An array of foreign languages blended into indecipherable babble. Then she heard a snippet from someone with an American accent, "…was sucked into an engine."

"What did you say?" Apple demanded.

"Somehow, a cat got caught in one of the engines," it sounded like they answered. Apple thought she must have heard wrong, but before she could ask again, the crowd reshaped around her and pushed through the corridors.

Once inside Cairo's overcrowded International Airport, Apple gained hope that the rest of her trip might not be as primitive as she had remembered. Flashing video screens announced, "Welcome to Egypt," a reception she had not expected. She was used to flying into small, out-of-the-way landing strips on her father's digs, where writing was in hieroglyphics and all structures looked like pyramids.

She spotted Dan in his standard, monogrammed, olive-green safari jacket and toothpick cocked to the side of his mouth.

He was rushing towards her through the crowd. Amanda, his surly and unapologetic wife trailed along, pushing a pram in obviously painful, too-tall, high heels. "Jaysus, it's Dan's 'mini-me'," Apple muttered under her breath. She had been given the impression Justin was a newborn, but this 'baby' looked to be at least two-years-old.

"Look, Justin!" Dan echoed through the airport, making Apple cringe, "Wave to your big sissy." The caramel-skinned toddler managed a floppy wave and flashed a big smile. All Apple could think was how this was living proof that Dan had re-scripted his life. He had a makeover just like his new wife. Embarrassment and rage flushed her bisque-toned cheeks to a cherry red as the trio hurried towards her.

Justin bore no resemblance to her father, who was a blue-eyed, California surfer type. Though he still considered himself blonde, his hair was fully gray and thinning. Nor did Justin look like her stepmonster, Amanda. She had Asian features, and hair laced with unnatural golden highlights and manufactured waves. Surprisingly, Apple felt tenderness when little Justin gleefully squealed "Appo," holding up his hand for a high five.

She smiled and gave him a soft slap before pulling out the stuffed leprechaun. "For sure, little fellow, this is from me mum, all the way in Oirland," she over-pronounced, shooting her dad a defiant look. Justin was overjoyed and hugged it right away, while Apple began a series of thoughts: So who is mum to Justin? Is he my brother, half brother, or stepbrother? It was all too complicated.

Apple stiffened, beginning her well-crafted mutiny by lowering her voice an octave, "Hello, Dan." She reached out her right hand to make clear there would be no hugging between them, and did not acknowledge Amanda at all, causing her to roll her eyes in exasperation. Dan acted oblivious to the tension between the two females.

Apple was insulted that no one brought up the fact that her plane had made an emergency landing. It was out of character for

Dan to remain quiet about his expertise in all pursuits: archae-ologist, gemologist, scientist, chef, artist, and, oh yes, even pilot. She was actually relieved not to have to listen to him describe at length how much better he would have handled the aviation crisis. Not wanting to appear 'dramatic,' as she had been labeled after their last visit, Apple concluded that he simply did not care that she might have died.

The two-and-a-half hour drive from the airport to the remote dig site was painfully silent. After several unsuccessful attempts at small talk, Dan gave up. The silence was awkward. Little Justin slept in his car seat, hugging his new leprechaun, the dashboard's green glow highlighting his runny nose. Apple stared out the window and envisioned a sarcastic dialogue: "So, Dan, how is your fantastic new home in California? Did you know we now live in a crumbling old flat? By the way, Dan, you missed my science project awards dinner…oh yes, I forgot, you had to take Amanda for a facial."

Facials were the least of Amanda's beauty treatments. Each visit, she morphed into a more surreal rendition of herself: bigger lips and higher cheeks, and now a thinner nose. She just keeps tryin' to be as pretty as Mum, Apple thought, as she twirled a long strand of her hair around her index finger. This was espe-cially clear at last year's visit. The two 'love-turds,' as Apple called them, had argued because Dan told Apple she was pretty, "the spitting image of her mum," he carelessly said at dinner. It was true. She did share her mum's saffron hair and sage-green eyes that leapt off porcelain skin, perfectly framing her dark-plum, heart-shaped lips (which she attributed to Makree's 'prisms and prunes' lip exercises, her Irish beauty secret). Apple never be-lieved it when people told her she had the face of a faerie princess.

It was ironic, even empowering, that the woman who broke up her family was the envious one. Apple decided she could use this jealousy to her advantage and defiantly rolled down her win-dow, pulling the clip out of her hair to let her red locks blow free. Amanda ratcheted around in the front seat and their eyes met.

Apple saw a sparkling ankh hanging around Amanda's neck. It brought to mind the mysterious cat at the church back in Dublin.

As if she sensed Apple's attempted coup, Amanda mouthed, "You will lose," and reached back, snatching Justin's leprechaun away. Amanda's cruelty was not new, like the time she cut Apple's long hair short like a boy, or when she hid her mum's letters. To Apple, the kind of person who would sink so low as to take a parent away from his children would have no problem taking a toy away from a helpless child.

"Hey Apple, the air is on and the sand's kicking up. Close the window, will you?" Apple ignored her father. "Now!" he barked, already out of patience. Apple pretended not to hear. Dan rolled the window up automatically from the driver's seat, almost smashing her fingertips, which she jerked off the beveled edge at the last second. Justin stirred in his seat and began to cry.

"Amadan, I think he wants his leprechaun back." Apple knew no one would notice she called her 'Amadan,' an Irish term for idiot, instead of Amanda. Reluctantly, Amanda gave Justin his toy, which he cuddled before drifting back to sleep, as Dan glared at Apple in the rearview mirror.

The car was silent again after that. Apple watched the moon-lit landscape pass outside her window. She spotted something out of the corner of her eye—a dust devil. Did that crazy wind follow me here? she wondered and sat upright. The sight triggered Apple's memory of Makree and her tales of gaoithe sidhe, the wind faeries who travel inside twisters, offering protection to Irish girls like Apple. Staring into the whirlwind, she thought she saw a shimmering faerie looking right at her, shaking her finger as if to say, "Don't do it." She decided to keep quiet and put her hair back up, feigning sleep until dreams finally overcame her.

CHAPTER 4

RASTA'S PRINCESS

The winds that sometimes take something we love,
are the same that bring us something we learn to love.

—Bob Marley, 1970s, Jamaica

As the morning sun spiked through the grey fabric screen of the spacious tent and pierced her closed eyelids, Apple had no recollection of arriving at the windswept field school. "Jaysus," she griped, "the sun must be closer to Egypt than it is to Ireland." The morning bustle of the campground, with smells of yeast-rich biscuits and full-bodied coffee, kept her from falling back to sleep. She stretched and yawned before noticing a second made-up cot with two army-green wool blankets neatly draped over the end. A lacy mosquito net hung down loosely around the cot, with a pair of fuzzy slippers on the floor next to it. She had a roommate, she surmised.

Rapidly changing her clothes, Apple tried to tame her curly hair with spit, achieving little success, then quickly unzipped the tent and stepped out into the hot Egyptian sun. Sluggish students in cargo pants and tee shirts, with bandanas around their necks ready to pull up for wind protection, wandered around in big floppy hats and gloves. They moved like zombies towards or away from the large, screened mess tent, lured by yummy scents. She could distinguish the staff by their kelly-green polo shirts and khaki shorts. Apple followed a stream of bodies without looking around. She was not a morning person.

"Jah blesses the late princess," said a staff member with a toothy grin, in what Apple viewed as an overdone Jamaican accent. He wore dreadlocks tucked into a striped, Rastafarian-style knit hat that contrasted with his preppy uniform. Apple winced. Dan used to call her "princess."

"Better get them feet moving before your whirlwind chases us all home."

How did he know about her wind issues? Then she retorted, "I am not a princess," thinking he was insulting her as stuck up, or advantaged.

"Ahh, things and things, free spirits are all Rasta princesses," he said, still wearing a big smile on his face. All this smiling was beginning to bother Apple. He handed her a bright blue, floppy cotton hat with a courteous bow.

She managed to squeak out a meager "Thanks, but if you'll be callin' me princess, I'll be callin' you Rasta," and then mumbled under her breath, "hump-off."

"Ah, you'd be very welcome to call me Rasta. Extra special, coming from a princess. Yes indeed, as good a name as any." Apple rolled her eyes, sorry she ever encouraged this grown muzzy.

She noticed a book tucked under his arm. "What are you readin'?" she asked, sure it was something she'd already read. She did not figure him for smart, since he was working as staff instead of being a college student.

"It's *Kebra Nagast*." Watching her and noticing she was actually interested instead of looking for a way to get rid of him, Rasta pressed on, "Dah sacred book of Ethiopia." Tucking it back under his arm, he gave her a wink.

"I've never heard of that," she said, gaining a bit of respect for him, "What's it about?"

Rasta's face lit up as he tossed his head back in a gruff laugh, causing his white teeth to sparkle like pearls against his coffee-toned skin in the bright morning light. "This book tells about dah romance of all romances, Queen Saba and the wisest king in all dah land, Solomon. His great-great-and-fifty-greats-more grandson was dah last emperor of Ethiopia. It is because of him that ol' Rasta joined this expedition. That wise king hid his treasure with Queen Saba, a golden chest covered in angels, and I aim to find it."

"What's in the chest?" asked Apple.

"Magic, princess—lots and lots of magic."

"Like what?"

"Well now, princess, there is a stick, a wooden stick, just an old chopped branch that grows flowers all on its own, with no water and no roots. There is food of the angels that never spoils, no way. And two stone tablets with the very words of Jah!" Rasta tucked two escaped tendrils of his dreadlocks back under his knit hat and smiled at Apple.

Uncomfortable with him just grinning at her, she broke the awkwardness by asking, "Is that where you're from, Ethiopia?"

He raised one brow and tapped his chest with his thumb, "Ah, little princess, Rasta is from everywhere." Although Apple's first impression of Rasta had been anything but good, she found she sort of liked him, but would need more time to size him up before making a true finding. Putting his book into a well-worn knapsack, which he closed securely, Rasta sang, "Time to go, time to go," in a reggae style as he headed for the vans.

Late for the meal and disappointed that there were no breakfast beans or beef pudding, Apple snagged a large muffin from a tray, wrapped it in two yellow napkins, and carefully placed it in her backpack before hurrying to the loading area.

The dusty trip to the site on a washboard dirt road was miserable, at best. Apple was glad she hadn't eaten yet. When her van came to a bumpy halt, Rasta was already there to open the door, and as Apple exited, said with a sweep of his hand and the bow of a footman, "Here we are, princess!" She ignored him.

Everyone climbed out and headed off to their section of the dig. Each assigned job was vital to the project. Apple waited for her task in the lopsided shade of the van as Dan sorted through documents in his briefcase. He finally looked up, feeling Apple watching him. Seeing her pouty grimace, he shook his head and mumbled so she could not hear, "Jeez kid, you are not a little child anymore. Don't you understand I'm working?" Dan was not able to face how his decisions had stunted Apple's development in many ways. He sighed, "Okay Apple, I need your help over there." He pointed to a distant tented area and hoped the bit of isolation might warm her interactions with him and the others.

Once he positioned her under a canopy with tools and drinking water, he said, "Need anything, just holler…and hydrate. You're not used to this climate." Then he watched in dismay as she threw her hat down and gave it a kick.

Apple recognized this job assignment as meaningless 'sandbox duty' right off, and it infuriated her. This was an area previously searched and ruled out as not having any relics. When she was ten, sandbox duty was fun. Now, as a teenager, she felt it was demeaning. "I'm nearly fourteen," she grumbled. Being assigned busywork only stoked her smoldering resentment of 'everything Dan.'

Shifting his trademark toothpick from one side of his mouth to the other, then back again, before taking it out to speak, he tried to calm her. "Now Apple, I can't have you flipping out in front of my students. I don't need you to have an attitude out here today."

Dan shrugged as he wondered if Apple purposely liked being difficult—it sure appeared that way to him. Sometimes he thought she was trying to get back at him for divorcing her mother. Well, that couldn't be helped. Maybe he needed to rethink her visits, like Amanda wanted. He had to put his new family first now.

While Dan and his students worked within sight and earshot, Apple sulked, feeling lonely, hot, and irritable. Setting her pack on the bright blue tarp laid out on the ground, she pulled out the muffin. Out of boredom, she began to stab her trowel hard into the crusty earth while she nibbled. Each successive and forceful jab provided an outlet for her smoldering anger, and the earth seemed to welcome the rage as it gave way more easily with each plunge.

While Apple lay on her stomach, snacking and poking around with her trowel, she flashed back to her family cat, Banjo. He had been the first casualty of the divorce. The veterinary nurse said he had passed from old age, but Apple knew that he died of a broken heart. He had been king of their block and never adjusted to life in a flat. He became confused and trapped. She could relate to the poor cat's feelings.

She stabbed her trowel into the earth harder as she remembered her old room with a window seat and canopy bed, family dinners, and fun vacations with everyone laughing together. Her anger increased. Thrusting again, even harder, she thought she saw the earth move, as if rising under her in a heaving breath. She was shocked when she realized that it was, indeed, moving! Was it an earthquake!? She had never felt one before, but had heard reports of them from Dan, who grew up in California. She looked around and saw everyone continuing his or her duties as if nothing had happened. "I guess not," she said aloud.

What Apple did not know was that she was digging very near a dangerous fiend, a monster that once set loose, could turn the tide of life on earth—the long-buried Arabian wind demon, Ephippas. His history of devastation had nearly destroyed the planet twice before. His catastrophic cyclones and hot winds had the power to raise global temperatures that would blight crops, wither trees, and eventually, end life on earth. It was his cold sister Ephima who had caused the ice age, killing the entire dinosaur kingdom. This was a very powerful wind demon.

Fortunately, at least for Ephippas, recent excavations and eroding winds made his once-deep resting spot now very near the surface. With another plunge of the trowel, Apple let out a moan of disgust at her father's running off to start a new family.

Then another at how unfair it was that her mother was left with nothing but toil and poverty. The ground around her shifted, rising up into a small mound right where she had been stabbing the trowel. This time she panicked and jumped up, thinking it may be a rare poisonous snake surfacing. Sudden blowing sand mixed with the hot tears that dripped like maple sap down her cheeks, blurring her vision. Apple threw the trowel down hard and heard a hollow "clunk." She wiped her eyes with her forearm. This was no snake. It could be a treasure! Apple looked up warily to see if anyone else had noticed. "Of course they didn't notice," she sniped sarcastically, "I am bleedin' invisible!"

Ephippas heaved. He was nearly free. All he needed was for Apple to remove the Magnificat Stone that held him in the ground.

Sweat beaded on her upper lip and mixed with her salty tears. Her heart raced in anticipation as she swiped her eyes again with her sleeved forearm. Tensely, lying back down on her belly, Apple began carefully digging and prying around the buried object using her fingers, like her father had taught her, so as not to damage it. Scraping around its edges, she worked painstakingly, her tongue poking the sides of her mouth, as if it was directing the extrication. Finally, she pried out a small clay box and set it carefully on the tarp alongside her, out of sight of any eyes that might stray her way.

A stinging blast of hot, mustard-colored steam erupted out of the hole, tossing her back several feet. She was blinded with cutting pain from the gritty sand blown into her eyes, and frantically felt for her canteen to splash water on them so she could see again. Before she could open them, the wind demon was free!

Apple was not aware of the escaped wind. Instead, she had only a single-minded anticipation of glory. "If treasures are here, I'll be takin' them home to Mum." She looked up and nodded towards the distant pyramids, as if turning her decision into a vow to the ancient pharaohs.

She dreamt that the money from a rare archaeological find

could buy her old life back, a grand cottage in Howth, overlooking the gulls and ruins, and out to the Irish Eye, a small lonely island off the east coast, where her mother would never have to work again at wearisome jobs. Karn would go to college and make Mum proud. Apple would never feel like an outcast again.

Apple picked up the box and studied it. It was made of some type of fired red clay, the size of a child's shoebox, but with rounded corners. She brushed away the rest of the gravelly dirt covering the lid and inspected it carefully. Examining the outside, she ran her fingers over its rough casing.

Just then, a hot blast of desert Khamsin wind spiraled up and around her from her feet to her head, before she could cover her eyes. She was not steady enough to prevent it from jostling her, and the box was ripped right out of her hands. It fell and shattered in pieces on the ground. A flat rectangular stone, about the size and thickness of a paperback novel, tumbled out. Rinsing the bluish-gray relic with a splash of water from her canteen, it became white, revealing small carved pictures—hieroglyphics?

When she looked back at what remained of the broken red-clay container, under the cornhusk-like fibers that had filled it she saw the image of a cat's paw stamped into a large bottom piece. As the daughter of a famed archeologist, she knew this box held something special. Cats were sacred in ancient Egypt, and protected under the law, even above humans. To kill a cat was an instant death sentence. Cats were often mummified and buried with untold treasures, protected by sinister curses.

She quickly placed the broken shards of the box back in the hole, using a yellow napkin from her muffin breakfast as a filler while she hastily covered it up with dirt. She tried to smooth the sand over it with her hand, but the swirling wind reopened the hole. Finally covering it as best she could, she tamped the earth hard with her foot.

Carefully, Apple wrapped the stone tablet in her remaining napkin and placed it in her pack. Blowing sand stung her bare calves like tiny pinpricks. She reckoned faeries were celebrating her discovery by increasing the wind. Unfortuntely, Apple was quite wrong about that.

"Hey App," Dan's voice echoed across the flat sand, "we're going to wrap this up. The winds are getting bad; looks like a haboob coming."

Apple looked at the horizon where her dad had motioned to see a swelling brown cloud rolling in like a fog bank, or a humongous muddy wave. She stood frozen by the sight, until Rasta shouted and waved her over to the van. That reminded her to pick up the blue, floppy hat he had loaned her out of the wiry dried-up plant where her kick had deposited it. She noted that Dan had shortened her name from Apple to App, "like a bleedin computer program he could turn on or off when it suited him," she snarked into the wind. "Well, he just can't delete me letter by letter," she continued with her one-track tirade about his new nickname for her. Right then and there, Apple decided not to tell him, or anyone else, about the stone tablet she found. She looked back to where she had been digging. Her yellow napkin had already become halfway unburied. That was okay though, she figured, it marked the spot so she could continue her excavation later.

Tucking her head and holding her hat on with one hand, she pressed her backpack to her chest and ran against the biting wind to join Rasta's already loaded van. His blue loaner hat shielded her face from the sand, and her guilt. Apple could feel him watching her in the rearview mirror all the way back to camp. She avoided his gaze.

As soon as the van doors opened, Apple raced to her tent and threw open the zippered flap, just in time to come face to face with her roommate, who had returned in the earlier van. She was brushing her hair and washing up in the small, round, water-filled basin, but stopped to greet Apple with a genial smile and outstretched hand. "Hi! My name is Rhonda. I'm from Canada," said the athletic brunette coed. As Apple reached to shake in greeting, her backpack fell to the floor, and the napkin-wrapped stone tumbled out at Rhonda's feet.

The student bent down to pick it up before Apple could react. She was petrified that the young woman would notice what it was, but instead, Rhonda politely handed the partially unwrapped stone back to her, and said, "Here you go. You'd better keep that pack zipped-up around here, eh?" Two other students peeked in to urge Rhonda to hurry to the mess tent for shelter from the coming storm. "I'll be right out," she told her friends. "You were asleep when I got up this morning," she said, addressing Apple again.

"Nice to be meetin' you," Apple said, turning her back straight away to slip the stone in her pack and zip it up.

Rhonda pressed, "You're aboot twelve-years-old, eh?" Then she asked politely, "Do you want me to wait for you?"

Apple ignored her, since she was obviously thirteen, and insulted, not to mention worried that the stone had been seen. Rhonda did not ask any more questions and simply headed out to join the group. Apple washed up and followed before the haboob hit.

Dinner consisted of dried fruit, brown bread, and a tasty soup, with lively discussions on what each observed at the dig site, trying to best each other. They were bragging about their discoveries, like fishermen do over who had caught the biggest fish. Apple knew they had nothing on her; she had caught a whale! She smiled smugly to herself. Rasta noticed, directing his attention towards Apple, "What did dah princess find, now?" he asked.

She iced up. Her thoughts raced. How does he know so much about me? He was nowhere near me or the relic. He watched her, waiting. "Nootin'," she quipped, as soon as she recovered her composure.

Rasta laughed aloud and tossed his head back, his heavy hair wobbling under his hat. "Especially for dah young, every footstep is a turnin' away from one life, and startin' towards a different one. Step carefully, princess," he cautioned, just before

Dan ordered everyone into the center of the large tent.

"Time to take cover, the full force of this haboob is about to hit," Dan warned. When it did, the strong tent rocked violently. Bouncing rocks and debris hit the side, and sand beat the roof like rain.

After the winds calmed from ferocious to steady later that night, Apple tossed restlessly, back in her tent. She dreamt of an Arabian king with pet cats on leashes like dogs, who snuggled with the monarch at night, keeping him warm. Yet, when the king was not near, the cats became frightening, yellow-eyed monsters.

Apple was awakened by a sustained cat-like hissing. "It's only the wind blowing around the outside of the tent," she soothed herself, then slowly sat up and looked around, hoping not to see cats filling the tent. She took in a long but shaky breath before lying back down. The whipping tent walls and her dream had her on edge. Her mind would not quiet down, going over her discovery of the stone endlessly. She did not get back to sleep for a long while.

CHAPTER 5

DEMON WINDS

And they were travelling along like the clouds
when they are driven before the attack
of mighty winds

— Is'haq Neburä -Id, *Kebra Nagast*, 14th century c.e., Ethiopia

It was still dark when Apple awoke on her second day at the field school to Rhonda's moaning. The night's windstorm had left fine silt covering her sleeping bag and specks of sand stuck to her skin, just as she had dreaded. She aimed her flashlight across the tent and saw Rhonda shivering with sweat. Not knowing what to do, and not wanting to go out into the dark windy night, she lay still until sunrise.

The camp began to bustle with lumbering, half-awake students, covered up like nomads to avoid the stinging sand. With her eyes still scratchy, even moisturizing drops brought little relief, but Apple was grateful because the redness hid any evidence of the homesick tears she would never admit to having shed. The staff had begun repairing damage and beating the dust off tent roofs with the stick-end of brooms, only to have the dust whip back in their faces, mockingly. Rasta called to Apple, "Catch this, princess," tossing a broom to her, smiling suggestively.

She caught it and then spotted her roommate wandering toward the nurse's tent and ran over. "Here ya go, roomie," she said, tossing Rhonda the broom.

Rhonda stared in disbelief at Apple's insensitivity as the broom tumbled to the ground, "I was sick all night, Apple!"

"How was I to be knowin' that?" smarted Apple.

The full effect of the blazing sun seared the desert floor. As the vans loaded, Apple stopped in her tracks before climbing in, realizing she had forgotten her hidden stone. She had removed it to shake out dust from her backpack, and left it under the pillow on her cot. Rushing back for it, she ran smack into Rasta. With no hat today, he wore his long dreadlocks partially pinned up in back. "Hey now, dah princess is late again?" Apple reversed course and ran for the van, not wanting to provoke any more of his nosiness. Besides, she was looking forward to finding more buried treasure and would need the extra room in her pack to store it.

The sluggish students, minus Rhonda, rode silently to the dig site in the rocking vans, balancing coffee and munching on pastries. They knew they had to rally for six to eight hours of digging before an afternoon of report work and lectures. Most were already fantasizing about completing their daily group briefings so they could relax.

"Hmm...what's going on here?" Dan remarked, looking ahead as the van slowed down approaching the dig site. This got everyone's attention. Dan removed his sunglasses so he could scan the area more carefully. He anxiously shifted his toothpick from side-to-side. "Who are those people?" The students strained their necks to see.

Apple, who had been unconsciously scribbling cat pictures on her notepad, lifted her head to see a small assembly of thin tall men ahead, in a watery mirage reflection. "What th...?" she asked.

Churning gusts whipped the men's galabeyas as they stood on the exact spot where Apple had been digging the day before.

Her heart sank and her feet went numb. Now she was grateful Rasta had prevented her from getting her stone. She might have been caught red-handed; though she was not exactly sure for what.

Piling out of the vans, the group, led by Dan, curiously approached the men who were wildly waving them over. Apple pushed past the others to peek out from behind her father, glimpsing her 'sandbox' now cordoned off with yellow tape and sandbags. Dan's assistants and students encircled a pile of clay shards outside a newly dug hole. Baffled, Dan exclaimed to three bearded men, in Arabic, "What is going on here?"

"What have you done?" the tallest man, wearing jeans and a white collared shirt, asked sternly of Dan, in English. "As director of Egypt's Ministry of Antiquities, I have been generous to you, Professor Standish. Even though our ancient burial sites have been robbed and our treasures withheld from us in museums of other nations, we still invite you to dig into the very soul of our land. You were given precise instructions regarding what you must do with what you find here. Why can't you Americans respect our wishes?"

Then another man, short and sporting a trim yellow beard, stepped forward from a nearby black SUV. With a stiff index finger pointed right at Dan, he shouted, "Majnoon!"

Dumbfounded, Dan knew he was being called a lunatic, but with a puzzled expression turned to the team and said, "I don't understand!"

Although Apple didn't know that word, she could tell these men were furious, not excited. They were not going to reward her for her significant find or thank her for discovering a sacred relic. Regarding Dan and his students suspiciously, the discussion intensified, as did the wind. Apple scanned the terrain quickly to see if she had left any trace of her digging, as the blond-bearded man bent down and picked up a potsherd. She noticed his other hand was holding her yellow napkin, as his piercing gaze intuitively darted to her. She slipped further behind her father. "Majoon!" he again snarled, shaking his finger at Dan while moving towards Apple and growling creepily in English, "Did you find something, little girl?" Apple peeked out just as the wind stole the yellow napkin and carried it up into the sky.

"No," she answered sheepishly, which surprised her. Dan flashed a shocked look at his daughter. Apple's answer fell stiffly, like breaking glass. It was a lie, and a tough spot to be in for a girl who hated liars, as she considered her father to be. Rasta pulled Apple gently back behind him by her shoulder, protecting her. The arguing resumed long enough for Apple to escape to the van and slink down into the back seat. The team joined her in short order as the wind reached a ferocious peak, slamming back the van doors as the crowd frantically piled inside.

Dan did not look at Apple, nor anyone else for that matter. He spoke in a controlled tone, the kind worse than yelling, "App, when we get back, pack up immediately. You are going home!" This was a bombshell. The students and Rasta gaped at Apple sympathetically, and Rasta suddenly understood Apple's cold disposition. The rest of the ride back was devoid of the usual student chatter. Rasta looked occasionally at Apple in the rearview mirror, hoping to offer her an understanding glance. Pretending not to notice, she continued scribbling cat pictures until they were back at camp, where she was first to scramble out of the van. Rasta watched her run to her tent as he took a sip of his lukewarm coffee and wished he could have broken through her tough shell before she left. He was an eternal optimist, and believed that everyone responds to kindness. Maybe he was wrong, he thought.

Rhonda's bedding was being bagged up by a woman wearing medical gloves and a white surgical mask as Apple burst in. "What are you doin'?" she asked curiously.

"Miss Rhonda fell sick and went to the hospital. Don't think she'll be back," the worker said nervously as she handed Apple a mask to don.

Apple put it on and hurriedly got to work collecting her

things. She lay on her stomach on her cot and reached underneath the pillow for the stone tablet. Tucking it between clothes in her backpack, Apple had just managed to cover it with yesterday's tee shirt when Amanda walked in with Justin.

"Time to go," Amanda announced gleefully before the attendant warned them away on her way out.

"Yep," quipped Apple from under her mask.

Looking around quickly to make sure no one could see, Amanda grabbed Apple by her upper arm and grimaced, then tightened her grip. "Hear me Aoife O'Hegarty," she seethed through clenched teeth. "There is an Arab proverb, 'Once you decide to hit someone, hit hard, for retribution will be the same either way.'" Then Amanda bit her own tongue in fury until it bled, and dug her red fingernails deep into Apple's arm, breaking the skin.

Justin reached out to Apple for a goodbye hug. Still stunned from Amanda's assault, Apple let him wrap his tiny arms around her leg as she patted his brown stubbly hair. She couldn't believe what Amanda had done, and right in front of her son. Was this kind of treatment something Justin was used to? Apple became very concerned for her new little brother.

Suddenly, even though she had orchestrated it all, and had even hoped for this exact outcome, her mouth quivered trying to hold back a sob that stuck like a lump of peanut butter in the back of her throat. Amanda rolled her eyes as if Apple were making a dramatic play and pranced away, her high heels wobbling in the gravel.

Apple knelt down to give Justin a big hug and a shirt she had brought from Ireland. It displayed the country's proper name, Éire. She picked it on purpose because of Dan's dismissal of so many things Irish. Justin grabbed Apple tightly around her neck and begged, almost desperately, "Pease take me wiff you…I want my sisser."

Surprised, she stiffened and stood up, and said what she always said to anything new, "No!" Then she added, "But you kin be comin' for a visit." Justin smiled. Apple never wanted to leave her mum, so if Justin wanted to leave his, there might be good reason. In three short days, Apple had come to like the little 'muzzy' after all.

Outside the van, Amanda stood innocently beside Dan. Justin clung again to Apple's leg. "Justin," Dan snapped, "get over here, now!" Amanda jerked the little boy by the arm, a little too roughly, and pulled him away kicking and screaming. Dan looked on in dismay at his wife.

He would not be driving Apple to the airport, and she didn't ask why. Rasta was already in the driver's seat and ready to go. Dan did not offer a hug, but instead put out his right hand as she had done to him at the airport. She refused it out of stubbornness, but was secretly sorry she had not hugged him at least once. Little Justin stood in the distance with his new leprechaun tucked under his arm, tear-streaked cheeks, and his thumb in his mouth. Amanda offered a 'princess wave' sarcastically, her cupped hand swiveling at the wrist.

Apple slid the van door open and climbed into the back seat. Dan surprised her when he said in Gaelic, "*Slán abhaile*," [have a safe trip home] as he closed the door for her.

"Dah 'little bitta fluff' wins, does she?" Apple saw Rasta's dark bushy brows move above his sunglasses in the rearview mirror.

What is it with this guy? she smoldered, as she wondered how he knew such Irish terms.

As they drove toward the airport, Apple stared silently out the van window at another gathering haboob, looming behind them. The low brown cloud darkened the horizon like a growing ogre, reaching for the highest point of the sky.

Rasta pulled to the side of the dusty road and stopped. She was nervous for a moment, having been warned by her mum about men in vans. He spoke slowly as he took the car out of gear, removed his sunglasses, and turned around. "Somebody woke up dah sleeping winds, princess. The wind is calling you. I have seen it before. The demon is awake. Look, look, child."

Apple shifted nervously and peered out the back window. Almost whispering, but with his low-toned voice still audible, he pointed at the wind. "See princess, dat wind, he is a demon." She hadn't noticed before, but now, when she looked at it carefully, she could see the shape of a face, a very angry face, quite plainly visible in the dust-cloud formation behind them. "Now, you listen to me, princess, you will be sent to the ends of the earth from such a wind as this!"

"Stop it, Rasta, if yer thinkin' yer hilarious, yer not. And yer not scaring me, neither," Apple sparked, after she had a second to collect herself. "You just want me to stay because I am the only one in the whole camp who even wants to talk with you," she jabbed.

Rasta tossed his head back in a belly laugh as he again faced the front, pulling his sunglasses down from on top of his head to rest on his nose. He put the van in gear and looked in the mirror, "Mark my words, princess, you will be leaving your home very soon. The winds are chasing you. Mark my words little one."

Apple considered lying or explaining, but remembered an old Irish proverb her grandmother used to say, "Don't let your tongue cut your throat." She changed the subject. "So Rasta, what will you be doin' after this class?"

He laughed, as he always did, with his white teeth gleaming. "I will be on to the next place, then the next, until I find what I am looking for."

"And what might that be, oh King Rasta of Everywhere?" Apple teased.

He raised his sunglasses and looked at her in the mirror. "Be thinking you know, princess. Be thinking you know."

"Oh, that's right, Noah's ark."

Again, Rasta laughed out loud, "Not that ark, not that ark at all. But if I stumbled on to it, that would be a good thing, too."

"Sometimes Rasta, I don't know if you're feedin' me rubbish or not."

Apple joined in the laugh as he flipped his sunglasses back down and they continued on their way to the airport. She even thought of thanking him for protecting her at the dig site, but instead, remained quiet.

Before she knew it, Apple was flying home to Dublin, her feelings of sorrow washed away by the hectic airport, where practically everyone pushed or shoved her. The anticipation of seeing her mum made her not even care. Once safely on the plane, Apple felt a twitter of exhilaration in her stomach from her brush with danger. Sabotaging Dan's dig was a bonus. The captain announced, "Sit back and relax folks. These tailwinds out of Egypt are exceptionally good, so we should arrive at Heathrow early." Apple pulled out her rosary pouch from her back pocket and gave it a kiss for good luck.

Chapter 6

Cat Dreams and Scientific Proof

Thank God men cannot fly,
and lay waste the sky
as well as the earth.

—Henry David Thoreau, *Walden*, 1854, Massachusetts, U. S.A.

Every night after Apple's return from Egypt, the wind howled and she dreamt of cats. Not ordinary cats, like one might find in kitchens mewing for food or licking themselves clean. These cats were a mishmash of curious feline creatures. She noticed Mum had been vacuuming the room more often.

Why 'flying over the moon' wizard cats and half-human cats were invading her dreams was beyond her. A skinny, golden-furred cat, wearing spectacles and reading from a dusty, old, medical journal, showed up most often. Seated in a stained and overstuffed chair, the pages he turned were so fragile they crumbled at the touch of his claw. The journal cover bore a picture of a sword standing on its tip, with a golden snake winding up from its point to the cat image carved into the grip. Every page was marked with one golden cat pawprint on the bottom outside corner.

An unkempt chocolate cat with coal black pupils that had

no sparkle stared at Apple while dipping its claw into a skull-shaped inkwell on a pale marble slab altar. The altar was not brick-red with lit candles and soft pads for kneeling, like in her parish. There was just a cold, grey, barren floor, where kneeling would hurt. The cat was writing, not on paper, but in mid-air. A large black 'M' sparkled yellow and lit the room. The cat's eyes stayed vapid.

One night, a cat flew around her room very slowly with a trail of sparks that changed colors from orange to green, to lavender, to blue. They crackled like twigs popping in a campfire. Apple especially remembered a bright white cat that placed its two front paws softly on her chest and then became a white-haired girl with mismatched eyes. Then she jolted awake.

There was some evidence that she was not dreaming at all. Like the time several huge cats with pheasant wings flew in and out of her room through a window sealed shut with paint from previous tenants. The next morning, Apple found the window wide open and in good working order. Another time, she swam in a blue lake with a bright orange cat wearing goggles, flippers, and a rubber swim cap, and awoke soaking wet with a fish in her bed. The most outlandish dream, by far, involved seven cats sitting at the foot of her bed, building a campfire, and fanning it with raven's wings. "Apple, there's a fire! We are getting out!" her mum yelled. She had smelled the smoke and called Fire Services. Apple decided not to tell her about the dream, especially after the neighbors had to stand in the cold in their pajamas for three hours while firefighters cleared the flats.

Apple had inherited her unimaginative mind from her father. She needed a scientific explanation before she was about to believe anything. Unfortunately, crazy-arse cats were not topics taught in her school.

The next morning, even the swaying trees and windswept grounds outside of her classroom window were more interesting than her teacher's lesson. She was daydreaming about her stone, hidden at home, as the teacher's voice droned on, when a headline on her computer screen popped up, catching her attention, "A Profound Discovery in Egypt; remnants of a 9,000-year-old mummified royal cat sarcophagus, older than the one discovered on the Isle of Cyprus." Riveted on the edge of her chair, she read on. "Archaeology students may be responsible for missing arti-facts in Egypt. The investigation by Egyptian officials has stalled due to severe haboob winds."

They're talking about me, she realized. Apple knew Egyptian history and could discuss with aplomb matters of archaeology because of her dad, so, when she read the word 'sarcophagus,' she knew that meant money, and money for Apple was the magic she needed to get her life back. Were her titillating thoughts of wealth and power possible? She could hardly wait for the school bell to ring.

As soon as it did, and she was dismissed, Apple rushed straight away home to her room, where she scrambled under her bed to ensure her treasure was safe-and-sound. The stone had moved! She panicked. Feeling around, she felt it a foot away from where she remembered placing it, maybe due to Mum's vacuum-ing. The thought of the stone being valuable overtook her and she considered again, just for a second, that if she were rich enough, perhaps her dad would come home. "But I don't want him home, ever!" She shook her head to chase that idea away.

Imagining her past lifestyle was a safe but sad place for Apple. Her second life (as she liked to call it) without Makree or her dad was isolating. Her daily routine was to get ready for school alone, then come home alone. Karn, her older brother, was in school sports and had a job at the nearby cheese shop, right next door to the Celtic ruins by the old parish. To pass the hours, Apple would usually go to the library to study exotic places and the latest scientific discoveries. Now, with this article, and after her discovery and dreams, she was invigorated to have something specific to study: old alphabets and odd cats.

While the hieroglyphics on her stone seemed indeci-pherable, a pattern did emerge concerning a certain sort of cat with wings, like those in her dreams. She discovered news reports of flying cats spanning 200 years, from Sweden, to China, to the Americas. Even Henry David Thoreau wrote of seeing a winged cat in 1842. She knew of him because Uncle Aden's favorite book, *Civil Disobedience*, was always on the dashboard of his pick-up truck. Thoreau wrote of his flying cat incident, "This would have been the right kind of cat for me to keep, if I had kept any, for why should not a poet's cat be winged as well as his horse?" He reportedly saved the wings.

Now Apple was on to something! There was certainly no scarcity of flying cat evidence. "Well, I'll be a flyin' cat on a faerie's wing!" she whispered to herself in amazement as she compiled as many news reports of flying felines as she could find from Wikipedia and other internet sources:

(1868) India: A winged cat exhibited at Bombay Asiatic Society

(1894) England: A cat with duckling wings exhibited

(1897) *High Peak News*; Buxton, England: A tortoiseshell cat with pheasant-like wings reported shot

(1899) *Strand Magazine*, London: A winged kitten was killed when someone cut off his wings

(1926) *Time Magazine*; Oregon, U.S.A: "curious cat…winged and thrice the size of a house cat," reminding old settlers of Paul Bunyan's 'minktums' and 'tigermonks'

(1934) Oxford Zoo: A winged black-and-white cat

(1936) Scotland: A winged cat was found on a farm near Portpatrick, a white longhair with wings 6" (15 cm) long and 3" (7.5 cm) wide on its back

(1939) England: Sally, a black-and-white cat with a 24" wingspan was sold to the Blackpool Museum as part of the freak show

(1949) Sweden: A farmer shot a cat with a 2' wingspan out of the night sky

(1950) England: A tortoiseshell cat named Sandy with 'sizable' wings was exhibited at a carnival in Sutton, Nottinghamshire

(1950) Madrid: newspapers reported Juan Priego's Angora cat, Angolina, had grown a pair of large fluffy wings

(1970)   Connecticut: J. A. Sandford of Wallingford saw an orange-and-white, longhaired winged cat in a neighbor's garden

(1975)   *Manchester Evening News* published a photograph of a winged cat in the Banister Walton & Co. building, with 11"-long fluffy wings. Workmen reported seeing the cat fly

(1986)   Britain: A winged cat was reported in Anglesey

(1995)   England: Martin Millner spotted a fluffy winged tabby in Backbarrow

(1998)   Middlesex: A black-winged cat was found in Northwood

(2004)   *Komsomolskaya Pravda* newspaper in central Russia reported a winged ginger stray, named Vaska, being drowned by superstitious villagers as a messenger of Satan

(2007)   Shaanxi, China: Mrs. Feng presented a tom with two very long and furry wings

(2009)   China reported another winged cat, with the story appearing on MSNBC

(2011)   Russia: A winged koshka [cat] was seen in Tatarstan, whose coat of arms is a winged cat from the Bulgar totem

(2011)   Siberian air traffic controllers were "buzzed" by a UFO who spoke in a female cat-like language saying, "mioaw-mioaw." Radar showed the cat flying at 6,000 m.p.h. and "rapidly changing direction in the early morning sky"

Apple found flying cats dating back to Spain's Tartessian kingdom in 700 B.C.E.; in Mesoamerica's Belize in 300 B.C.E.; and on and on it went. This convinced even skeptical Apple that there very well could be such a thing as magical flying cats.

In between tall bookshelves in the library's mythology aisle, where no one ever was, Apple liked to sit cross-legged on the floor. Right out of the sky, an old worn volume fell in front of her with a thud, almost hitting her in the head. She looked up, thinking she might see an empty space where it came from. The shelved books remained tightly pressed together. Hesitating to pick it up, she tentatively fingered a few pages when a yellowed, torn (not cut) scrap fell out. She had just started to unfold it when the church bell rang in the distance, signaling she was late going home again. "Gobshite!" she reprimanded herself.

Apple tossed the old book and the paper into her backpack and dashed out without even checking it out. She wanted to beat her mum home from her job at the antique shop, so they could heat up the colcannon they made the night before for a rare family dinner together before Mum had to go to her other job.

While she was foostering through her backpack for her keys after she ran the two blocks home, Karn opened the front door of their flat. "What took you?" he asked. She had expected the customary smart-mouthed jab from him for being late, but then he hugged her hard, smashing her backpack painfully against her budding breasts. Over his shoulder, Apple spotted her mum on the sofa with Uncle Sean from Galway. She was dabbing a tissue to her swollen eyes.

Panicked, Apple broke away from Karn, "What's wrong, Mum?" Apple bristled as her mum motioned for a hug. "No, tell me what's wrong first!" she demanded.

Uncle Sean, her mother's oldest and least fun brother of all twelve of them, rose to his feet and began to ramble on about how Apple "would have opportunities…" and "you are often alone…blah, blah, blah." What he was saying did not compute, as anxiety overtook her.

Seeing her daughter's alarm, Mum patted the cushion next to her, "Come sit, mo ghrá. Let me explain sometin' to you." Apple plopped down, folded her arms like crossbones warning of a poisonous concoction one dare not touch, and stared at her feet as they bounced nervously off the edge of the sofa. Her teeth clenched while an avalanche of words tumbled off Mum's lips about doctors and her having medical treatment in Galway. "I won't be able to work for some time Apple, and that means money will be tight."

Then KAPOW, the bomb dropped: "You will have to go live with your father in America." She barely heard the rest of what her mother said about Karn staying with Uncle Sean.

It felt like the kind of explosion Uncle Aden described during a fiddle playin', where he lost his hearing for three days. Mum let loose unrestrained tears at her daughter's frozen face, and tried to embrace Apple to comfort her. Apple pushed her away. She couldn't breathe—really couldn't breathe. Lunging over the coffee table, she shoved her brother out of the way and bolted out the door with her backpack swinging over her shoulder.

Running directionless down the drizzle-slick Dublin streets, she remembered Makree telling her that "Rain is really faerie tears, sent to wash away sadness." For the first time in a long while, watery tears poured down Apple's red cheeks. Without even thinking, she arrived at the one place that always gave her comfort, the old parish, where she'd seen the odd cat on the day of the wee wild wind. Trying the main doors, she found them locked. Dashing around the building to the small adoration chapel, she was happy to find it still open.

A red-faced, tear-streaked Apple peeked in to see a couple of blue-haired folks, one wearing a scarf, silently praying. Pausing to calm her heavy breath, she quietly entered the warm silence, dipped her fingers in the marble bowl, made the sign of the cross, and knelt before the simple altar in the sparse room. It held no grand statues or icons, only a lone crucifix on a discolored wall and eight metal folding chairs.

As Apple moved to a seat in the back, she thought of how Jesus must have felt when no one came to save him. Apple did not notice Tak's oval-shaped, yellow eyes peering out from a wide crevice in the chapel wall, watching the young girl's every move.

CHAPTER 7

SIR THOMAS O'FERAL

The naming of cats is a difficult matter,
It isn't just one of your holiday games;
You may think at first I'm as mad as a hatter
When I tell you, a cat must have three different names.

—T.S. Elliot, "The Naming of Cats,"
Old Possum's Book of Practical Cats, 1939, England

Thom's hammock swung in the rafters as he jumped down to scratch off his claw shrouds on the shredded burlap stool. His thump woke Tak, who had drifted off to sleep at sunrise again, right at his desk.

"Top o' the morning, Tak," chirped Thom, the light making his orange stripes especially bright. Tak bristled. He often felt overwhelmed by Thom's constant gusto, especially right upon waking.

"Good day to you, Thom," he replied politely, but in a tenor suggesting he was not in a chatty mood and hoped to nip any jibber-jabber in the bud. With his usual swagger and lighthearted countenance, Thom threw on his tartan scarf and slipped out through the spit to regard the morning sun with his one good eye.

Tak had been up all night doing calculations about the prodding winds. With the recent activity, he determined that he would need help from all the Clouders to understand what they were saying. Since he could not fly, and he needed to send a classified message fast, he would create a zephyr to seek out his friend Polaris, the polar bear wind of the north, to assist in carrying his summons.

The Clouders consisted of six elected elders, all eight-life wise or better, and each assigned to a different continental region of the globe. They served as ambassadors and watchcats to keep Tak informed of what was going on in every part of the world.

Because relationships with some of the Clouders could be taxing, Tak was thankful he had Thom around. Thom was uncomplicated. Tak would never admit it, but he respected the lighthearted common cat more than many of his Clouders. Thom understood loyalty and obedience.

Unrestrained breeding by his Magnificat Scottish Rex father and Irish common cat mother left Thom a stray—without magic, name, or tartan. In spite of that, he lived slapdash and carefree, as if he had a hundred lives. Tak admired that, though he could never live that way himself.

Tak met Thom one fateful night while pursuing a thieving Feral queen. In her fleeing wake, Tak found Thom in the vicious fangs of three male Ferals, who had snatched the poor cat hostage while he lounged on the docks of the Irish Sea. They threatened to slice his throat with one quick gnash if Tak pursued their queen one paw further. In most instances, Tak would have bowled them over in his pursuit and not given the hostage cat a second thought, but when the scruffy Irish cat said. "Go after her. Never mind about me, you cannot be trustin' these thievin' Ferals," Tak was moved by Thom's courage and like-mindedness towards the wicked Ferals and lunged. The five cats snarled and fought like a pack of feeding wolves before Tak ripped the Feral's faces with his powerful swipes and tore their bellies open, leaving them as food for a pack of nearby, ravenous dock rats.

"I will take you to my lair," he said, dragging Thom home in his powerful, blood-frothing jaws, like a rabid mother carrying her kitten.

Severely wounded and barely conscious, Thom moaned, "T'anks old fella," just before he passed out cold. Tak treated Thom with Egyptian medicine. It was, after all, his specialty.

It was touch and go, and fearing Thom may not make it, Tak decided he deserved honor for his bravery against the Ferals before he died. Inside the parish, behind the holy statue of Heaven's Archer Queen, Tak held a solemn commissioning in a church alcove, already lit with candles and adorned with flowers. "In the name of Silvestria, our feline mother, and in the shadow of the Archer Queen, I hereby dub you Sir Thomas O'Feral." Then he laid his sword next to him.

Thom gained the 'Sir' for bravery, the customary 'O' as an Irish grandson, and a surname to reflect the Feral blood he spilled in the fight. Miraculously, instead of a burial in the Viking tombs below the parish, Thom was marred, but recovered.

In gratitude, the now one-eared, half-sighted Thom devoted his life to Tak. "Ah, devotion, a quality rarely seen in cats or Archers," Tak sighed as he watched Thom stretch and yawn outside in the afternoon sun. Though the imperious Tak often responded to Thom's foolery with superciliousness, he thoroughly enjoyed his humor and clever Irish wit. Chatty as a Siamese, Thom added color to Littern Tak's grey world.

However much Thom respected Tak, he feared him doubly. After all, he had witnessed what Tak was capable of firsthand. Unpredictable and territorial, Thom found it difficult to gauge what may set Tak off, or when the Littern might tolerate playfulness. In spite of Tak's volatility, Thom often laughed covertly from his perch in the rafters when he observed Tak puffing up his chest and pulling tight his sagging skin in order to appear younger as he reviewed himself in the old framed mirror that leaned against the wall. All the while, Thom anxiously anticipated the moment Tak might shape-shift again, changing into his half-Archer Bastet form, with mountainous rippling muscles emitting joules as spectrums of light. Thom knew Tak did not have many transformations left in him, and he dreaded the day when his friend would set out on the Crystal Sea without him.

Tak also had lingering concerns about Thom's health since the attack, especially about the cross of blood from Feral to cat. Mewing cats like Thom had been known to degenerate into ferocious Ferals after their blood was mixed. Thom's wounds were deep, and if the Feral blood was queen blood, one could verily imagine what might happen. Only time would tell. Tak pushed it to the back of his mind. If a dark turn in Thom were to occur, he dreaded what he would have to do to his mate.

Tak stuck his nose out the spit and meowed to Thom, still sunning himself. "I must consult the Clouders."

Thom was taken aback. This was the first time Tak had mentioned the Clouders to him directly. He had overheard conversations between Tak and other Magnificats, like former Clouder Ming Fang or Tak's godkitten, Felene, but Thom always pretended to know nothing, "What you be sayin'—Clouders?" Thom played dumb.

"I need to get a pulse on the winds of the world," Tak declared. "Something big must be going on somewhere that is causing these winds to hammer at my door." Rather than responding, Thom busied himself with the sun-soaked rocks that he had begun to roll into the lair to provide warmth for the chilly night ahead. He was adept at avoiding Magnificat matters, and liked it that way. He and Tak did bat ideas around like cat toys at times, but for the most part, Thom wisely avoided Littern business.

Impatiently, Tak hissed, "You and I have come too far for you to pull this tomfoolery now, mate. Like it or not, your help is needed to send a Clouder message."

Thom set down the warm rocks, hopped in through the spit to join Tak, and crouched in submission. He saw in Tak an apprehension he had not witnessed before, and a weariness. "Why do you keep on like this Tak? I'd be on tropical oilands instead of stuck here in this old choich, if I were you."

Tak paced upright, with his forepaws folded behind his back and his tail down, "I took a job, Thomas, and that job is here." (He rarely called Thom, 'Thomas.') "Magnificat Litterns have always been stationed in Ireland, where Mother Nature has little wrath, so we can get the job done with few distractions: no earthquakes, hurricanes, rarely a blizzard, no tidal waves, nor the like. Litterns can focus on their work instead of heading off calamities. There are not even any snakes here, since St. Patrick drove them out," Tak laughed. "There is not such a land as Ireland in all the earth, Thom. Here, even Archers respect magical kingdoms—faeries, trees, and such."

"Well Tak, I never thought of it that way, but right you are, 'tis bewitching, this Ireland."

As night fell, the unusual winds kicked up dust bombs outside, which made ramblin' Thom stay inside for a change. Tak worked on coordinates for Polaris, the great bear wind of the north, until he could no longer stay awake. Thom snagged the nearby rat-skin quilt to cover his snoozing friend. As he did so, the leaf Tak had brought in after the sheegee wind fell to the ground. Stooping to sniff and investigate it, Thom noticed the first few letters, written in Ogham tree language. Although Thom was a common cat, and common cats did not have the skills of Magnificats, Ogham was a language all Irish cats knew. They never lost their ability to communicate with trees. When he saw the tiny willow and ash leaves imprinted on the larger leaf, his fur stood on end. They spelled out: "Warning!"

CHAPTER 8

EMPRESS MING FANG

Nothing in the Universe can travel at the speed of light,
they say, forgetful of the shadow's speed.

—Howard Nemerov, "The First Day," 1977, New York, U.S.A.

Happy daydreams embraced Thomas O'Feral as he watched sunlit rainbows dance on the wall from the stained glass overhead. In his usual way, Tak had over-explained how colors emanating from the crystal prisms had healing properties, based on the work of Sir Isaac Newton and the renowned Magnificat, Spitface. His lectures bored Thom and took the fun out of just making shadow puppets with his paws that chased the colors across the ceiling, but they did introduce him to the 'splendid and brilliant Spitface.'

Thom had become fascinated by his perception of this particular Magnificat. He admired her like a young sailor would a pin-up girl, and playfully imagined the moving rainbows on his wall as her dancing with him in Sir Isaac's study, where the design for the first cat-sized door flap, the 'spit,' had been drawn just for her. That spit had saved Thom's tail on more than one occasion. The invention changed his life and gave him real independence.

Archer doors were no friend to cats of any sort, with slick round knobs that no claw could easily grasp.

Gradually, an overpowering and bittersweet aroma made Thom's back fur twitch. He leapt up to the stained glass octagon ledge above his hammock to peek out of the small chip, hoping it was not who he feared. "Uh oh, it'd be the empress," he warned. There she was, waddling right towards his freedom-launching spit, the plump and disheveled Magnificat—her majesty, the imperial empress and former Clouder, Ming Fang.

"She's full o' wind oilright," he chuckled as he watched her trying to hold on to her fan in the blustery weather. She was up on her two back legs, sashaying her way towards the lair, carrying an oat-colored scroll, tied with a crimson thread. She never brought good news, as far as Thom was concerned. He pretended he was not home, keeping very, very still.

"Open the spit, you fool!" she demanded, whipping her tail back and forth impatiently. Thom stayed quiet, hoping Tak would break away from his work and let her in. "Thomas, I saw you laughing at me, and if you expect me to wait out here, you had better make another plan."

Thom heaved a defeated sigh. "How does she be knowin' these t'ings?" he wondered aloud, and then zigzagged down from the window to the bookshelf, to the stool, to the spit, where he held the flap up as she squeezed her round body through the narrow entry. Her noisy Siamese entourage snickered as they fussed over the bamboo litter in which they carted her, until she waved her fan three times out of the spit with her pudgy paw. The litter and Siamese attendants disappeared.

Ming Fang's white feathered fan was an auspicious possession. Like Tak's pipe, it shielded her flying litter from Archer view, since she was too large to fly herself anymore. The fan came from Magnificat Ming, an alchemist who worked with the chubby Archer, Zhongli-Quan, who became one of the famous eight immortals after his experimental batch of the 'Elixir of Life' exploded. That recipe, along with all of the others listed on the scroll she carried, would go into the Magnificat *Book of Secrets* that Tak wanted to complete in time for the upcoming centennial summit. Ming Fang was proud she shared her mentor's plump and cheery characteristics, and his gifts in alchemy.

"To what do we owe this honor, Empress?" Tak asked jovially, as he rose from his desk chair to his four paws, hiding the pain in his stiff haunches.

"I came to see my warrior friend Tak, you old tomcat," she teased while plucking an extra long chin whisker and sizing up Tak's appearance. "And what is this I see instead, a stiff old sack of fur? I would be eternally young if I had your abilities at skin-walking." As she chuckled, only half-kidding, a rat scurried across the floor and into a hole in the wall. In earlier days, Tak would have dispatched that rat in a flash. Ming Fang noticed and remarked sympathetically, "Ah, those pesky rats would eat everything if not for we cats. Oh, the plagues they have caused this world. If only Archers knew what Magnificats have done for them, we would already be living among them as counterparts."

"Some do," Tak replied with a knowing smile.

Once a fierce sleek avenger, Ming Fang was far too fat now. Yet, when she heard snideness about her weight, she was flattered. To her, size indicated power and lineage. Of true Dragon Li ancestry, she carried the traditional dark head stripes and smile dots around the mouth. Along with being a former Clouder, Ming Fang carried the title of Grandmistress of the Chinese Medicine Scrolls. She was quite fond of titles.

"Now seriously, Tak, I am here on an urgent matter with no time for cat-chat," she said, while simultaneously unrolling the packet of scrolls. Pulling out the small one on top, she read, "Honorable Ming Fang, I lament that the guardian Magnificat Stone has been taken by a red-furred Archer child."

Tak shuddered at the words. His fur stood on end. He swore he could hear the wind outside laugh because he had not known. Instead of reacting, Tak hissed suspiciously, "Who sent you this scroll, Ming Fang?" His tone relaxed her defenses and she answered without thinking.

"Magnificat Miz, the Mayan dreamer in Mezo-America."

Tak lit with ire. He was incensed that a younger Magnificat should have important knowledge before him. And not even a Clouder! Ming Fang could sense this and quickly moved a step or two away, then snapped back. "It is not uncommon for Miz to contact me Tak. You forget, I was a much beloved Clouder."

"How did she learn of this before the rest of us?" demanded Tak, slamming his paw on old Terence again.

Ming Fang jumped back with a start and immediately backed down. Her voice softened in pacification. "From her dreams, Tak. They have become stronger since the Archers uncovered the Mayan temple carvings."

Tak began pacing.

"Now don't get all worked up. You know I told you all about the sculpted wall of the Triad of Cats, the ones with fire in their eyes and expansive wings. Remember, it was discovered near her village in Belize?" Tak had a blank expression. "Well anyway," she continued, "those same dreams told her of a red-furred Archer holding the Magnificat Stone. She just…"

"No, Ming Fang, I was not informed of the Triad of Cats or the missing Magnificat Stone!" Tak cut her off and leaned further in at her, with saliva dripping off his fangs onto her feather fan.

Min Fang ignored the dribble. "Well, I know for certain that Miz had informed the Americas' Clouder, Moosa, because she told me they are both of the same mind about earth as a mother, and all that nonsense that Magnificats of the earthy sort like to…"

"Stop talking!" Tak butted in again. Ming Fang's incessant chatter was giving him a striking headache. "What hubris!" Tak wondered if Moosa really could sink to this new low, intentionally withholding information to embarrass him. "This act will not go unchecked," he mumbled.

Ming Fang started to retort, "I told…"

Thom caught her eye with a long claw pushed to his pursed

lips, "Shhh."

Tak insisted, "You told who what?"

"I told Thom to tell you too, Tak. It was the day before the..."

Tak threw a stern look at Thom, who ducked. "Ming Fang, you know he is not a Magnificat. That is like giving a Magnifikitten one of your Chinese medicine recipes."

Ming Fang and Thom shared a knowing glance. Tak had obviously forgotten that they had both told him of Miz's dreaming and of the Triad of Cats in Amazonia. But she steered the topic artfully, "Anyway, to add to Miz's dreaming, Archers reported finding an empty Egyptian cat sarcophagus," she garbled on without taking a breath.

Tak hissed, his fur rising, this time all along his spine to the end of his tail. "So what you are telling me is that a Magnificat Stone could be in the hands of an Archer child? Gads, Ming Fang!"

Finally getting pushed too far, and puffing up to match his indignation, Ming Fang snarled, "The Archers in Egypt think only a cat relic was taken, so calm down. No one has any idea a child may have anything important. But," she continued on with the second part of the disaster as if she were telling him it was time for dinner, "you know that old devil wind Ephippas was being held down by that stone, and, well, he may have been released and taken to the skies."

All at once, the strange wind, the scents, the memories, everything made sense to Tak. He was alarmed, but somehow relieved. At least now he knew what all this wind haunting was about. The release of the demon wind would be devastating to the environment, but the discovery of the stone could have even worse consequences. "If the Magnificat Stone's code were to be broken, like the Egyptian code was after the Archer discovery at Rasheda, oh my!" Tak put his paw to his brow and massaged his aching forehead. "If Archers decipher the stone and gain nine-life powers, they will create hell on earth. No one would be safe from their surge for ultimate control." Tak paced and his paws trembled. He quickly clasped them behind his back, hoping Ming Fang would not notice. "There is no time to lose," he decreed.

Thom sprang to alert and dashed up the wall to his hammock when a course of electricity and booming thunder rocked the lair. The flash revealed Tak's righteous blaze. He was transforming! Thom peeked out from between his paws as Tak's body filled with lavender light and his fur lifted from the static that sucked it horizontal, so strong it even pulled away loose tufts. Thom extended his claws for stability as his hammock swung wildly out of control. Ming Fang shrank back into a corner for shelter, wishing she had held her tongue. The room became electric, creating its own cosmic environment. Static continued to pull at their fur and whiskers, causing blue sparks.

A wind swirled around Tak, sweeping up anything not held down, as Ming Fang dug her long claws as deeply as she could into the floor. Her jewelry pulled parallel, outstretched towards Tak as if he were a magnet. The intensity held steady for a good three minutes, as Thom gripped the rafter overhead for dear life. Ming Fang's claws scraped deep ridges into the floorboards. Then, in an instant, all went still. Her jewelry fell, and objects previously swept up by the wind dropped flatly. Ming Fang plunged off the wall with a plunk, smacking her nose on the floor. "Yeow!" Thom clutched his hammock while it swung to stillness.

Before them stood a new Tak, morphed into his Bastet half-Archer form, in all his beauty and power. His yellow eyes burned red like the fresh blood of a young rat, as remaining sweat dripped down onto his furless skin. Tak was no longer the old tired cat. He looked up at Thom and spoke in a deep, almost alien-sounding voice, "It's time. We will need extra power sooner than anticipated. The Clouders need to be here—yesterday!"

Tak snagged Thom like a plaything and flung him over his now broad shoulders. Moving a large, square floorboard, they descended into the catacombs towards the River Liffey, winding through the underground route where Vikings once held fiendish ceremonies, and Catholics reclaimed their treasures from churches commandeered by the Protestants.

The catacombs led to the cat towers. Archers never recognized that their high-voltage boom towers resembled cats seated on hind legs, ears alert. In general, they missed most magic right in front of their eyes, due to their busyness in acquiring this or that. But then again, being born without a stitch of fur could cause insecurities and lead to hoarding behaviors, Tak had always believed, sympathetically.

Tak and Thom traveled underground below the city. They wound through the gruesome, cold corridors until finally reaching a metal grate near the outside of the fenced-in high voltage facility. Summoning her Siamese helpers with a wave of her fan, Ming Fang followed by air.

The sun was setting and the towers hummed as they arrived, causing an immediate rise in Thom's fur and making him purr uncontrollably. He could not help it. Tak selected the tower with the tallest ears and widest shoulders. There was no fanfare. Even the wind stopped, watching and waiting to see what Bastet Tak might do.

Once the Siamese dropped off Ming Fang, they made haste away to a safe distance, while she, Tak, and Thom purred together to join the electrical song and raise the frequency of the towers. They could even feel it in their teeth. "Purr, Thom, purr like you will die if you don't," demanded Tak.

"Aye Tak," Thom said in obedience, thrilled to experience something a common cat rarely had—Magnificat magic. Electrical winds began to rip around them.

"Duck Thom," warned Tak. Thom did, and then closed his eyes tight to avoid the intense light burning in, and through, Tak, which began to overtake the dark, isolated site. Tak drew his ancient metal wand, a gift from Celeste's father, a relic from a Fourth Dynasty pharaoh's tomb.

Silhouetted against the darkening sky, Tak's large body

knelt and he raised the wand. Its tip lit with a pink glow. "Tak, your necklace is burning you," Thom yelled as he watched the ankh singe the bare skin on Tak's chest from the radiant heat.

"No time for that now Thom, brace me! The heat and the wind will take us both down if we don't stand firm together."

Against the current, Thom clawed his way to Tak's side, steadying his kneeling body from behind. "I gotcha me friend, I gotcha," Thom hollered loudly, to be heard above the buzzing. Leaning into the current together, they purred harder, raising the vibration until it reached the necessary voltage frequency.

Raising the wand higher, Tak yelled, "*Ventis exsuscito!*" He was creating a wind to serve as his emissary to carry the message, first to Polaris, and then to the Clouders. The increasing pressure tossed Ming Fang aside. THUD—she tumbled like a kicked tin can, until pinned against a nearby chain-link fence.

Keeping their paws aligned together on the wand so Thom would not become a conductor and be killed, blue waves of electricity rippled rhythmically across both Tak and Thom's bodies, up and down and back and forth, narrowing into a snakelike arc of light that zapped the tip of the iron wand and shot rocket-like up the metal tower to meet the heavy lines with a loud, "bwee-pop" sound.

"Get off me now, Thom!" Tak yelled as he shoved Thom away. "The power is coming." The arcing beams danced between the wand and the tower until they funneled into one pinpoint shaft of crimson light at the tip of his wand.

Abruptly, the wind spun all around them, but where they stood was untouched. "We are in the eye of the electrical storm Thom, anything can happen here." It was silent and still. Even gravity did not exist, so they bobbed, weightless. Around them, sheets of gold radiated off the wires, floating down and hovering. Using the wand like a stylus, Tak inscribed his command to the Clouders in the air, letter by letter: "Clouders of the Great Lands: Arrant winds are stirring. Come at once. Signed, Littern Tak."

As soon as he finished, the arc of light dissolved to a fluorescent falling mist, and Tak's newly created wind emissary, Zephyr, took his order and rushed the fiery words away to Polaris in the far north. "Watch out Tak," Thom howled, as wires snapped when the calm center of the storm collapsed upon the two wind masters, tossing Tak to the ground beside Thom.

Then, in an instant, the cat tower crackled and all of Dublin went black. Transformers popped and sparked, one after another, down street after street. In the distance, emergency sirens erupted. "Phew," Tak wiped the sweat from his brow and nodded to Thom, "Respect, Sir Thomas."

Thom beamed, "A wee bit shell-shocked, but I have never had so much fun in all my life."

Tak stood and turned to bow his head in gratitude to the powerful tower. Thom mimicked him and bowed, though not sure why. When he looked up, Tak was his old self, fully a cat again. As Tak set down his wand, unexpected sparks flew that sent him tumbling. "Hang on Tak, I'll be getting you,'" Thom howled, laughing as he grabbed the wand in his teeth and chased the plummeting Littern down the old power-line road. Tak landed in a field, sitting open legged with a half-dazed expression and a dandelion stuck in his ear.

"Aye, Tak, you o'right, old fella?" Thom snorted, unable to control his eye-watering laughter.

"Yes, yes, a few tumbles aren't so bad if you know how to roll with them," Tak chuckled as he haphazardly got up on all fours. The two limped slowly home.

"Help me up, you motley crew," whined Ming Fang to her Siamese, as she unpinned herself from the fence. Snickering, the Siamese helped extricate her. "Shut up, you mangy mutts," she groaned, but even she could no longer resist laughing as the skinny troop retrieved each of her two-inch wads of fur from the fence. "Never leave your fur behind," she always taught, "for fear of witches stealing your essence, making you a part of their spells."

With the Zephyr wind on its way, Tak, Thom, and Ming

Fang reunited at the parish for a well-deserved rest. Thom retired to his hammock while the two Magnificats spoke quietly. "My next stop is to see Felene and to begin processing the Chinese medicine scrolls for the *Book of Secrets*." When Thom heard Ming Fang saying she was on her way to visit Felene, he frowned. He knew every time someone made mention of Felene (or her mother, Mariah), Tak sank into a moody state for several days.

Tak had not seen or heard from Felene for some time. Although he was happy his godkitten was an independent sort of cat, sometimes, especially on dark, foggy nights, he wished he had not taught her so well to fend for herself. It would be nice if she needed him on occasion, or even thought that he might need her, once in a while.

Thom tucked his face under his paw in an effort to re-capture the night's thrilling magic. "I am the luckiest cat alive, Spitface, wherever you are," he said aloud to his idol. By sunup, Thom's memory of the powerful Bastet faded, as Tak's more ordinary snoring began. Together, he and Ming Fang formed a duet of "zzzs" as Thom tossed and turned, trying to invoke some soothing prism images to help put him back to sleep.

Awake by noon, Tak sat sullenly by the hearth, with Mariah's warm rat quilt wrapped around his shoulders, puffing on his pipe. Tak never pulled out the old quilt unless he was di-gressing to, and wallowing in, a darker part of himself. As Thom had feared, Tak's melancholy was setting in.

Murmuring to himself in a deep mimicking voice, Thom counted on his claws, "Number one: Tak will start out with, 'Yes, I have Thom for company, but he is not a Magnificat, and there are certain things he just does not understand.' Number two: 'I will never see my loved ones again,' and three: 'I am too old to finish my work as Littern.'" This was how it always went when Tak got depressed. As Tak wrapped Mariah's blanket more tightly around himself, Thom dared not move. "He'll likely rip my head off, just because," so he feigned sleep.

Sunset found Tak still sitting in the same spot. Centering

sandalwood smoke wiggled through the crevices from the evening's mass. The aroma revived Tak and reminded him he had missed his three-o'clock tea. He set the water to heat on the back of the alter, bellyaching, just as Thom predicted, "Why does it matter? Thom does not really understand the magic of tea. Oh, how could he, the mewing cat that he is." Thom's ears perked. "Loneliness is the guest of leadership," Tak opined as he put in the teabag. Then he looked at Terence, filled with unfinished projects, "I will never be able to finish all this work," he whimpered as he poured the steeped tea into his blue cup.

Rising with a downward cat-stretch, Tak casually passed the jagged mirror and, catching a glimpse, hardly recognized himself. He had to stop for a moment, and sit. "Look at my golden coat, now peppered with gray. I could swear my legs are shorter, and I'm certain my neck is. My word," he moaned as he looked over his shoulder, "I believe my tail used to be straight." With thinning fur no barrier to the hard floor, he shifted his hips to prevent the cold air from penetrating his bones. Shaking his head at the thought of the work ahead, he hissed dispiritedly, "Even nine lives are not enough."

Thom was counting each of the three steps of melancholy as they occurred, just waiting for a moment to escape.

Outside, the yappy Siamese packed for Ming Fang's departure. She was primping to leave when she saw Tak staring at himself in the only mirror. She nudged him over with her round hips to smooth on some lipstick, and Thom took that opportunity to run outside for fresh air. He watched in awe from up in the faerie tree as Ming Fang, barely able to exit through the spit, finally burst out with a grunt. She gestured to the Siamese, waved her fan, and they were gone. Thom wisely, stayed out of sight.

CHAPTER 9

FETCHING CLOUDER MOOSA

Yonder sky
that has wept tears of compassion
changeless and eternal,
may change.
Today is fair.

—Chief Seattle, Nez Perce Treaty Oration, 1854, Northwest, U.S.A.

Tak's message had flown off Ireland's western coast, stirring midair ice glints into diamond dust over Iceland's brown waterfalls and Greenland's sea. It splashed right onto Greenland's subzero desert, where a local, glacial 'Coho' wind helped it up and over the 'top of the world' mountain. The secret message reached the Brobdingnagian paw of the polar bear wind, shattering the purplish-green aurora into shards and cracking open the ether world; the portal that allowed Magnificats, angels, and even some Archers, to enter other realms. Most only dared to do so in their dreams.

Polaris took the message from Tak's Zephyr and barreled south over Kanata towards Clouder Moosa, spinning a herd of flying reindeer in his wake. Trailing Magnificats snagged the fractured aurora's medicinal light particles to take to Magnificat Stubbs in Alaxsxaq, where the feline mayor was recovering from a vicious dog attack. Polaris' wind brought early winter to a swaggering wolf pack, treading single file across the rocky tundra below, and they howled in protest: "We have not prepared our dens yet." The sudden frost over the steep hillsides angered bears for the same reason. Polaris was unmoved. His cold wind pressed southward over Turtle Island's elk-filled, brown grass prairies, to the red-earthed Land of the Sun, where condors with eleven-foot wingspans made passage over the aqua waters of the regal Grand Canyon. Finally, Polaris settled at the top of the aspen and pine covered San Francisco Peaks, the seat of Moosa, Clouder over the 56 nations of the Americas. The sudden wind caused the white underside of the aspen leaves to dance like butterflies.

Clouder Moosa sat cross-legged on his javalina-skin rug, eating a tasty grey quail. "Ah, Polaris," growled Moosa, "did you really think you could surprise me?" The ancestors had been visiting his dreams, warning him, and he had been having visions of the promised Tiponi child. The mountain huk had spoken to him of an Archer unearthing. "Even rats know what is buried should remain buried," Moosa complained.

Moosa's lair was located deep inside the tree-covered mountain that housed the Hopi Stone Tablets, which were under the protection of the Kachina dancers and bringers of storms, who saved Archers and Magnificats alike from the first world destructions by leading them underground and teaching them to sprout beans for food. Juxtaposed to Moosa's mountain, through the center of the earth, was Mt. Meru, the lair of Clouder Billi. That mountain was sacred to one-fifth of Archerkind.

Moosa was unimpressed with any message from Tak, who, to him, was an unworthy Littern. He made no bones about this. "Tak has no ability to fly! He jeopardized dear Mariah, uses his position for personal benefit, and lives with a common cat in the belly of an old church with Archer comforts," he chided.

Nearly the size of a raccoon, with finger-like paw dexterity, Moosa was a true Maine Coon cat. Being native to the Micmac lands in the cold northeast, his naturally weatherproof fur and thick ear tufts made him a good candidate for transfer to this two-mile-high mountain home. With an extra-deep scruff, laced with eagle feathers about his neck, he had a chiefly look.

The entry to Moosa's lair was through a post-volcanic cavern that snaked behind a forgotten, four-storied, ancient cliff dwelling; the hand-tied ladders leading from level to level pillaged by Archers long ago. There was also a secret Ant kingdom entry. If not for Moosa's floating clavicles, the broad-chested coon cat could never have squeezed through that narrow entrance.

A fallen and petrified tree created a bridge over a blackened ravine to the opening of his den. At one time, that chasm had been alive with orange and blue lava bubbling 1,000 feet below. Currently, only soot-charred rock remained, pocked by boulders tossed upward during Humphrey's last volcanic eruption.

Painted over the doorway of his lair was the Cherokee Morning Prayer, "Wen de ya ho [Our spirits/hearts are strong]." Moosa sang it faithfully each morning when he stepped outside to greet the new day and the Great Spirit. His bed was on an overhang of stonework. A 'dream catcher' dangled above, insuring only true dreams, so that the coyote trickster could not fool him, essential for a talented dreamer like Moosa.

In the far corner, carved into a yellow rock, were the words of the Hopi *Fifth World Prophesy*, warning of the next disaster to befall mother earth. "There have been destructions of the first three worlds, one by sinking, one by freezing, and one by flooding. The fourth world's destruction shall be by ashes, if peace and balance are not preserved." Moosa aimed to lead Magnificats with this knowledge one day, to ensure peace.

After his meal, just as he had decided to ignore Tak and take a catnap, Polaris poured into his lair with fury and a stench of burnt fur, making his eyes narrow and stomach turn. It forced him to the surface, where Tak's message appeared in the sky, "Clouders of the Great Lands: Arrant winds are stirring. Come at once. Signed, Littern Tak."

Moosa grabbed his cottonwood drum, intending to send a

message back to Tak that he had no interest in a meeting, but a cold wind slapped his muzzle with a fresh pine scent that filled him with the irresistible urge to fly. He had never been able to refuse the call of the wind, even as a Magnifikitten.

He drummed: one, two...three; one, two...three. The coming storm's distant thunder harmonized with the slow steady beat, and reverberated into his broad chest and down through his paws. His heartbeat synchronized to the pounding. Cumulus clouds gathered like white buffalo stampeding, as monsoons formed along the Mogollon rim. They were heading his way.

"I hope my efforts are appreciated this time," he grumbled, as he tied the Sinagua medicine bag made of prairie dog skin around his waist. It held sage sticks, along with antelope hoof powder, copper pigment, feathers, plant roots, corn pollen, and a turtle-shell rattle. It was a rare thing to have, since the Sinagua Archers mysteriously disappeared before the last Millennial Magnificat Summit. He would give Tak a gift of sage. Gifts to the Littern were customary.

"Caw, caw, caw," called the ravens clustered among the bending aspens saying, "Fly, fly, fly." In surrender, he set down the drum, raised his forepaws, and created lightning that sparked fires in the dry forests below, sending up smoke in orchestrated puffs spelling "alsink," his homeland's word for fly. His round eyes squinted into determined slits as the wind forced back his ears and fur, exposing chiseled features usually masked by his thick coat, displaying his powerful fangs, squared jaw, and high cheekbones. The eagle feathers braided around his neck whipped his face.

Overlooking the Painted Desert, Moosa began a weighty-pawed dance to the rhythm of the distant thunder until it pulsated through his dense fur, awakening his sleeping wings. In an instant, he took flight. Sister ravens followed until he reached a safe altitude, flying towards Turtle Island's Great Lakes, over Nova Scotia, around the southern tip of Greenland, to Ireland, and Tak.

CHAPTER 10

KRYSTAL KAY KENNER

For I'se still goin', honey,
I'se still climbin',
And life for me ain't been no crystal stair.

—Langston Hughes, "Mother to Son," 1922, Missouri, U.S.A.

As Polaris continued south toward Clouder Rose in Antarctica, the storms set off by Moosa's dance brought drenching rain to the humble home of Krystal Kay Kenner. She was named Krystal by her mother, not because of her frosty eyes or her vanilla hair, but after the toxic substance her mother constantly craved.

Intermittent lightning strobes filtered through tattered mini-blinds in Krystal's bedroom, which she shared with her little brother LB, tinting the sleeping twelve-year-old's blonde hair purple with each flash. Her family's run-down apartment in Phoenix was also home to her troubled mother, who wrestled with demons she could not tame. Torrential sheets of rain battered the window. The crack of heart-pounding thunder rumbled heaven into her room, a heaven that always seemed to be just out of her reach.

"LB!" Krystal screamed as she was jarred awake from the hypnotic sleep that only children know. She groped in the darkness for him. "Thank God," she said, as she felt his warm body, still sound asleep.

Hopping up to flip on the light switch, the power was out, so she ran to tell her mother, but, as was often the case, the fold-out couch was unopened and empty. Krystal felt her way in the dark along the wall to the hall closet, where she fumbled through the shelves for the flashlight, only to find the batteries were dead. Intermittent lightning provided momentary clear-sightedness. It allowed her to grab a kitchen pan to place under the drip, drip, drip from the leak above the window next to their blow-up mattress on the bedroom floor.

Looking through gaps of missing blinds, Krystal watched lightning charges compete with the red and blue police car lights in the street below. Several emergency vehicles created a haze of steam in the pouring rain. Police visiting her neighborhood was as normal as the scent of desert chaparral. The officers always drew folks out. Residents wanted to know why they were there— again. In fact, in Krystal's neighborhood, this was how neighbors usually met.

Looking out at the gathering crowd, she laughed, "Oh, Ms. Coleman, you are a sketch," just as a sudden wind gust flipped umbrellas and blew off an officer's hat, sending him chasing after it, leaving Ms. Coleman pointing her finger in a lecturing manner. Ms. Coleman insisted on being called "Ms. Coleman," not Miss Coleman or Mrs. Coleman, but Mzz. Coleman. She was a bear-hugging woman that sang all the time and had skin the color of caramel candy, just like LB's. Her hair always seemed to be in the making, in curlers or under scarves.

Krystal often saw magic in her bleak world. Police car lights, reflecting on glass-littered asphalt, became a ruby and sapphire path that led to a palace, complete with a handsome prince. The low, dark clouds were an elevator straight to Jupiter, where she was the queen. Kindly thunder was a muffler for the hunger growling in her belly.

BOOM-CRACK! Another bang shuddered in Krystal's

chest and catapulted LB straight into her arms. "Kwissy," he cried, pressing into her and covering his ears.

She hugged him and tried to sidetrack his fear. "Look LB, there is nothing to be afraid of. See Ms. Coleman down there?" LB peeked out from between his fingers and began to laugh, as a big, pink-headed woman was still pointing a parenting finger at a young officer, who hung his head in regret. The distraction worked. BAM!, went another thunder clap. "Don't worry LB, its just clouds kissing." Then she showed him her two fists banging together. "Clouds love to kiss," she chuckled. So did LB.

That last thunder smack loosed a torrent of grape-sized hail, causing the people assembled below to scatter. Ms. Coleman's retro, pink hair curlers rose like alien antennas in the scurrying crowd. Steam came out of her mouth and her arms signaled orders, as she spouted off to the police officers, whom she saw as making things worse. A missing piece of glass in the corner of their window allowed the two children to hear the banter, but also let in sprays of tar-tinged water, which was pouring off the roof. They giggled watching Ms. Coleman's foam rollers bob up and down, until even she finally raced for cover.

Ms. Coleman was a towering, Rubenesque woman. With her dated, faux leopard fur slippers and lime-green, too-small-around-the-middle bathrobe, she looked like a cross between a cartoon character and a giant insect. The two children rolled back onto their bed in laughter.

Larger than life, Ms. Coleman was the only stable force in the children's lives. Much more than a nice neighbor lady who informally babysat, she had been a professional foster parent for over a decade, since a work injury had caused her to lose her job as a nurse. "I know all about babies," she would tell Krystal. "I helped to deliver hundreds of babes." In the past 15 years, the soft, squishy woman had cared for more than 60 children as a foster mother. The State would not let her adopt any of them because she had been almost 50 years old when she started—too old they said.

Now in her mid-60's, she would say she was "just learnin'" how to be a decent parent. If she could have, Ms. Coleman "would have kept 'em all," she told Krystal.

Each one of their pictures was on top of the rickety buffet in her over-filled living room. Every so often, one or another of the kids she had cared for, now an adult, would stop in to say hello. "You are so lucky to have Ms. Coleman," they would tell LB and Krystal.

After she hurt her back, foster parenting was a way she could afford to live on her own. That was when she had a nice big house, before the city government took it to build the metro line. "Sometimes ya gotta look at the bigger picture, Kryssy," she would say, not bitter about the loss at all. Krystal wondered how many people like Ms. Coleman were rendered homeless because of that train through town.

Krystal and LB watched the scene outside until the police cars pulled away. Then she set LB down and covered him before peering back out the window until even the orange lights of the tow truck faded into the distance. LB pulled his "blankey" up over his curl-framed face to deflect lingering lightning sparks. His long locks often led people to think he was a girl. Even at only two, this made him furious. Squeezing her beanie baby, a white-and-gold stuffed unicorn that she was really too old for, Krystal positioned it gently beside LB. She looked forward to Ms. Coleman making a special mini-pancake for her Uni in the morning. She never let LB know she was scared.

"I was born in the Bible Belt," Ms. Coleman would proudly say, which meant Alabama to her. If she knew their mom did not come home, Ms. Coleman would let them sleep over. They would make a big bed out of couch pillows on the floor while she told stories of Alabama and Africa.

One story of Alabama that Krystal requested repeatedly was about an old courthouse where an innocent man was hung from a tree for a crime he did not commit. "At the moment of his hangin', lightnin' struck that courthouse window, and forever marked his face in it, like an old camera glass plate, as if God had sent his judgment for all to see. No matter how many times folks done changed that glass, his face stayed etched in it. Hand to God, true as I am sittin' right here," she declared, pointing her long knotty finger at the chair in which she was seated.

Ms. Coleman often told about her great-great-grand-mother, her Bibi, a famous medicine woman taken by force to America. "Now listen here children, once the healin' women were taken, a curse took over the land, bringing drought and disease that remains to this very day. My Bibi came from Africa in chains, and got her chil'ins ripped right from her arms." Krystal understood how that felt. Social workers had ripped LB from her arms before. She was always relieved when Ms. Coleman got to the part of the story where a kindly farmer saved her Bibi. "He and his missus helped her find her chil'ins, and they sang for three days, thankin' the Lord Jesus." Then Ms. Coleman would say, "See youngins, that's why you never give up hopin'. No matter what it looks like. No matter what anyone says to you. You never give up hopin'. Ya hear me?"

"Yes," the children would nod, or she would get very excited, even mad.

"Sometimes, I wake up and smell the African elephants on the grass," she told them. "Even though I ain't never been there before, I swear I can taste the land." Krystal swore she could taste it too when Ms. Colman told about it. The woman often sang old spirituals, the code songs of her plantation ancestors, until the children drifted into a peaceful sleep.

Ms. Coleman would pull out her black, licorice bead neck-lace and fiddle with it like a rosary when she told Bibi stories. Those beads were a tie to her Bibi. Ms. Coleman had always hoped that one day she would go to Africa, and step where her Bibi walked the land free, but she never had the sort of money needed for a trip like that. Krystal loved her stories. She could hear them again and again. They swept her away into a world of possibilities. "Without storytellers, there ain't nothin' beyond the horizon. No, no, nothin'....," Ms. Coleman would sing while she did the dishes.

Most days, when Krystal got home after school, Ms. Coleman made her Mexican jamaica tea from the flowers of the hibiscus bush that grew in her rooftop garden, and they would sit together and just talk about the day. "Tea's better than med'cin' to cure what's ailin' ya, child," was her favorite thing to say whenever she made sun tea, steeped tea, or any kind of tea. She tended to repeat herself, and Krystal benefitted from the predictability of their conversations. It comforted her. Ms. Coleman had a tea for everything: one made of valerian leaves, for calming; another made of lemon balm leaves, for 'energizing.' Krystal learned that Ms. Coleman was right. Sitting down for a cup of tea did make her feel better, every time. A sip of tea made the clock stop.

After the storm passed, Krystal drifted off to sleep, but was soon awakened by LB tugging on her pajama pant leg. "I hungry, Kwissy," he whined. She smiled to see he was still holding Uni. As they passed through their small cluttered living room, she was relieved to see the couch still empty. Sometimes, she would wake to find creepy people with tattoos and scarred faces leering at her as she passed by.

The two children wandered downstairs to Ms. Coleman's ground-floor apartment for breakfast, as they did almost every morning. She was still in curlers, but had added a flowered scarf over them, tied at the top of her head. She was dressed in a floral Hawaiian mu'u mu'u and wore an especially vivid pink lipstick.

The morning brightened as Ms. Coleman hummed while flipping buckwheat pancakes in a cast-iron skillet with one hand, like a skilled chef, and resting the other hand on her round hip as gracefully as a movie star. She said that cast iron was "the only metal to be cookin' on. Makes your blood strong," she insisted. A 1950's diner-style metal table in the corner carved out enough space for a breakfast nook. It was set with two places, each with a glass of orange juice and a bowl for cereal, of which several choices were available.

"Why, hello chil'in," Ms. Coleman said cheerfully, as she patted LB's curly hair with a big smile. "How'd ya'll sleep last night?" Without waiting for an answer, she began to go on and on about the police causing a big commotion over some "teenagers joyriding and runnin' smack into a fire hydrant that spewed more water than poured out of the sky. Don't those police got better things to do than wake up the neighborhood with those danged sirens?"

Sitting down at the table, Krystal said nothing. She was groggy from lack of sleep and happy to let someone else do the talking. That was something at which Ms. Coleman was very adept. "Well, you don't worry none honey, you'll be goin' to school today, and then it's a holiday weekend." Krystal dug into the pancake on her plate. LB impatiently awaited his special topping, with his feet hopping like rabbits, dangling off the chair in mid-air. "Appos, appos," he gleed. He liked applesauce instead of syrup. It was how his mother made them. Ms. Coleman brought him his applesauce and laid a small pancake on a tiny plate for Uni, while Krystal wolfed down another big fat one with lots of butter.

It was a joy and good company for Ms. Coleman to have Krystal around her apartment before and after school. Krystal enjoyed doing things Ms. Coleman's old back injury made difficult and painful. She was also a big help in the rooftop community garden. It took up nearly half of the two-story apartment complex's parapet roof. All sorts of food grew up there, along with herbs and flowers for Ms. Coleman's teas. Krystal was fascinated by the plants Ms. Coleman raised to make medicines. She had comfrey for healing wounds; elderberries for colds; citrus, palms, roses, and chamomile for sleep; peppermint for tummy aches; and sage for "clearing folk's negativity," whatever that meant.

The bigger-than-life woman had declared herself "blessed with a green thumb." That was why she was able to grow non-native plants in the desert climate. Krystal thought it was far more likely it was Ms. Coleman's singing that made her plants thrive. She had the voice of an underwater angel.

After breakfast, Krystal got up, as was customary, to go and tend to the garden. "I got something for ya, Kryssy girl," Ms. Coleman said, preventing her from darting out the door. She held out her Bibi's long necklace made of wild licorice seeds, "From the great continent of Africa." She claimed it had protected her and all her relations for generations. "My great-great Bibi wore this when she came into port at South Carolina, bound at the ankles," she said again, for the twenty-thousandth time.

Ms. Coleman had brought that shiny black necklace safely all the way to Arizona when she came to be near her fiancé's Navajo relatives, after her former home in notorious Tornado Alley was destroyed. She said she "weren't interested in a husband, only a fiancé, because they didn't leave messes around the house and had someplace else to go when football came on the TV."

"Why are you giving me this, Ms. Coleman?" asked Krystal, palpating the cool, smooth beads.

"Well, child, I gots no one else to give it to. And the Lord's been showin' me there's a changin' wind comin'." Then she went back to opening cans of cat food at the counter for all the strays she fed daily. Clearly, she was not interested in talking further on the topic.

Krystal shivered in concern, but was afraid to ask any questions. "Thank you, Ms. Coleman. I will guard them with my life," she said sternly.

"Oh, child, you done guarded enough already. Those beads gonna be guardin' you from now on," Ms. Coleman said, her voice nearly cracking with emotion. Krystal held the beads to her heart, then wrapped them in a tissue, put them in her shirt pocket, and started to head up to the roof again.

The rooftop garden was cluttered with rows of plant-filled mismatched pots, rusted old coffee cans, and homemade wooden planters set on two-by-fours stacked on cinderblocks, which formed an unceremonious labyrinth. Air conditioner units, pipes, and wires were woven into the aesthetics as trellises and sculptures. It was "Eden in the middle of the dry desert city," Ms. Coleman would say to her church friends. One section was set aside for her church "ministry." She and a bunch of brightly-dressed, wide-hipped ladies would huddle in a circle, holding hands and praying loudly, shouting about the wonderful things they were expecting from the Good Lord. Every Sunday, they gathered to pack up vegetables in bags tied with ribbons and delivered them to neighbors who were not feeling well, or were out of work.

The roof's western corner held a special magical garden for Krystal. It was all her own. Ms. Coleman had helped Krystal build it, in exchange for the morning watering. She filled Krystal's garden with plants to lure faeries, mainly, but butterflies loved the milkweed and hummingbirds enjoyed the sweet, bright-colored blooms, too. Krystal's garden included flowers that opened at night, like jasmine and primrose. "That's because," Ms. Coleman said, "that's when the crystal stair rolls down from the clouds for the faeries, who, like me, can't fly due to injuries and sickness, so they kin enjoy the flowers, too." She also made sure to meet the basic needs of the fey: foxglove for hats and (obviously) gloves; tulips were for wing covers and baby beds.

A sign over the entry quoted Hans Christian Anderson: "Just living is not enough," said the butterfly, "one must have sunshine, freedom, and a little flower."

Angels and faeries were a big part of Ms. Coleman's decor, both inside and out. She had a grand collection of children's faerie tale books. Krystal's favorite was *Peeps the Sunshine Fairy*, who slid down rainbows to make children happy on rainy days. As much as Krystal wanted to believe that the stories of crystal stairs and faeries were true, she was equally afraid they might not be. Nevertheless, she always hoped to spot some evidence of magic, like some broken shards of crystal from tiny faerie stairs.

Once, while digging around for gardening tools under

a splintery raised bed, Krystal had found an old rusty Hills Brothers coffee can with a plastic snap-on lid. Inside was a fat roll of money wrapped in a red, ready-to-crack rubber band. Krystal figured it was the "husband divorcing" money that she overheard Ms. Coleman joking about whenever her church friends stopped by. Unable to hold it in, Krystal blurted out, "Ms. Coleman, why is there money in this old coffee can?" She raised it up.

Ms. Coleman laughed. "Why Kryssy, you would be the one to find that ol' can."

"Why do you say that Ms. Coleman?"

"'Cos money is attracted to pretty—like butterflies to flowers, especially the bright green and yellow colors in gardens. I leave that ol' can here and it just grows more money all on its own, then it will fly away easy as it came in. Jest the way it is, that's all, jest the way it is. Ain't no rhyme why some folks got money, and no reason why some don't…" Ms. Coleman's voice trailed off to a mumble as she got back to gardening. Krystal did not ask any further questions and began digging, looking for any evidence the magical creatures had been there.

At least nine cats lounged in that garden. The exact number was unclear because so many came and went. Just like the money, Krystal thought. Both Ms. Coleman and Krystal loved to take care of things—children, animals, but especially cats. Ms. Coleman was always "doctorin'" them. She gave them cranberry leaf tea "for the bladder" and bathed them in pinecone tea to "rid 'um of fleas." Stray cats having kittens were laid on a warm cloth diaper soaked in chamomile flowers, "to ease the curse," as she called it. Once, Krystal asked her what the curse was, and Ms. Coleman told her a story of the Garden of Eden, of people eating a magical apple that made everything die. Nothing died before that; not animals, plants, nor people, Ms. Coleman taught. The pain in having babies came along with all the other bad stuff. "Women were never meant for sufferin'," she would often say. Krystal was scared and saddened by the tale.

To address pain, Ms. Coleman made a special poultice for

"unloadin' blood," to treat swelling and bruising. Krystal recalled her saying once, "Since I had no chil'ins of my own, Kryssy, I aim to teach you all I know about cat med'cin'. Danged if I am gonna let my Bibi's secrets leave this world with me." Krystal concluded the gift of the beads must have had something to do with that. She quickly decided she would be like Ms. Coleman and have no children of her own. She felt, deep down, like she already was a mother to LB anyway.

Just as Krystal headed for the door and up to water her faerie garden, Ms. Coleman said, "Here now, child, don't you be runnin' to the roof. Mix up in here some flax, bran, slipp'ry elm bark, charcoal, and those chopped carrots over there," as she pointed to the sink. "Make a thick paste, not dribbling, you hear? Then pack it in jars and write this on the label: 'Rub lard on skin and put poultice under cloth over the pain.'" Krystal obeyed and worked away while LB played with his pancakes. She enjoyed the work.

Ms. Coleman pulled out a couple of old books on healing. "Child," she said in a more serious tone, "you got a mind for learnin' and a knack for healin', hot hands and a tender touch. I've seen it only a couple times. Ya'll need to be careful about that. Don't go telling folk, you hear? I may not always be around to protect you."

"Why shouldn't I tell people?" asked Krystal. Ms. Coleman never answered the question.

She was right, though, and Krystal knew it. For as long as she could remember, animals, birds, fish, even insects who were hurt or sick would show up wherever she went. In Ms. Coleman's rooftop garden, injured birds were always flying in. Beat-up cats, after a night of fighting, would rub against her legs while she watered until she cared for them or took them to Ms. Coleman. She was frustrated by not always knowing how to help—so much so that she had an unspoken desire to become a veterinarian one day, if she could ever afford to go to school. No one in her family, at least the family she knew of on her mom's side, ever went to college. Krystal never told anyone about her aspirations. She was afraid that saying it aloud would jinx it.

While mixing up the poultice recipe, Krystal heard a crash and a loud crack. She turned to see Ms. Coleman on the ground, her leg twisted behind her. "Kryssy girl, I done fell while reachin' for that dang cat food. Ya'll get me some of that paste you're mixin'; the one with the carrots." Krystal stood still, her aquamarine eye fixed in apprehension. Her green eye filled with tears. She knew this was going to take more than a poultice to fix.

Seeing the terrified look on Krystal's face, Ms. Coleman said, "Come here then, child, bring me that phone." Krystal instead dialed 911. It was not her first time. She had called many times for her mom.

"Ms. Coleman fell and I heard a loud pop. I think she broke her hip," Krystal told the dispatcher. Ms. Coleman knew she was right.

"Would you mind holding these knotty old fingers until the ambulance come, Kryssy?"

Krystal took the strong woman's hand as LB rushed over and squatted next to them on the floor, patting the scarf covering Ms. Coleman's curlers until it slid off. Krystal tried to block him from touching her, but she saw the comfort on both their faces and let it be. Somehow, Krystal thought older people were never afraid, that they had mastered their fears during their years of living. She hurt for Ms. Coleman, and worried about what she and LB would do without her.

A strange wind blew the kitchen door open, causing the curtains to fly in the living room, and blowing the front door shut. Within minutes, sirens howled and a yellow-haired paramedic pulled the kitchen screen door open as a large dust devil stirred and ripped it out of his hand, slamming it backwards, tweaking the hinge. Sand and paper bits brushed over the walkway as the small room filled with a wall of blue uniforms, edging Krystal and LB out of the way. Ms. Coleman reluctantly released Krystal's hand.

"She'll be all right now, little lady, I promise," said a fire-fighter, pushing her aside.

Within moments, Ms. Coleman was loaded onto a gurney and wheeled to the ambulance, with Krystal running alongside to hold her hand. "Little lady, would you like to ride in the ambulance with her?" the medic asked. "Yes!" she chirped, forgetting her brother would then be alone.

"I'll be fine, child," Ms. Coleman said knowingly, in her soothing tone, releasing her grasp. "You take care of LB." The ambulance door closed. With one hand on Krystal's shoulder, a lady EMT hit the back door three times with her fist, signaling all was secure in back. The siren howled like a mournful cat as the coming winds of a threatening haboob began to blacken the western horizon.

Before she left, the medic warned Krystal to get inside and stay there during the dust storm. Ms. Coleman had always said this was "'cos them storms carry the Valley Fever." The disease lay dormant, like many buried things, deep in the dirt, until the winds blew and Arizona desert dwellers became sick. Most of them had the disease to one degree or another. Krystal rushed her crying brother into Ms. Coleman's apartment. She lured the cats inside with freshly opened cans of food, and hoped the garden would survive the spattering desert rocks and sand. She and LB huddled on the couch, afraid. Neither would be going to school that day. Krystal blamed the prior night's storm for the whole mess. But she was wrong, Polaris was long gone, along with Tak's message. These new winds were calling her to a destiny that she never imagined.

CHAPTER 11

THE REMAINING CLOUDERS

Showing up is 80 percent of success.
Sometimes it's easier to hide home in bed.
I've done both.

—Marshall Brickman, 1977, New York, U.S.A.

By the time Krystal locked her windows in Arizona, Polaris had already passed over Popocatepetl and his princess, Iztaccihuatl, two lovers who became volcanos in Mexico. He gave the pair a respectful pass of the snow dusting he brought to the rest of the Meso-American mountains, before weakening over Colombia's warm Chocolate Islands. There, Thunderbird, the west wind, blocked the interfering trade winds, allowing Polaris clear passage to ascend the Andes glacier, the mother of the Amazon River. Waving her long, striped tail from atop Machu Piccu was Magnificat Miz. Her jaguar-like coat nearly camouflaged her as she trilled and blew a kiss. She had been expecting the big old bear.

Finally reaching the tip of South America, over Magellan's frigid straights and 100-foot waves, Polaris spun off a whistling williwaw's sea-foam twister, splashing clusters of elephant seals and sea lions who had been basking sleepily in the fish-fragrant tide pools. They barked at his rudeness. Next stop, the Crystal Desert, Antarctica, the land no Archer dared to claim. Ten thousand chattering penguins welcomed him onto the world's coldest, driest desert. Mt. Vinson glowed green and amethyst in the southern aurora's light, but when Polaris' dampness hit the dry mountain, the skies lit up with red sprites and blue jets, which usually occurred only above thunderstorms.

This light show slipped past the attention of international Archer research stations, but not Clouder Rose in her laboratory. "Come, come team," called Clouder Rose. All the cats leapt to a line of telescopes before the clear sheets of green basalt that formed windows to watch the rare sky show. Outside, the great bear wind wound-up like a pitcher and hurled Tak's message right to a speck of brown rocky nanatak that stood like a catcher's glove in the frozen white at the foot of Thiel Mountain, the entry to Rose's subterranean research lair.

While it was autumn in Ireland for Tak, it was spring on the White Continent. With no plant life, constant twilight draped the land in plum tones, casting powder-blue shadows over the endless ice.

Archers considered Antarctica uninhabitable, and instead of any of them owning it, nations set up research centers along its coastline. "If they could, Archers would make this a seaside resort, for heaven's sake," Rose would mock, "where they could fritter their green magic away on a pile of ice. What a waste, an utter squanderance of magic." Green magic was the Archer's greatest magic, according to Magnificats. It could manifest almost anything.

"Calm down now," stoic Rose mewed to her team as they raised their backs and hissed and growled at the in-pouring wind.

"Look, look, Dr. Rose!" the cats frantically howled.

"Th-the w-w-wind is b-blowing snow like an avalanche off the p-peak," whimpered Tobias, a former 'volunteer' Chilean test cat. He was only suited for calm places now, previously having who-knows-what injected into him.

Polaris' wind gust had to descend the icy entrance and take a sharp right at a rose-quartz backlit candle (named for Clouder Rose, of course) to reach her spotless laboratory's white calcite walls and shiny gray hematite floors, which appeared as smooth stainless steel to the untrained eye. Eight-inch thick, highly polished silver slabs formed sparkling jagged-edged tabletops. An under-lit onyx cabinet displayed sterile crystal vials and some glass and metal instruments, which Rose had 'borrowed' from various Archer stations.

The rush of wind toppled bottles, doused flames, and even knocked Magnificat Macak's scroll off the wall—basically, wreaking havoc. The ominous blast carried an Archer fragrance right into Rose's sanitary atmosphere. It lingered on her whiskers like sticky goo. If there was anything that made pure-white Rose angry, it was untidiness. She hissed and reared up. "Enough!" she shouted as she batted the wind with her out-stretched claws. "What is it you want?" she demanded. An inscription began to appear on her magnetic wallboard, like a text on a cell phone, letter by letter. "Clouders of the Great Lands: Arrant winds are stirring. Come at once. Signed, Littern Tak." Now Rose understood the stench and shivered. She still carried the scars of a 'volunteer' research cat herself: prodded, poked, and injected. It had affected her nerves. She had no desire to go to bustling Dublin.

Though she enjoyed the cold, Rose was not native to the South Pole. As a Siberian Forest cat, her lineage had exclusive ancestry to all longhaired cats, and was the undisputed national cat of the Red Land, that which the Archers called Russia. She took the assignment to the South Pole precisely because of her Siberian heritage. Her waterproof triple coat, which shed according to changes in light, not temperature (unlike most breeds), proved extremely helpful. Designed to keep her warm in cold and cool in heat, her fur allowed her to stay comfortable during the long dark season, regardless of the temperature. A green-eyed feline, she was not vulnerable to snow blindness, like cats with blue eyes. Her chubby, fur-filled paws acted like snowshoes.

Appearing much younger than her nine lives, Rose held her large bust out and bushy gray-tipped tail up—like a real lady. She had charisma, and broke Archer stereotypes about females (never understood or practiced by Magnificats) as both a distinguished scientist and powerful hunter. She held her own with the most brilliant Magnificat scholars, memorizing entire libraries, and speaking most Archer dialects, as well as Feral and common cat. She had been teacher to Archers and to animal kingdoms alike. She could even speak the language of angels, a skill usually reserved only for Archers.

Rose and her cats monitored the continent's various Archer research stations through a series of tunnels, naturally formed by slow-moving glaciers meeting warm springs deep below the surface. Her network of interconnected routes wove inside the entire land mass, some nearly vertical, allowing her to slide from level to level. By these same channels, Rose rescued cats from experimental torture and mutilation.

Light studies were her specialty, both in science and magic, as they were for her mentors, Clouder Moira and Clouder Macak, both master lightworkers. Clouder Moira, an alchemist, captured sparks to produce gemstones, a process Archers were learning to mimic, but not all that well. It would be millennia before they could transform the essence of light into an authentic diamond, as Moira did. After her retirement, Moira relocated to the North Pole, where she trained reindeer in flight and light alchemy. Her students, Silvershod and Rudolph, reached notoriety even among Archers. Rudolph led the way in infrared light technology, while Silvershod reigned in gem transformation. His son, Silverson was continuing that work in the north.

Macak studied electricity and, like Tak, formed deep bonds with Archers. His fondness for an autistic child, Nikola Tesla, has been well documented. They had a deep and lasting relationship, and did many experiments relating to alternating current electricity. Macak tried collaborating with the pioneer of the other kind of electricity, direct current, but found Thomas Edison to be a grave disappointment. "Edison betrayed every Magnificat," Macak would rant. After working closely together and sharing many Magnificat texts, Edison publicly tortured and electrocuted cats, demonstrating the supposed dangers of Tesla's work. Because of this deep betrayal, Macak refused to teach any more Archers, retired, and left his volumes of work to Rose.

Rose picked up the scroll the wind had blown off the wall. It was a tribute to Magnificat Macak. Its true meaning was lost to Archers, who saw the letter only as an old man's fond memory of his pet cat. Magnificats knew better. Rose read the letter once weekly to her team for inspiration:

Macak, the finest of all cats in the world. I wish I could give you an adequate idea of the affection that existed between us. We lived for one another. Wherever I went, Macak followed, because of our mutual love. It happened that one day the cold was drier than ever before. In the dusk of the evening, as I stroked Macak's back, I saw a miracle that made me speechless with amazement. Macak's back was a sheet of light and my hand produced a shower of sparks, loud enough to be heard all over the house. Is nature a gigantic cat? If so, who strokes its back? It can only be God, I concluded. I strained my eyes and saw that his body was surrounded distinctly by a halo like the aureole of a saint. I cannot exaggerate the effect of this marvelous night on my childish imagination. Day after day, I asked myself, 'What is electricity?' And found no answer. Eighty years gone by…and I still ask myself the same question, unable to answer it. —Nicola Tesla

"Any one of you could be the next Macak," she would encourage her team.

Rose had mixed feelings over work and family, even though her partner, Koshka, preferred a playful life in Russian forestlands, nurturing the home fires, and snuggling young ones. Most male forest cats took care of the kittens. Koshka stood twice the size of the average cat, and terrified those who did not know him well. In reality, he was a tender, cuddly father and friend. He and Rose bonded while very young, still being close to their wild state, as was common among their breed.

While Rose's cats launched into action cleaning up the wind-rushed lab, she prepared a report to Tak on the rock-eating microbes Archer researchers had found while drilling half a mile into a deep glacial lake. Rose had taken a sample from her last sortie, after spotting them glowing in a darkened corner. She packed them tightly into a water-filled container with two small rocks for their food and tucked them into her mountain pack. Rose added the many antarctic medicine scrolls she could now deliver to Ming Fang. They included the cure antarctic Magnificats had given to a Phoenician captain to carry home for his dying son, 2,700 years earlier.

The multitude of insecure lab cats crowded around Rose to say goodbye and wish her safe passage, when, in a cross between a cats meow and a sheep's bleat, Rose spoke, "Now, don't look so glum. You all have plenty of work to do to keep you busy. Tobias will be in charge." Donning her mink ushanka, frustrated she had to leave her important work and needy cats, she clenched her paw in the air, and with tears in her eyes, she stated emphatically: "Archers think they own this earth. If this giant ice cube belongs to anyone, it is Magnificats! We shed blood here." The lab cats applauded and cheered.

She stretched her claws out like tiny spikes to prevent slipping as she made her way up to the surface. Her feathery fur whipped as she drew near the opening and inhaled the cold air, feeling like her lungs might collapse. At that moment, Rose took off her ushanka and waved it as if for a cab and was caught up by a blazing jet stream. The fiery ball, with a tail like a comet, traveled upward 50 miles and north, into the warm thermosphere, towards the brightest morning star. There would be no time to stop and see Koshka until her return trip.

"ROARRRR...cough...choke...hack." The mighty north

wind had spewed the last of his southbound cold and was ready for some well-earned recuperation, when Blue Whale, the wind of the antarctic south, splashed a "Goodbye Polaris, I will take it from here" gesture with a wave of her fin and flip of her tail, creating a gigantic northerly gush to push Polaris back towards his home.

"Your tail is still pretty quick for an old blue whale," Polaris joked tiredly as he eased into his turn.

Blue did a double midair flip to show him she still had that (and more) in her, accidentally sending a surging sea wave towards Oceania. "Oops'" she giggled, in hopes the icebergs she sent rolling would go unnoticed. In the past, Blue had swept away entire populations of animals and Archers with her 'innocent' wakes.

Barreling through the sky, Blue pressed the tips of gentle swells into 60-foot whitewater waves, with a twist here and a zigzag there. She was avoiding resistant air pockets with summersaults when she came face-to-face with Ephippas, the wind demon Apple had unleashed. He had settled over the Southern Pacific Ocean, slam-bang in the middle of some 300 Fijian islands, the first land to see the sun every morning. When her dry antarctic cold met the hot demon's clockwise spiral, a cataclysmic spin-off of four additional storms resulted, each carrying a clone of Tak's message.

The first storm moved toward the nearby lands of Clouder Alkina of Oceania; the second raged west over the Coral Sea towards Africa, and Clouder Makeda. The third wind sped northwest to India and Clouder Billi. The fourth jetted north to Clouder Neko in Japan.

As the first storm wreaked havoc over Australia's abandoned prison for 'young Irelanders,' Tak shivered all the way back on the Erin sod. Blue Whale rose high into hiding, pretty sure she would be blamed for the whole mess.

"What now?" Alkina complained as a wind whipped up. He was altogether unprepared for Tak's message. He had no dreams, no visits from heavenly sorts. "Awk, a-another m-message from T-Tak, I'll bet," he stuttered. He had been avoiding Tak's requests for an update on his region. He muttered, "Well, there is no report—not my b-bowl of rice anymore. How's that T-Tak?" he muttered. Truth be told, he had given up and lost his will to fight for his land anymore. Cats were being killed in Australia by the thousands. Day rolled into day, each one consisting of a dingo's breakfast; "a yawn, a leak, and a good look 'round (no breakfast)."

With uniform, dark gray, stiff, short fur that became bronze at night, Alkina (named for moonlight) was a Behemoth cat—huge. He had rounded ears and a carved opal hoop pierced between his shiny black nostrils, the mark of a bush-healer. His breed's usually husky build did not describe Alkina anymore. He was skinny from dearth of nourishment—too skinny. His once brawny tail that resembled a cedar tree swaying slow and weighty in a strong wind now hung limp. A descendent from the large breed of Ngariman, his bigness made life even more dangerous in a land that rewarded Archers for killing cats. He was often confused with a panther, or a roo, which added further threat to him from Archer hunters. For some reason, his size made every-one expect more of him, as if he had a greater responsibility to the world because he was gigantic, for a cat, that is.

Of Pogeyan lineage, originally from the Indian tribal regions, Alkina was a Mystifier—able to engender a mist-like covering through his skin, allowing his fur to change like a cha-meleon. He could project images out on his fur, like a television screen, to trick the eye. This skill ingratiated him to the Jawoyn Archer tribe of the north, who divided into groups by 10 differ-ent skin types. They placed high importance on markings. He could disappear in the shadow of a golden wattle flower as easily as he could blend in with the blue sky.

Autumn in Ireland meant Jungalk in Australia, the hottest of its six seasons. The ground burned Alkina's paw-pads, and the hatching of crocodile eggs and ripening of green plums came early, as he made his way beneath a blanket of shimmering stars onto the still warm yellow boulder outside his lair. It was the very boulder where Magnificat Ngariman, the giant cat of legend, unintentionally caused all cats to be forever despised in the Land Down Under.

Alkina followed the dream-lines, the maps that recorded songs of all who passed that way before. Before the cat killings, when he had been feeling better, he used to croon on his walkabouts:

> *Without singing, singing, singing,*
> *nothing at all exists.*
> *By singing, singing, singing,*
> *all the land exists.*

Now, he had acquired a stutter, and did little more than complain. "How is any Magnificat, no m-matter how large, supposed to manage 25,000 islands, including N-New Zealand and N-New Guinea?" With the Archer-supported cat genocides, Alkina had broken under the pressure and literally gone to live in a cave.

His lair was an eerie, cluttered, labyrinth of oversized limestone chambers, made of what appeared to be oozing foam. Otherworldly and enormous, the tapering stalactites growing downwards from a dripping ceiling were mushy looking. One needed to touch them to prove their firmness. Tall stalagmites came up from the floor like the walking dead. A yellow cloud lingered from the murky thermal ponds, bubbling like a witch's cauldron in need of a stir. This is where the giant cat felt safe, his panic and nightmares under control.

Studying local medicinal plants, his most recent work had involved finding an antidote for the poisons used to murder Ferals, who were decimating native marsupials that Archer's wanted to protect. Some of those tasty poisons had caught the noses of more than just Ferals—even two beloved Magnificats who had come to visit him had died. He never thought he would witness such barbarism in his eighth lifetime. He had hoped the world would have progressed beyond that.

Tak and Alkina had not always had differences. They once shared many fun times playing chess, while Tak enjoyed his Irish tea, and Alkina his vodka (a Behemoth trait). Both were strong leaders and understood the concept of command. Tak's refusal to send Alkina help during these treacherous times had caused their current rift.

When Tak's message appeared above the bubbling pools, Alkina reluctantly determined he would go to him and try once again to convince his one-time friend that in order to save Magnificats, Ferals must be protected too. He knew it would not be easy to overcome Tak's hatred of Ferals.

Alkina packed a dilly bag loaded with fire-sticks, water, and some goanna oil for Tak's well-known achy muscles, and left his lair to sing his way to Ireland. Following the notes towards the rescue helicopter refueling station at the foot of the mountain, he became masked in his own mist and blended into the red and white of the helicopter. Then the big Magnificat straddled the tail of the chopper and sang to the rhythm of the whirling blades all the way to Canberra Airport. There he would change planes for Ireland. "I am too tired to fly myself," he moaned.

While Alkina was dangling from a helicopter, the second splinter storm reached the east coast of Africa, after giving a powerful show of strength over Flying Fish Cove, Diego's Footprint, and terrifying a bale of green sea turtles off Coco Isle. The storm brought an early start to the rainy Krempt season, as the Guinea winds rushed in from behind.

The rain reached Clouder Makeda in Ethiopia at a most inopportune time. She had just begun demonstrating to a group of Magnifikittens how to roast the world's most colorful seeds to make haze medicine. Makeda's Magnifikitten school was the most important thing in her life. The world was dying for lack of knowledge about cat medicine, and she aimed to set that right. Her Africa was rapidly losing its precious things, including medicine secrets, because most of the Cat Women were gone;

taken forcefully to other lands by evil Archers.

"Never disclose the name of a plant," she was lecturing, as the first rain spat against the smoldering rock-hard berries. "Once the name is spoken it loses its power…." She didn't have time to finish with "…until the end of your ninth life, and, then only to a worthy Archer" part of the lesson, before the sparse splats became darting pellets, snuffing out the eking flames of the fire for her demonstration and sending up steam. Instead of the usual trip to the medicinal garden, she and her brood of Magnifikittens darted for cover under a nearby elephant fern.

Makeda was a debtera, a healer. Ethiopian Archer healers had been generally male since the great abduction. Females were always far more powerful. Any remaining healers were such a threat to the males of the land that they were often declared witches and killed, just so the males did not lose business to them. To Magnificats, these Archer women were among those known as Cat Women.

Like Ming Fang, Makeda had begun efforts to catalogue Ethiopian plant cures for the *Book of Secrets* before all the healing recipes were lost. Their medicine had lived in stories from generation to generation, and since Africa had not had a true Cat Woman in more than 150 years, documenting the cures was imperative. Only some great-great-granddaughters, who were lucky enough to hear the secret recipes, could share them now. And as far as anyone knew, no African Cat Women of deep knowledge remained in the entire world. This is why Makeda's lair had become a school for Magnifikittens. She was training them to carry the knowledge into their futures, to eventually teach the medicine secrets to a new generation of Archer women, something she wished her cousin, Tak, would take a more active role in supporting.

Clouder Makeda's lineage went all the way back to the Nubian Black Pharaohs. Without moving once, her Magnificat line had lived in Kerma, Nubia, Kush, Aksum, Sheba, Ethiopia, Abyssinia, and again, Ethiopia. Her roots went far deeper in

Ethiopia than Tak's. His family left during the great famine. For 3,000 years, her lineage taught Archer pharaohs, emperors, empresses, kings, and queens, about Magnificat magic. She herself trained the lions that guarded the great storm-caster, Haile Selassie, the last emperor of Ethiopia. His storm skills were unmatched, and even sparked a new religion: Rastafarianism. She, along with all of Ethiopia, fell into despair after his passing, and the return of the drought. With no sitting Cat Woman in the territory to nourish and balance the land, even Magnificats could only watch as Ethiopia's lush landscape dried and cracked into broken craters. The medicine withered, causing Archers and Magnificats alike to suffer the lack.

Makeda was a black, medium-sized serval breed, a small African wild cat. Her extended, slender frame was offset by too long of a neck and rather curt legs, with ears that were too close together for her small face. The size of her head however, had little to do with her aptitude. She was brilliant. Her tail and legs were short for a cat, and despite the fact she was not a large Magnificat, she was taller sitting up than any Magnificat Clouder, other than Alkina. She had a black nose, black eyes, and even a black tongue. Fortunately, her fur was not in demand by Archers, as was that of her not-so-lucky spotted relations, whom she rarely saw because she was too busy with her students.

When she received the message from the wind, Makeda packed a traditional gift for Tak; a bit of sand (to sprinkle mountains), a chicken feather (to scratch valleys), and herself—a black cat (for pleasant company). All three were required to create earth, or any new venture for that matter. In addition, a bag of Ethiopian coffee would be a special treat. "There, that will do it," she said.

Without hesitation, she raced up a tall tree like a squirrel and stepped off the tip-top branch into…nothing! Her wings did not spread. She just stepped off.

"NO!" gasped the Magnifikittens below in unison.

Always teaching, Makeda shook her finger at the little magicians, "Never doubt yourself, and a way will come." Then she blew a kiss and instantly, a round flat stone, covered in green moss, appeared. With every step, another stone emerged. If she did not step out, no stone manifested. The steps climbed through layers of clouds of varying thickness, some like cotton and others like wool, until she was above the storm, where a rainbow greeted her. Transformed inside a weightless bubble, she sailed gently to Ireland.

Meanwhile, far below Makeda's bubble, and to the east, the third storm caused by Blue's clash with Ephippas limped towards Clouder Billi, by way of Jakarta and Sri Lanka. It had slowed and bowed in the Bay of Bengal to honor Bangladesh's sacred river, as all storms must do, at the mouth of the Ganges River. That river is a healer. In fact, even saying her name, G-A-N-G-E-S, can make the sick well. Unfortunately, storms pausing in reverence to the great river caused problems for Archers living there. The makeshift Archer villages were repeatedly leveled; submerging and reemerging in the tangled swampland by such storms.

In Dublin, Terence's oak swirls showed Tak a vision of the stalled storm as he sat at his desk. Leaping out the spit onto the drizzle-misted stacked-stone wall, he lit his pipe, and with a huge breath, blew his magic smoke towards Ramstail, the wind of the east. He went back inside to his writing, but instead, fell asleep again.

As soon as Tak's smoke reached Ramstail's nose, the east wind strengthened towards Bangladesh, and the storm spun again, garnering enough strength to crest the rocky slopes of Mt. Everest, 'Goddess of the Sky.' With two-hundred-mile-per-hour crosswinds at her peak, she was the tallest mountain in the world, the only one to pierce the stratosphere. Tak's message broke through those crosswinds, shattering horizontal icicles and fast-forming flag clouds at the summit.

Only a few Archers had ever been that high. When caught off guard, a number of Archers had fallen to their deaths in the climb. Geese and Magnificats flew in the next sphere upward, but some, sadly, had been sucked into jet engines while flying up there. Thankfully, only a small number, in contrast to the regularity with which they flew beyond the peak.

Blue's spin-off storm winds gently wove through the tall Himalayas towards Tibet, passing over the mystical singing lakes of sun and moon. Lake Manasarovar sang, "I am round like the sun, come bathe in my healing waters." Her crescent shaped brother, Lake Rakshastal, overwhelmed her sweetness with a menacing threat, "Come to my brackish waters, and I shall kill you." Blue's splinter wind skirted away from him.

Tak's message settled with a sigh in Clouder Billi's high lair at her pyramid-shaped mountain. She liked to tease when being introduced, "I live in the 'Bellybutton of the World,' the 'Jewel of the Snow,' the 'Mother of the Ganges,' Mount Meru." It had so many names.

She was quietly yogi-posed in penance, a prayer of her body for a special favor, when the wind settled in. "*Namaste*," she whispered to the wind as she untangled her contorted body, her paw over her ear, bowing to the mountain while praying Hindi's five holy syllables, *namah shivaaya*, to clear her thoughts. Smudging ash upon her forehead and with no possessions at all, without question, she spread her tiny wings and flew west to Tak.

The fourth and final storm message had roared over Micronesia, Guam, and Saipan, before it whirled north to Magnificat Neko, located on an insignificant atoll in a string of small Kuril Islands, surrounded on all sides by sea. This was not the kind of isle where one might like to be marooned, snacking on coconuts and crab. Neko lived amid freezing volcanic islands stretching from the farthest extremity of Japan to the tiniest edge of Russia, where the living is easy only if you reside underground.

This group of islands had been the domain of Neko's Kurilian Bobtail lineage long before the first Archers lived on them. No one, not even cats, knew how this bobtail breed got to this location, but they had been alongside all the noblest Archers there throughout recorded history, right up to the present day.

Neko lounged in his bedchamber on an imposing round pillow covered with silks of red, orange, and brown. Barely visible with all the pillows layered around him, he was reading a book when he calmly peered over the top rim of his glasses, asking the wind, "Have you ever read it—*The Boy Who Drew Cats*?" Then he tossed his head back in a deep laugh, which he rarely did. Waving a paw, he said, "Welcome" in a good-humored tone, as he did to every wind, in case it was Kamikaze coming for tea. Neko sniffed, "No, you are not Kamikaze, the divine wind of warriors. Perhaps you are his lovely daughter wind, Shinatobe, come to visit?"

A scent of Egyptian mint overtook the room. "Ah, Tak, my worrisome friend, I sense this message is from you." Neko had mastered worry, and had little tolerance for it.

He sat back down cross-legged on his large pillow, placed a cloth napkin on his lap and brewed his tea. He waited patiently for the message to appear in the whistling steam, as the teapot lid danced from the pressure. Tak's message finally formed, "Clouders of the Great Lands: Arrant winds are stirring. Come at once. Signed, Littern Tak."

Clouder Neko tied a silk scarf behind his short lynx-tipped ears and began to dance in big sweeps, eventually rising into the air and dancing on until he shape-shifted into the Bakaneko, sprouting a hard shell like a tortoise with wings from underneath, and even a second bobbed tail. Neko floated outside, where his scarf became a kite that followed a ribbon of Qi to Ireland, his obi sash trailing in the breeze. Soon, all the Clouders would meet at Tak's lair.

CHAPTER 12

ORPHAN WINDS

An' little Orphan Annie says,
'When the blaze is blue,
An' the lamp-wick sputters,
an' the wind goes woo-oo!
An' you hear the crickets quit,
an' the moon is gray,
An' the lightnin'-bugs in dew
is all squenched away.'

—John Whitcomb Riley, *The Elf Child*, 1885, Indiana, U.S.A.

Krystal stared out the car window at the Arizona desert. "Ms. Coleman is not coming back," she feared, under her breath. Her mother had, but became sick again, seeing spiders and scary things. An ambulance came and her mom tried to latch onto Krystal's arm as the police officer firmly peeled off her fingers.

Krystal missed Ms. Coleman's usual plea, "These young'ins are stayin' with me, right?" nodding her head up and down at Krystal's mom until she mimicked her, "See, their mama says it's okay." Then she would whisk them inside "until things were sorted out," usually in about three days. That is how long the hospital would keep their mom for observation.

Perfume lingered in the car as the manly-dressed social

worker urged her and LB to talk. They were not about to. The woman had hurriedly tossed a few of Krystal and LB's belongings into paper bags and jammed them into her trunk, rushed the children into the backseat, then simply drove off. Krystal had taken off her seatbelt. She wanted to turn around and pound on the back window, screaming as the distance separated her from home.

"Put your seatbelt back on," ordered the social worker. As usual, Krystal obeyed. Adults might be able to make her obey, but they could not make her talk. She had control of that.

It was dark, late, and the parking lot at the emergency child placement center was empty. "Hurry up, its pouring." The automatic light went on as soon as they approached the large, green metal door. "Press the buzzer," demanded the worker holding LB, angry that she was getting wet and would be home late for dinner again. A loud buzz and then a click—"Open it!" the impatient worker snapped at Krystal.

The three entered to find a rectangular glass window with a sleepy employee, sporting purple and green streaked hair on the other side. "We got a full house," the girl waved, showing her poorly tattooed arm. The social worker scowled and flashed her identification. "Bzzz," another door opened. Krystal looked up at the worker for a signal, she nodded, and Krystal turned the knob to enter the secured area. LB flinched when the door clanged shut and locked behind them.

The shelter separated children by age, and LB's two-year-old arms stretched out in panic to his older sister as he sensed the coming separation. His nappy hair was still glistening with mist as they shifted him into the arms of another facility staff person. His car-print pajamas were damp and he shivered. "Kwissy, I want Kwissy!" he cried as he was taken away screaming and kicking.

Krystal tried to yell, "No!" However, all that came out was a cough. Her sense of authority choked as she watched LB carried off, leaving her alone. She clutched Bibi's beads for comfort and strength.

Hours became weeks. "When can I see LB?" became her mantra. A lavender-haired therapist she was forced to talk to finally told her, in the softest way possible, that no foster family would take her and her brother, since they were different races and ages, and that was not what people were looking for as they planned a family. They mostly wanted a long-term placement, which meant an infant. Since Krystal was older, she should think of what was best for LB, and hope he found a 'forever home.'

"What did that mean?" she seethed, "A 'forever home?' We have a home. I have been doing a fine job of taking care of him. We love each other and that's all we need." It seemed to Krystal that to adults, a good home meant money. Poof!—like magic, things like a big house, nice schools, and tennis lessons made for a perfectly happy home. As if being poor was a crime and a reason some should not have children. Krystal did not want stuff. "I want my family together," she raged to deaf ears.

A whirlwind of judges, foster parents, and teachers became routine. Krystal shifted homes and schools weekly. She stopped asking for LB. The only remnant of her family was her stuffed Uni. "Who would make him a special mini-pancake now?" she pouted. She carried him in her pocket at all times, along with Grandma Bibi's black licorice-seed necklace, since she never knew if she might be yanked right out of school, or be taken to a new foster home in the middle of the night.

"Your honor, these children are difficult to place together because of their age difference. The mix of their races further complicates the attempt to keep these siblings together. We are lucky to have found a nice pre-adoptive home for LB, out of state," a new social worker argued in court.

"Is that his full name?" asked the judge.

"Yes sir, it is."

"Where is the mother?" The bailiff rolled her eyes, realizing once again that this new judge, cycled in from traffic court, was not at all up to speed on the dependency system.

"The mother was in the hospital your honor. She was released and is now unavailable, not returning calls or letters."

The children's state-provided attorney piped in, "It appears she has abandoned the children your honor."

The social worker added, "This is her second failure to comply with the reunification plan for the family." With that, a true finding deemed the children dependants of the state, parental rights removed. Krystal and LB were ordered into separate placements; she for long-term foster care, and he towards adoption. She sobbed as she hugged LB one last time.

Krystal traced the outline of a short-lived dust devil that trailed alongside the van as it traveled north on the windy road. It picked things up and dropped them like a chess game. A young social worker, Jenny, sat next to her, texting on her cell phone. It was twilight when they arrived at an exclusive gated community near Moosa's mountain. "You are so lucky Krystal, don't mess this up, okay?" whispered Jenny when they arrived at the elegant, terracotta-colored home. Krystal did not feel lucky at all. She had no idea where LB was. She might never see him again, or her mom, or Ms. Coleman. It was a dark day for Krystal.

The initial meeting was awkward, to say the least. Jenny chatted with the foster mother like a salesperson—pitching the child like a pet. Krystal was surprised they didn't check her teeth right then and there. "She is a lovely girl, likes to cook, and does well in school, for her situation." Mrs. Fairmount tried to warm up to Krystal but became frustrated when treats, toys, and even the family dog did not elicit so much as a smile. "Give it some time," Jenny advised.

A princess room and pink dollhouse awaited Krystal. Diapers were stacked neatly on a changing table under a window. It was clear the Fairmounts had expected a younger child. Mrs. Fairmount showed her the room and a closet full of lovely dresses and outfits, all too small. "We thought it best to wait until you could try things on yourself. We can go shopping tomorrow, if you like." Krystal chewed her thumbnail raw, not knowing what to say or do. She had never worn clothes like these, or slept in a room that seemed like a fabricated palace.

Krystal's sulky silence exasperated Mrs. Fairmount, who looked puzzled and started to leave the room, just as the social worker came in. "What's the matter, Kryssy?" she asked, concerned.

"My name is Krystal," was all she could spit out, but her thoughts raced on in her mind. *Only my brother and Ms. Coleman can call me Kryssy. And how can you not know what is wrong? I'm not a puppy. I'm a human being that has been torn from my home and family, for god sakes!* The adults scurried away whispering, leaving Krystal alone in a room fit for a princess. She flopped face-up and spread-eagle on the big bed, sinking into deep, downy softness. Above was a canopy with white lace and hanging crystals. She stared at them until she fell asleep, which was quickly.

A few days later, when Krystal began adjusting and was going to start school, she thought there might be a chance to start over for everyone. After all, it had been a rough time for her, and a long wait for the Fairmounts. They had hoped to adopt for three years, but they had wanted a baby. Still, they had decided to give her a try, despite her advanced age of twelve.

Then, just as Krystal was feeling more at ease, it became clear that Mrs. Fairmount was not pleased with the situation. On Krystal's way downstairs for breakfast, wearing her new pink hoodie, she overheard Mrs. Fairmount on the phone, "You have got to come and get this child, she does nothing but sulk. She is miserable here. She is antisocial, for Pete's sake! Well then, you can pick her up at school—we are done." The phone slammed down on the table with a crack. Mrs. Fairmount began to cry. When she noticed Krystal peeking through the half-closed door, she screamed "You little eavesdropper!" then slammed the door shut. Mr. Fairmount drove Krystal and her packed-up belongings wordlessly to school. They neglected to pack Uni. Bibi's beads however, were still in her pocket, thank goodness.

Krystal was numb, and had no idea what to expect. She went through the school day with little hope. Some nice Latina girls asked her to sit with them during lunch, and she enjoyed that. After class, kids, buses, and grown-ups rushed in all directions until the parking lot emptied and the last bus left. With no friends yet, and teachers who did not even know her name, Krystal went unnoticed.

No Fairmounts picked her up. No social worker was waiting for her. Sitting alone on her new rolling duffle bag, she could see the distant lightning of a storm approaching. "I wish the wind would just sweep me away and get it over with," she said, pounding her fist on her knee and biting her lip in determination. "I'm not moving for you, storm, I am not moving for anyone anymore."

Slipping down to the sidewalk, resting her back on the duffle, the winds began to kick up. Thunder drummed. "You can't make me move, you stupid storm, no matter what you throw at me." She refused to take cover when the first large drops fell. When hail battered her, she pulled her pink hood up over her head, then wrapped her arms around her bag and sat firmly, refusing to move. When the stinging hail became torrents of slanting rain, she finally gave in, and with her bag over her head she ran for cover, hiding under a juniper tree. The kindly tree took the brunt of the rain, but she was still getting drenched.

Krystal had a strange sense of oneness with nature that she had not experienced before. The storm, she realized, brought her what she needed. It made her comfortably invisible, provided a bath for her salty tears, and thunder to muffle her sobs. She looked up just in time to see a flash of purple lightning. A split second later, a bolt struck and cracked the tree she was under, forking to the wet ground, sending what looked like a bright electric snake towards her feet. Then her world went black.

When she first opened her eyes again, if the ground had not been hard and wet, Krystal might have thought she was back in her soft bed at the Fairmount's house. The storm had passed and stars shown above her like the crystal canopy in her princess room. She lay flat on her back as she stared up at the night sky and realized she had just been dreaming of a white cat sitting over her, with its paws on her chest. At that very second, Krystal experienced a very grown-up thought, "I am not an orphan. I am a daughter of the wind. I am free." She did not know where the thought came from. It seemed to come from the place between waking and sleeping, but wherever it came from, it was true. She was as free as any adult walking around. She just didn't have her own money.

"Perhaps the lightning really was a snake!" One that bit her, and strengthened her with its venom, to face the almost unacceptable truth; that she, at twelve and three-quarter years, had to make it on her own.

Slowly becoming aware of her surroundings, lying on the ground in the dark, Krystal got up dizzily and noticed illuminated, fluorescent pawprints glowing on the asphalt. leading down the street, away from the school. Curiously, she tapped the first print with the tip of her shoe. It lit up to a bright violet. She touched the next one. It lit up, too. Bending down for a closer look, she confirmed they were indeed cat pawprints, "Maybe that dream cat?" she guessed. Step after step, each print responded to her toe touch as she followed them.

The city lights grew brighter and traffic increased. Her clothes dried. Nightlife began. The cat prints led to a hectic bus depot, where they ended—right at an outgoing bus. A family with two young children boarded with lots of luggage. Krystal blended into the group unnoticed. "Swoosh," the bus door closed, and when the air brakes let out a sigh, so did Krystal. Not caring where she was going, she curled up in a double seat while the rocking motion and humming motor lulled her to sleep.

It was early morning when she arrived at a dirty southern California bus station. Everyone exited the bus and she followed the family, still unnoticed, until they boarded a taxi and she was left alone. She saw a group of children at a school bus stop down the block and hopped in line, again blending in. She watched as children said embarrassed goodbyes to their parents, shaking her head at their foolishness for not appreciating a caring family, when she was bumped by a tall redheaded girl as she prepared to climb the steps into the school bus. "Watch yersalf," the girl warned in a funny accent.

Where am I? Krystal wondered.

Neither of the two girls, Krystal nor Apple, had any inkling that this simple brush was the first signal of a fate they were to share; a fate that would inevitably unite them.

The bus continued along a winding road, edging high wasting cliffs that looked out to the Pacific Ocean. A sign marked an overlook, "Point of Light." A few more stops and the bus arrived at a small neighborhood school, with part of the playground on the beach, including volleyball nets and lines of surfboards. Children shoved their way off the bus and marched towards the single-story, sea-foam green buildings. Krystal snuck away and headed for the cliffs. Apple noticed, but got distracted when someone else bumped into her. "Hey," she snapped, in her usual ready-for-a-fight response.

Wandering around her new American middle school campus with a huge chip on her shoulder, Apple was disoriented and just plain miserable. She didn't like Mrs. Russell, her homeroom teacher, who seemed to be either texting on her phone or droning on and on to a class of idiots, unable to answer one single question she asked.

A California history lesson was extended for Apple's benefit, and to her embarrassment. "I know you are new to America, Apple, and might not know about the natives who lived peacefully here, until the Spaniards, the Padres, and the Mexicans displaced them, and then one another." Mrs. Russell taught how the discovery of gold built the state. Her teaching style consisted of the memorization of dry facts, and Apple could not stand it. It was not like her school in Ireland.

When Mrs. Russell wrongly instructed that the person on

the Great Seal of California was a conquistador, Apple could be silent no more. "Wait a bleedin' minute—ere you foolin' with me? Everyone knows that's the mythical warrior Queen Califia, from Garci Rodriquiz de Montalvo's novel, written in the 1500's." Mrs. Russell stood stunned at her outburst.

Apple had learned about California from her father. He did have a way of making boring history into epic fantasy. His California stayed with Apple because it was exciting. "Imagine Apple, a beautiful coast, with giant women in charge of the richest store of gold and pearls on earth."

"That is an interesting story, Apple," Mrs. Russell said in a dismissive manner, changing the subject. Apple was furious. She could now see that what her Uncle Aden always said about Americans was true: "Yanks removed all of the magic from the land."

Suddenly missing her mum, Apple realized just how much she hated living with her father, in his spacious mid-century-modern home that overlooked the ocean. A girl other than Apple might have been grateful to have a private room over the garage, far away from the rest of the family. To Apple it was isolation, as if she were diseased. She decided God was punishing her for stealing the stone—her sentence: California. Between classes, Apple stood alone, daydreaming and kicking soft dry sand on the beach, where she stood out. Her bright red hair, gleaming white skin, and Irish accent didn't do much to help her fit in. She was the only ginger student, or "canela," as the other children called her whenever she gave them dirty looks, which she did a lot. All this caused her to seem 'a bit off' and most steered clear of her. Apple welcomed the wind that kicked up suddenly off the ocean as she lagged behind when morning break ended.

"Someone stole my lunch, Mrs. Russell," screeched a chubby boy named Miguel, causing a disturbance as everyone returned to class. The children murmured suspicions of who could have done such a thing, when Veri, a slender Latina student with tightly waxed curls and broad painted brows, accused Apple: "We never had anything stolen in this class until SHE got here." All looks flew to Apple.

This was the last thing Apple needed, and it was the final straw; she was not going to stand for this assault on her personhood, her integrity, and her right to be different, for one more second. Without thinking, she lunged at Veri, who lit up with fear and surprise as the fiery-headed lass took her down to the ground in a tumble that resulted in mutual hair pulling, fingernail scratching, and screams. As the class began cheering the fight on, Mrs. Russell had each girl by one arm and up on their feet, marching them directly to the principal's office, with sweat staining both their red faces.

"App, I don't know what to do with you," her dad scolded as they drove home. "And stop biting your nails. You're down to raw skin!" swatting her hand away from her mouth a little harder than he needed to. Apple knew he was angry, and she was glad. If he got mad enough, he would send her back to Ireland, to her mum, where she was not the only red-haired kid in the entire school. "We should look at a private school for you, App. Maybe this is too much of a culture shock."

No dad, I want to go home, she thought, but could not say aloud because there was no home for her to go to anymore.

"Well you are suspended for a couple of days, so we'll take a look at other options," he continued. Her heart sang when she thought of no school for two whole days.

Banished to her room, she was elated, especially happy to realize that her father thought this was a punishment. She pulled out the old book that fell from the shelf in the library in Ireland. Immediately, a windblast blew through her opened window, scattering loosened pages over her bed. Scrambling to close it and gather papers, a small, yellowed note showed in the mess of white. "I wonder why I never noticed this before," she murmured.

Smack dab in the middle of the paper was a cat's pawprint. Excitedly turning it over, she read; "There shall arise a tempestuous wind, called Euroclydon." Apple sat for a moment staring at it. The cat sarcophagus, the cat dreams, the howling cat at night, and now, a note signed with a cat pawprint was all too obvious for even her not to notice.

For a second, Apple worried that someone was playing a well-orchestrated prank on her. Then she quickly realized that to pull it off, they would have had to cross an ocean. If only she was not on restriction, she could research the Euroclydon wind on her new tablet, currently repossessed by Dan because of the school fight.

Days passed, and finding no immediate opening at the private schools in town, Apple returned to public school, to a class sorry to see her back. Veri still had a bruise on her cheek and hatred in her gaze, which quickly switched to fear when Apple glared back even harder. Veri avoided all contact with Apple after that. It seemed other classmates were afraid to look her in the eye as well, in case she might attack them. Apple enjoyed the power it provided, no longer caused by her difference, but by the dread she struck in their hearts.

At lunch, from her now private corner of the school grounds, she recognized a pink hoodie entering the vacant classroom. "Hey, that's the girl that bumped me at the bus, the one that wandered away from school," Apple muttered suspiciously. She headed in that direction, only to find no one there.

Then she heard Miguel yelling, "Mrs. Russell, my snack is missing from my backpack, again!"

No one dared accuse Apple this time, even though she was the only student they thought had been near the room. She went inside, plopped heavily down in her seat, and waited for school to end.

Off restriction, she could return to her usual first choice, the library. The order and sameness of libraries, no matter where one was in the world (a lot like churches, quiet and uncluttered), made her feel at home. Googling Euroclydon on a library computer, she discovered it was a stormy northeaster from the coast of Syria. That wind had caused Saint Paul to shipwreck two thousand years before, "Hmm, what could this be meanin'?" She reread the passage, "'There shall arise a tempestuous wind, called Euroclydon.' Maybe, a storm is coming?" she wondered, just as the corner of her eye caught a blur of bright pink passing to her left. The girl wearing it sat down right next to her. Apple leaned over and scolded, "I seen you go into class, you know," in a voice a wee bit loud for a library.

Beneath the pink hood peeked two light-colored eyes— one green, and the other blue. "You did?" asked Krystal, quickly averting her gaze.

"Surely I did. I ought to give you a swift kick. I got in a lot o' trouble on your account."

Krystal shifted and unzipped her sweatshirt, taking it off and tying it around her shoulders loosely. "You did?" Krystal asked again, with more strain.

"That all you kin say? And what's wrong with your eyes? They don't match at all, they're actually kinda' creepy." Krystal put her head down shamefully.

"Ah, m' gosh, a sensitive thing, are you?" Apple regretted saying this as soon as she spoke, glancing down to notice Krystal's dirty fingernails and muddy shoes. The girl stood up and bolted for the door. Apple ran after her, and though she was not nearly as fast, the intermittent pink flashes kept Krystal in sight. Veering onto a dirt path leading to the old lighthouse, the bushes whipped Apple's face as they bounced back in Krystal's wake. Just ahead, the pink sweatshirt lay on the ground. "Oh, no," said a breathless Apple, "I've lost her." She was hoping to force a confession to Mrs. Russell and had missed her chance.

A hot, dry, Santa Ana wind was blowing from the desert to the sea, instead of the usual breeze coming in off the ocean. In Arizona, a wind like that would precede hard monsoon rains, so Krystal ran for cover and would look for her sweatshirt later. Out of breath, she felt relieved to be back in the ramshackle shed in the canyon that she had fashioned into a home for herself. When she first arrived, it had been full of trash. There were blankets, as if someone had lived there before, but the decay in the waste showed no one had been there in some time.

As Ms. Coleman had taught her, Krystal fixed it up with curtains and pictures she found in alleyways behind the nearby mansions that lined the ocean cliffs. "Every one of us chil'ins got orders from the Man upstairs to keep Eden beautiful. And Eden is wherever he puts you," she could hear Ms. Coleman say.

She had discovered a nearby patch above the ocean where she collected plump blackberries. It was as if all of nature wanted to help her. Every Friday, a white cat would lay a fat dead dove at her doorway. She used it to make a soup that would last her for three days, thanks to Ms. Coleman's lessons. Most meals started with hot water she heated in a thin pan on a small fire. She added packets of ketchup and chopped onions she gathered at the fast-food restaurant near the library. Then she pulled off the feathers, put in the meat, and let it stew.

After school hours, so as not to raise suspicion, she went to the library to read about how to cook, identify wild edible plants, and create remedies for her new animal friends. She was happy, but a deep sadness still crept in when she thought of LB. She rarely thought of her mother, and felt guilt for that. She wondered often about Ms. Coleman.

This was the first sense of control of her own destiny Krystal had known. She luxuriated as she curled up on a blanket with the snack she had stolen from school, along with the book on Benjamin Franklin and his fascination with electricity she had "borrowed" from the library. Ever since she was struck by lightning, she, too, had a great interest in electricity. Now, whenever she was around a clock, it ran backwards. Krystal did not like stealing, not from the kids at school, nor from the library, but she would pay it all back one day, she reasoned. In the world that had so completely deserted her, she finally felt safe and content.

"Hello, you in there?" came Apple's raised voice right into Krystal's haven. She sat up with a start.

"Oh no," she whispered, trying to be perfectly still and quiet as the rickety door creaked open. She had forgotten to roll the large rock against it.

Apple barged in, sizing up the situation in an instant, "Is this where you've been livin'? Aren't you lucky as a leprechaun? Look at this place, no folks, no school." Apple was both envious and perplexed, plus still annoyed at being blamed for the stolen lunches.

"I'm Krystal. Yes, this is my house and you were not invited," Krystal said defensively as she stood up. And why do you talk so funny?" Krystal had never met anyone who spoke with an Irish brogue.

"What do you be tinkin' now?" Apple said in an overdone accent. "Most folks call me Apple, I am from Oirland, don't you know?" Apple was an expert swordswoman with words and quickly gained the upper hand in the discussion.

"Would you like some?" Krystal offered Apple half of the stolen egg and potato burrito.

"Sure," said Apple, grabbing it and biting the soft treat. "No wonder Miguel gets miffed when he loses his lunch. This is amazin'. Whatcha be callin' it?"

Krystal laughed, "It's a burrito." The two girls shared marigold flowers Krystal had salted and dried like chips, to Apple's admiration. It was the first time either girl was comfortable with anyone in a very long time. They made small talk until Apple could wait no longer, "Tell me Krys, what are you doin' here? How can a kid be livin' all by themselves?"

"I was a foster child."

Apple looked puzzled.

"That's where you live in other peoples' homes. People you don't know. Do they have those in Oirland?"

"I don't know," giggled Apple. "You don't have to say it like that. Here, look, this is how it is spelled," and she used her finger to spell it out in the air; I-R-E-L-A-N-D. "It's with an 'i' not an 'oi' sound."

"Then why do you say it like that?" Krystal asked.

"'Cos, I am from there, so I kin say it that way. Other people only sound foolish when they do." Then Apple got right to the burning question, "So, what happened to your family?"

"My mom had problems and social workers took me and my little brother into 'protective custody.' They call it that but it isn't protective at all. We were doing fine with Ms. Coleman, our neighbor lady in Phoenix, who fell and went to the hospital. After that, they took my brother away, and sent me to a family that didn't want me. So, I took a bus and came here." Krystal left out the facts about the lightning and cat prints.

"Where's your mom now?"

"I don't know. She never came back for us. She gets sick a lot."

"Could she be dead?" Apple asked in a whisper, afraid for her own mum.

"Maybe, but more likely, she is not in her right mind again. That was a mean thing to ask me, you know?" Krystal then turned the conversation, as she passed the crispy flowers, "What made you come to California?"

"Well, me mum got sick and sent me to live with my dad. I hate it here," she said kicking at nothing.

"At least you have a dad to go live with Apple," said Krystal, hoping to encourage her.

Honestly, Apple had never even considered not having parents who could take care of her. She mostly wanted to get away from her dad. For just a second, she thought maybe she was not so bad off.

The girls giggled and told stories about their lives before California, things they liked to do. Krystal shared about her faerie garden and Ms. Coleman's cats back in Arizona. Apple told a more than curious Krystal all about how faeries pretty much run Ireland. The two seemed to suit one another. Krystal needed a protector, and Apple's pent up indignation needed someone to protect. They were a good match as friends.

When Krystal told her of the animals she helped and the food left at her door, and how Ms. Coleman taught her cat medicine, she regretted it, remembering Ms. Coleman telling her not to tell people that she had a way with animals. She didn't mention that ever since she was zapped by lightning, she could see colors around different parts of an animal's body, and by placing her hand, or even a certain flower, over a dark spot, animals would miraculously become well.

Apple dared not tell Krystal of her strange cat goings-on, or the stone. Before they knew it, the sun was almost down. Apple said a quick goodbye, grabbed her backpack and jetted out the door, forgetting to return the pink hoodie she had picked up in the chase.

The dry electric wind had followed Krystal from the Arizona desert, sparking the air and igniting fires in the land, carrying her scent to the sleek white Magnificat Felene, Tak's godkitten. The young Archer fascinated her. Felene made her home nearby in the blackberries, protectively buried amid sprawling prickly pear cacti, above the ocean.

Covertly, Felene had been stalking and looking out for Krystal. She was the one leaving her food, and had watched Apple's visit, and even overheard some of their chatting about cats. Felene was trying to understand what the winds wanted her to know about this homeless Archer child. She sniffed the air, but no answer came. Apple was another story. Felene did not like her one bit.

During the short time since Krystal's arrival, Felene was amazed to see an injured pigeon and other assorted hurt and disabled birds, and even reptiles, drawn to, and healed by, the mysterious child. What interested Felene most was the Archer girl's strange healing power in her hands. She could also see a gold circle around Krystal's head when she worked, like a halo.

"Could this be a Cat Woman?" Felene wondered. Her secret wish had always been that she would be the next Magnificat to find a Cat Woman. They were the missing link for the evolution of Magnificat medicine. Some recipes could not be prepared without Archer assistance, and some materials were nearly impossible to get without them. Felene was curious if this young Archer, with unmatched eyes like her own, could be her Cat Woman. She would need to collect more evidence.

Krystal's reputation quickly spread throughout the canyon's animal population. Despite the notoriety, and the fact that Felene was stalking her, no one noticed when a large, scraggly, black Feral cat, in a troubled labor, stopped at Krystal's door for help. Finding the scar-covered and dirty cat at her doorstep, Krystal asked quietly, "Oh my black cat, may I pick you up and carry you inside?" The cat hissed a warning, then got up on her feet, walked in of her own accord, and lay down on Krystal's blanket with a low moan. She growled when Krystal tried to approach her. Krystal backed off in respect. "If you want me to help, you have to let me get near you." Slowly she reached out to hold her hand over the wild cat, pacifying her. The black cat lay her head down as if to agree to Krystal's terms.

Cautiously massaging her abdomen, Krystal whispered, "Oh, I see the situation, mama cat. I am happy to help. Me and Ms. Coleman birthed a bunch of kittens."

In short order, three black kittens came, one after another. The scruffy and scarred mother cat fell asleep, exhausted, while Krystal rubbed the wet kittens to stir their circulation and promote breathing. Then she cleaned them with a cloth and placed them at their mother's side to suckle.

When the scraggly mother cat awoke, she let out a loud growl, which appeared to summon several motley cats who howled outside until Krystal opened the door. "You must be friends of the mama cat. She is doing fine and her babies are hungry and healthy." Without acknowledging Krystal, the cats leapt in and thanklessly carried away two kittens. Krystal did not interfere.

"You are a good mother, fine black cat," Krystal said as she watched the mama cat rise, stretch, and pick up her third kitten, joining the group as they slithered into the darkness. The large black cat looked back, with the one kitten swinging in her commanding jaw, and for a moment seemed to say, "Thank you," with her eyes. Word spread soon to Felene that Krystal had saved Tak's nemesis, the Feral Queen Phoebe!

Unknown to Krystal, she was being watched; not only by the cats, but also by the winds that blustered outside.

CHAPTER 13

DRAGONS IN THE CLOUDS

Roaring bears and howling dragons roused me—
Oh, the clamorous waters of the rapids!
...Clouds on clouds gathered above, threatening rain;
The waters gushed below, breaking into mist.
A peal of blasting thunder!
The mountains crumbled.

—Li Po, 700's C.E., China

Change was coming. Felene could feel it. Most Archers and ordinary cats would not notice the unfolding calamity, but to Magnificats like Felene, the winds spoke, usually quietly, in hisses. Today was a roar! As the static in the air charged her platinum fur to spark electric blue, Felene sped towards the ocean bluffs for a closer look. This was no ordinary storm approaching. Dark cold battled for the dry hot shore. Her pink nose twitched skyward, whiskers reaching like antennae, as her stiff, perked ears strained seaward to decode the mounting winds. Fighting her innate urge to chase the birds and rodents fleeing the rocks along the cliff line in preparation for the storm, she braced herself by curling her claws firmly into the earth.

The tempest brought disturbing scents from distant shores and upper skies, which awakened her drive to take flight to new adventures. That desire had been dormant in Felene for a long time. Leaning harder against the shoreward winds from the overlook, mist coated her fur tips and a sudden chill squirmed up her spine, as her tail fur stood on end. The cotton clouds morphed into steely dragons, breathing thunderous fire on the churning waves as they slapped the unstable cliffs, unleashing small rivers of sand.

Lightning torched a small Torrey pine a few yards from her; an omen of her own fate, should she remain. Felene watched the snake-like lightning bolt seize a nearby metal sign warning of unstable cliffs. As the rain came down, Felene twirled around and scurried home, the sudden hail stinging her hind legs.

In spite of her choice to live alone in the wild, Felene's cat lair in the blackberry patch was anything but primitive. Tucked cleverly above the cliffs beyond the main Archer trail, an under-sized entrance beneath three cat-shaped rocks led into an old tapered drainpipe, which submerged for several feet and resurfaced directly beyond a sprawling prickly pear cactus. It was a tricky path to navigate without pricks. Bright-white shattered seashells formed a quaint manicured path, lined with yellow-flowering ice plant. The blooms folded and puddles began to overtake her walkway by the time Felene reached her gated yard, bordered by a driftwood fence fastened by seaweed that looked slippery in the rain. A spiky bougainvillea plant formed the front of her lair, large enough to veil the small three-prop windmill she had built in the rear.

She rushed in through the waterproof, gull-feather door curtain as it swished and slapped in the turbulent wind, shielding the fur-lined walls of the interior. Rabbit pelts offered superior insulation and made the room cozy and feminine, with their blush hues. To the left, her mother Maria's teacups dangled on a twisted branch, bleached to a soft gray by the sun and sea, mounted over a kitchen sink fashioned from two white, still-joined giant clamshells she'd dug up during a blue moon. The back of her small lair burrowed underground. In the furthest corner lay an assortment of soft chewed pelts. This art she learned as a young Glaring from Apache moccasin makers. She had spent vacations with Moosa, visiting his mountain before her mother went missing and Tak and Moosa had their falling out. Navajo sand paintings of Mariah and her godfather, Tak, hung on the far wall above the double sink. Her father's image was noticeably absent.

A multicolored Persian rug sealed the rough sand floor. It might have led some to believe Felene was a Persian breed. On the contrary, she was a White Thai Jewel Magnificat, altogether different from her Persian cousins with their long fur, so prone to knotting, and bulging eyes pressed out by flattened noses. Felene's white fur was stiff, with diamond tips that quivered prominently under alert, and her nose was longer and more gracefully shaped.

Tired of Magnificat demands, Felene craved seclusion and rest. She had come to love the gentle existence she had scratched out of her sometimes violent past, which included the conflict with Ferals, particularly Queen Phoebe's lot. She despised the queen, who took her mother away, though that trauma rarely infiltrated her dreams anymore.

Tending gardens, knitting, and hunting unique items with which to fill her home was all that interested her now. Her lair had been a haven for the past five years, and she killed only for food. However, that night, as the storm raged and the wind pounded on her roof, loneliness bruised her heart. She trembled like a kitten when the thunder rumbled through her belly, until finally drifting off to a one-eyed sleep (a knack she had perfected in her fourth life).

By morning, birdsongs and sunlight replaced the storm. Whiffs of aloeswood crept through the feather door curtain, still dripping from the night's bucketing rain. "Wait," her nose twitched, "Oh, no!" This fragrance Felene knew all too well. "Oh, no," she said again, scrambling to neaten up the place. Aloeswood was her mentor Ming Fang's signature scent. "Ah," Felene hissed, "now, the dragon clouds make sense."

Ming Fang's siamese entourage mangled the morning quiet as they toiled, hoisting her up and over the cactus, since she would never fit through the drainpipe, and there was no place to land the litter inside Felene's yard. "Pay attention, you fools!" the empress snarled, "or I'll use your skinny hides in my next batch of liniment." The Siamese were perplexed by how they would negotiate the buxom empress over the last section of the sprawling prickly pear, as she primped and filed her nails while raucously hissing commands, "No talking, only drive."

There was no doubt Ming Fang was difficult; nevertheless, she had stepped up to be a mother to Felene when Mariah went missing. Her unsolved disappearance continued to rock the Magnificat community. Ming Fang had ensured Felene's edification in the Dragon Li gift of Archer languages. Littern Tak had assured Felene retained her mother's Thai gift of reading and writing as well. As a result, Felene was distinguished as a Magnificat who could read, write, and speak all cat and Archer languages.

"*Ni hao*, Empress Ming Fang," Felene said with a bow.

"*Wo hao*, my jewel. *Hao ma*, on this lovely day?" Ming Fang panted as she wobbled to stand on her two hind paws, while the Siamese dusted her off annoyingly.

"I am well now that the storm has passed," answered Felene.

"Did you enjoy my stormy entrance?" Ming Fang beamed proudly, "Chinese Magnificats certainly are the greatest wind conjurers, my dear Felene." This, of course, was not true. All Magnificats could manifest wind with a flick of an ear or a puff of breath. Felene smiled in agreement anyway. She had learned very young that there was no use arguing with the empress.

Tossing a suspicious glance back and forth, Ming Fang signaled her words were not for the ears of the impulsive Siamese, who busily unloaded silk satchels filled with scrolls. Then she put her six-flanged paw on Felene's shoulder, indicating she was ready to be escorted into the lair.

Huffing, she entered the fur-softened thorny home relatively unscathed. Her shiny black nose sniffed in scrutiny, "Well, my jewel, I am pleased to see you've kept an air of civility." In the past, she had made no secret that she was not at all happy with the 'down-to-earth' lifestyle Felene had chosen.

"What have you to offer me to eat?" Ming Fang's meal was always her first order of business. The two nibbled on lizard jerky and sipped blackberry leaf tea in Mariah's cobalt-colored teacups, when, after perfunctory cat-chat, Ming Fang pulled out seven scrolls from their satchels. "The Chinese medicine secrets," she whispered, as if the walls had ears, motioning for more jerky as she continued. "As I told you before, according to the Dragon Li Scrolls, all medicine is of the same source; it is the preparation that creates subtle, yet powerful properties. Some chew or smoke the medicines. I prefer medicines as soup, stewed slowly together for rich fragrance and cross-purposes." Then she jokingly patted her fat, dotted belly, finally full, indicating that this was part of the reason for her well-endowed figure.

"Honestly, Felene, even with my many lives of studying healing, I cannot say whether it is the ingredients that heal, or the love with which I infuse them while stirring."

Finally stopping her paper shuffling, Ming Fang leaned back in relief, "Ah, here it is; Goddess Yifan Zhang's recipes." Felene's ears perked in anticipation. The sacred Goddess' formulas were legendary. She was the reason Magnificats spoke the Archer languages at all. Her healing elixirs had been hush-hush for centuries, and Felene drooled in expectation.

"Now listen closely, Felene," sitting cross-legged and leaning in towards her, Ming Fang cited the poem, for the hundredth time, of how her lineage almost lost their magic:

Four thousand years ago,
Cats learned how to talk,

Which made them all laze,
While rat kingdoms played,
And Archers ran out of luck.

Felene knew the rest of the story. When the rat population increased, it brought plagues and epidemics. Archers blamed the goddess and plotted to kill her and destroy her cats. A few escaped, but soft beds easily lured most. The goddess disguised herself as a common cat and slipped away. A kindly Archer took her in, but she was ill with rat disease. In gratitude, the goddess shared her most hallowed 'elixir of healing' to save the woman.

"That recipe is in these scrolls. Protect it!" demanded Ming Fang.

The Archers who collected the goddess' cats became proud of their talking pets, and wanted more. They bred them with any old cats they could find, not knowing that took their magic out of them. Soon, Archers took fancies to one trait or another, a long tail here, an eye color there. They created mutant cats—domesticated shadows of the Magnificats they once were, like taking the smell out of a rose. "We remaining magical Magnificats, as you know my dear Felene, have lived cautiously."

Felene nodded, acutely interested…finally.

"My jewel, You were born for such a time as this. I received permission from Tak to have you transcribe the sacred medicine scrolls. This task must be completed in time for the Centennial Magnificat Summit."

Exhilaration and panic overcame Felene. She sensed her quiet, well-ordered life slipping away. Her claws clutched the Persian rug beneath her. "Don't worry," Ming Fang reassured her, "You will have Jaibon as your assistant."

Felene tried her best to continue listening. Her brain replayed Jaibon's name in a loop of anxiety. But…but, she thought, Jaibon and I are simply incompatible. He is an arrogant, repetitive, know-it-all!

Spreading more papers over the rug, Ming Fang shot rapid-fire orders; pointing at one papyrus, then a list, tapping her claws sharply here and there. "These are the recipes that were buried with cats of the Yellow Emperor," shifting topics in rapid succession. "Oh, and here, these are the sacred teas," whispering, "the ones tea masters hid from the Archer Polo. Remember that story, my jewel? The poor fool purchased tea swept off the floor and never knew it. Archers still believe they drink good tea today," she snorted smugly. Dragon Li Tea Masters guarded these teas with their very lives.

"And finally, these are the Egyptian Papyrus Scr…"

Felene cut her off mid sentence, "But I thought those were lost?"

"Stop interrupting, my jewel," Ming Fang hissed. "You isolated yourself in this dreary place and have no idea what is happening, do you? An Archer child has uncovered the sacred tablet, awakening the demon wind Ephippas from his tomb in Egypt. The Triad of Magnificats were discovered in the Americas, followed by Glarings discovering the Egyptian Scrolls while snowboarding upon Mt. Ararat. All signs are converging. How can you not know? I thought Tak and I raised you better than this."

Felene remained quiet, not lifting her gaze. She really should have known. Have I silenced the world so much that I no longer hear the mysteries? she wondered.

Aloeswood spread its intoxicating effect as the day rolled into night and Ming Fang's droning became a sedative, transporting Felene back to her mother's giggle and Tak's sweet catnip pipe. The stories he told by the fire came back to her, with his descriptions of shape shifting, and how Egyptian Magnificats were equal with humans. Even back then, Ming Fang would interrupt to tell her goddess stories. Good-natured Tak would give a wink and take another puff. Felene and her mother would purr together in the safety of their love.

Suddenly, Felene's fur bristled at the sting of unbearable loss. This is why she avoided Ming Fang. She was a reminder of a past that Felene chose to forget. So was Tak. She reeled in her feelings as Ming Fang tossed a paper from the heap, snapping her claws, "Stay with me Felene, and translate this. This formula is essential: Elder's Soup for Dizzy Feeling." Felene wrote furiously, jotting notes in the margins. "Slow cook shark cartilage, shell-fish, and sea cucumber in salty water for eight hours, then let them sun dry." Ming Fang explained, "In China, the brain is the 'sea of marrow.' Without bone in food, the brain gets hard and shrinks. Marrow keeps the brain soft, protecting the memories of Magnificats when they are old." Tak needs some of this, she thought to herself.

"Are you going to tell me why the dragon appeared in the clouds before the storm last night?" Felene asked.

The old empress stopped fiddling with papers and took a deep breath, "It was to remind you the time is near—remember, my dear? The past, present, and future can be seen in the image of the dragon, like a map." She took a feather out from Felene's door and scratched the thick end of it in the air, drawing a dragon shape. "All of China's dynasties are in this map. Starting in the tail, the oldest, the Shang Dynasty; moving up to the hips, the Qin; then the Han; Five Dynasties; Jin; Yuan; and up to the dragon's shoulders that represented the Ming Dynasty, which was the last one. Having all passed now, we are in the time of the head of the dragon. China's turn at ruling earth has come again. This is one more foretelling of the White Stone Child, the Tiponi, as Moosa calls it."

Felene tilted her head. She was disappointed she did not receive a clearer answer, but was not surprised, since Ming Fang thought China was supreme at everything. She sorted through recipes in the soft light as Ming Fang rambled on until falling asleep, still holding her cobalt blue cup. Felene carefully removed it and continued scouring the documents.

Unlike Ming Fang's Dragon Li lineage, Felene's Thai Jewel lineage did not consider food to be medicine, so some of Ming Fang's ideas seemed old and outdated to her. Her mother, Mariah, had served in the palace of Thai King Rama V, where she was so valued for her beauty and eyes of two colors that he assigned her the honor of caring for his son. She even slept at his feet in the royal bed.

Thai Jewel essences, made via extracting the spirit of plants by distilling them, seemed so much cleaner and scientific. But the discussion of food made Felene hungry, so she snuck out for a quick hunt during Ming Fang's catnap. She returned with a tasty little squirrel for a late night snack, while the empress' snoring vibrated the remaining teacups hanging on the sun-bleached branch.

The next morning, as unexpectedly as Ming Fang blew in, off she flew with her noisy entourage. Felene waved goodbye and blissfully headed towards her bed. Napping would be the order of the day. She was so tired she was almost happy about Jaibon's pending visit. As she curled up on her squirrel-fur stuffed sofa, a Santa Ana wind blew in from the east, carrying any lingering scent of Ming Fang far out to sea, and setting off more fires in the region.

Chapter 14

A Magnificat Ceremony

I know a man caught up to the third heaven.
Whether it was in the body or out of the body,
I do not know.

—Apostle Paul, *2 Corinthians*, 1 C.E.

As the Clouders assembled in Ireland, the winds continued their unpredictable patterns.

"Lovely to see you, Clouder Moosa," Rose said as she reached out her white paw for Moosa to kiss. He took a deep breath of the Irish air, so as not to say what he was sarcastically thinking—Her Majesty Rose. Instead, he stood up on his two hind paws to give a reluctant kiss, deciding it might help to be diplomatic in the event he needed her vote, should his dream come true and there was a coup. Rose removed her fur scarf and ushanka, and was hanging them on the coatrack near the spit when Alkina poked his head in.

"I don't think I can f-fit in this humpy," he announced, trying to be funny by using a common Irish term. Four of the summoned Clouders were at hand and accounted for. Alkina, who made five, was present by the fact of his head jutting in through the spit. Because he was so large, he was never going to fit through that opening. Moosa barely made it himself, only his shifting clavicles allowed passage. "T-Tak has a nice p-place for himself here," Alkina continued, his head poking inside and his body outside, swinging his tail. Everyone noticed his new stutter.

"Tak, should have thought of this and had us meet somewhere you can fit, Brother Alkina," Moosa growled, still trying to form alliances early on, while not-so-subtly criticizing Tak's leadership.

"Welcome to the land of the green," Tak sang a tad too jovially as he arrived outside behind Alkina, who was slowly backing out of the spit. "Please follow me Clouder Alkina, I will show you in through the chapel."

Moosa heard from inside and rolled his eyes as if to say, "Now you tell us."

Neko was the last Clouder to arrive, floating in on a Qi ribbon to sleepy Dublin, settling his silk kite very near the faerie tree. Twirling slowly, his shell and wings disappeared.

Thom was hiding with his paws over his head in his hammock.

Tak and Alkina entered, and with an overhead wave of his paw, Tak signaled Thom to come down to meet the Clouders. Thom wanted no part of this meeting. The Magnificat Clouders terrified him.

"C-C-Can I get you's somethin'?" Thom asked with an unexplained stutter, more exaggerated than Alkina's, as he made his way down. Alkina looked at him compassionately. He knew Thom was in over his head. That was exactly how he felt all the time, lately.

"Can you find some of that black bass, that prehistoric-looking Irish fish Tak sent me some time ago?" piped up Rose in common cat-speak mewing, with her pinky claw up in the air as she took another sip of tea.

Anxious for a chance to get out of there, Thom meowed back, "Aye, I know where they have some just a wee bit from here," and out the spit he bolted.

The Clouders sat on the floor in a circle around a smoldering bit of peat that Thom had gathered for the meeting, snacking on salty fish bits. They would have a proper dinner later. "The ceremony has begun," Tak announced. All the Clouders muttered and bowed their heads. "Clouder Neko, might you do us the honor of interpreting the message of the tea?"

Neko nodded to Tak and removed his obi from around his waist, placing it over his shoulders like a priestly vestment. The teapot came to a fast boil and the lid danced in the steam until a puff of it spelled out a message over their heads in bold white letters that only Neko could read. He refilled Rose's cup. "Please, pour tea not for yourself, but for your neighbor, then allow yourself to be served as well." The pot passed around the circle with each Clouder filling the teacup belonging to the Magnificat seated to their right.

Neko put his paws in a prayer posture, "The tea has spoken. She has instructed us that we should begin this meeting as strangers contemplating cherry trees." Then he glanced up towards the rafters, where a dark puff of steam had settled over Thom's hammock, and a gloomy expression came over him. Collecting himself, he continued, "Familiarity will not be productive, according to the tea." Neko replaced his obi back around his waist. He looked up at the menacing cloud still hovering over Thom's bed.

Not noticing this, Tak broke the silence. "This is wisdom. Hear then, comrades, this is where we will come to know each other anew, who we are now, in this present life," Tak continued in a formal, even eloquent manner. "I will begin."

Moosa became tense, but held his tongue. He believed it inappropriate that Tak would not have his guests go first. Attempting to catch Neko's glance to share his opinion about Tak's rudeness, Neko purposefully avoided his gaze.

"I am Magnificat Littern Tak, a true Abyssinian. My mother, Miw, was of Ethiopia, and my father of Egypt. As a Magnifikitten, I was raised in England, the first Abyssinian to live with Archers in the British Isles. This is my ninth and final life. I have no heirs other than my godkitten, Felene. My gift is shape shifting; my knowledge—Archer behavior; my symbol is the key of life, or ankh; my medicine—Egyptian."

Tak nodded to his right, to Clouder Billi, signaling it was her turn. The tiny Magnificat's long, buff-yellow fur glistened in the candlelight, sparkling off her white tips. Her extra-long tail wrapped around her elegantly like a stole, and highlighted its brown rings, reminiscent of a raccoon. Billi, no more than seven pounds, sat in a perfect yoga pose with her paws formed together and her striped head bowed. She cocked her low-set rounded ears thoughtfully, considering what was most important to point out. Unlike most felines, Billi was not nocturnal and had round pupils, not diamond-shaped. She was crepuscular, a lover of silver mauve twilight. It was hard for her to stay awake in the dark, warm room.

"I am Clouder Billi of Tibet; a Pallas cat by breed, the smallest of all Magnificats. I was born on the Sacred Mountain of many names. It is my eighth life and my kittens are all proudly serving Magnificats. My gift, along with my small size and clandestine work, is as a wind exorcist; a chantress. I wear the agate dzi stone with its twelve eyes to protect against evil. My mountain is connected to Moosa's by the forbidden channel straight through middle earth." Billi looked at Moosa then folded her paws and bowed to show she was finished.

Moosa held an abalone shell in his lap as he sat cross-pawed on the floor. Tak bristled at what he might say. Lighting a bundle of sage from the peat flame, Moosa clipped off a feather from around his neck to distribute the smoke rising off the sage in the shell. "Who holds the sage is the one who speaks. This is the Turtle Island way," he spoke in monotone.

His deep voice rumbled, vibrating in little Billi's chest, "I am Clouder Moosa, forced from my home to the Sacred Peaks," as a jab towards Tak. Then looking at Billi, "I am of your brother mountain, home of the Kachina tablets, that lies opposite Mt. Meru. I, too, am in my eighth life. My medicine is the four directions, and the Turtle Clan symbol is worn for my Mother earth, and all that grows from her shell."

He passed the shell and feather to Alkina, who, in a weak, almost shivering voice, said, "I am C-Clouder Alkina, of the Unnamed Land along the Magnificat song line. I once had k-kittens and a mate, but no more. I am in my eighth l-life. My medicine is in p-plant smoke, and my gift, a m-mystifier. I wear the Dreamtime opal, from where the Creator's foot first touched the earth, when dirt clods came alive with all colors." All Clouders noticed that Alkina's stutter stopped when he told of the opal stone. He touched the stone around his neck with one of his enormous paws as he passed the shell to Neko.

Neko passed it on right away to Rose, refusing to partici-pate in Moosa's obvious insubordination. As a Samurai, he found Moosa to be a typical eighth-lived blowhard, not yet seasoned by true leadership, always thinking he could do everything better.

Neko bowed before speaking. His black and white spotted fur appeared orange and brown in the firelight. "I am Neko. This is my ninth life in the volcano steppes to Japan. I proudly don my short tail as the mark of a warrior. Evil Archers believed our tails had the magic to transform into serpents, so they cut them off. To defy the Archers, we continue this practice to show our bravery. It is an honor to sacrifice a tail to show our strength. I am a Samurai of Samurais, and a Tea Master. My symbol is my obi that encircles my belly, my hara, the source of my power."

The council sat silent, even stunned. Neko was usually so mild. This vigor was an unexpected departure. He folded his paws in completion.

Rose, who held the smoky shell, bowed her head and be-gan, "I am Clouder Rose, of the Crystal Desert. I have kittens and a mate in my homeland of Siberia, in the Red Forests of Russia. My medicine is snow lion's milk. I wear the ushanka to remind me of home." She handed the shell to Makeda.

There was an uncomfortable twinge among the group before Makeda spoke. She had only recently filled the empty

Clouder position in Africa that occurred when Mariah went missing. It had been empty for too long a time, according to many Magnificats. No one spoke of it to keep from upsetting Tak. He still believed that Mariah might return, against all expectations. Makeda had big paws to fill. All were nervous about what she might say. She was not one for sugarcoating things.

"I am Clouder Makeda of Africa," she spoke proudly in a throaty voice, as if to say, *this is my place now, the grieving must end.* "My lair is beside the mountain that hides the sacred Arc, deep within Ras Dashen's peak. This is my ninth life. I am a distant cousin of Littern Tak, though my ancestors come from the Nubian Kingdom of the Black Pharaohs. I use bush-haze medicine and my sense of smell gives me visions. My symbol is the gold trinity of the Order of the Queen of Saba." Makeda handed the shell and feather to Tak, who laid them down in front of him.

Tak nodded in thanks to Makeda, not showing any discomfort in her statement. "Thank you Clouders for coming so quickly, we have not met for a long time."

Moosa corrected, "Eh-hem, for many moons."

"Yes, thank you Clouder Moosa, for many moons," he replied so as not to show any annoyance with Moosa's ongoing attempt at injecting his own traditions.

"Not all that this council has to discuss can be addressed here. I know there are problems within each of your mountain lands. However, we have another, more pressing need. A rampant wind, Ephippas, has been released by the hand of a child, as reported by Magnificat Miz, of Mezo-America." Tak could not resist the temptation to shoot a look to Moosa. "It might be helpful for each of us to report what we know about this wind." There was silence.

Billi spoke first. "I come from the land of Jinn, and in meditation, I was told this wind demon Ephippas is a hot wind. He wants retribution. I am certain I am correct, but will entertain challenges to my intercession," she said, escalating her tone at the end, as if to dare another Clouder to do so.

All began murmuring at once, in side conversations here and there.

"Eh-hem," Tak interrupted from the back of his throat. "Thank you Billi. Who else has knowledge of this wind?"

"It is a wind of evil, but not a wind I have known," chimed Moosa. Noticing a spider, he picked it up and put it in his open paw to show the group. "Welcome spider," he said. "Spider medicine has come to the meeting. The spider wants to help us." To Moosa, a spider showing up was not happenstance. Then he knew; "We must seek out Spider Grandmother to destroy this wind. Her cluster brought fire to the Archers by carrying it from the dark side of the earth, after spinning a worldwide web and then crawling over it. Perhaps, we can capture this wind in a great net. Spider Grandmother might help."

Looking directly at Tak, Rose interjected, "This is not a wind of the south, yet it has settled in the southern oceans. I say we bid the wind here, for a meeting." Rose was an eternal optimist, who thought everyone could be reasonable.

Neko hissed, "Moosa is right, we must rain fire down on him!" His warrior-like stance, upright on his two back legs with his front paws on his hips, again surprised the Clouders.

Great disagreement arose that caused some debate before Alkina stood, towering over the group, his shadow casting an ominous feeling. "This wind is nearest my land, a land where Magnificats are already under siege. I think Ephippas selected this location because Magnificats are weakest there. Our forces are non-existent. Even Ferals can be of no help there."

"Ferals!" erupted Tak. "You would seek council and aid from rats and skunks as well?" Alkina sat down. "There is no way working with Ferals will ever be an option as long as I am Littern." The room became so quiet and the air so filled with mixed feelings, that even Tak had a rush of blood fill his cheeks. That was when he decided to let them know the rest of the story, "Our stone is in the hands of the Archer child who freed the demon!"

The Clouders raged, "This could mean the end of all we know—our way back to the Garden would be lost forever!"

"How can a child have the stone?"

Tak answered, "The proclamation made when Ephippas was buried was that only by the hand of an Archer maiden, filled with righteous anger, can the Magnificat stone containing him be loosed. It must have been a perfect storm of coincidence, unless she was looking for Ephippas. We do not yet know the intentions of her heart, and remember—we cannot take the stone from her by force. She must willingly surrender it, or it will lose power. If other Archers take it from her, they will be sickened."

More gasps and concern, "If Archers gained the secret to nine lives, all would be lost!"

"Evil Archers will use it to destroy all they do not want in the world with them!"

These and more comments echoed in the chamber. Moosa shook his head in disgust at this disorder happening. He blamed Tak, of course.

Tak reared to his haunches and patted his paws in midair in a buoyant, downward-bouncing gesture, "Calm Clouders, calm. We must not react out of fear, but out of strategy." He did feel a sense of relief that the Clouders had not gotten wind of the Magnificat Stone being in the hands of the red-haired girl before he had. "Ephippas is loose and bent on destroying us all. What we do not know is where the stone is, and what is in this Archer girl's heart."

"I can tame a lioness, as well as a lion," interrupted Makeda, both to establish her strength, and to preempt unproductive arguments. "My ancestors stood in that same temple where Ephippas was enslaved by the Archer Solomon, guarding Queen Saba. If this is the very same Ephippas that held up the temple's pillar, I will recognize this wind!"

"That is exactly why you should not go near him," interrupted little Billi, to everyone's dismay. "He will surely recognize you too, and since he does not yet know we are onto him, we must plan well." Makeda, diminished by this little Magnificat, hissed at her loudly.

Billi did not back down, "Clouder Makeda, this is no time for division!"

Makeda's eyes sparkled in the firelight as she softened and smiled, admiring and respecting this tiny Clouder. Billi continued, "Ephippas is of the Jinn, of fire and wind. I know them to be cunning, fiery tricksters. They are as common in my land as faeries are in yours, Littern Tak. A young lioness is ferocious, but her milk is sweet and wet." Then she looked to Rose, "That sweet milk can quench the demon fire, can it not, Rose?" Rose nodded cautiously, not sure yet where Billi was going with this.

"We are considering a net, but the hot demon could melt any net. We need snow lion milk from Rose's Siberian forest to help cool it," said Billi. "With a bit of luck, this child has a good heart. We can all attest to the fact that the strongest force in nature is the true heart of an Archer." The Clouders agreed.

"I recall it was an Archer boy who entrapped Ephippas after he escaped the last time," said Makeda, "by luring him into a lambskin flask. Then he was buried deep in the earth with his tomb sealed by the Magnificat Stone. I recommend that be our model, since it is proven to have worked in the past. This wind demon must be captured by the hand of a pure-hearted Archer child and again secured in a lambskin flask. We must capture him before he heats up the entire globe, as he tried to do before."

"My colleagues in the north may be able to help," reasoned Rose. "Rudolph and Silvershod would surely assist us to stop their icecap from melting. If we need extra power to strengthen the net, their gems and lights would be a good option. And Koshka knows the snow lions near our home."

"Let me find this red-furred Archer! I will determine if she has a pure heart," challenged Makeda.

Alkina whined, "I doubt there is one pure Archer heart left in the world."

"Let us seek the council of the flames," a more cooperative

Moosa suggested. He did not want it to appear that he was not a team player. Tak remained silent, happy to see his Clouders united.

Moosa tossed twigs onto the still-smoldering peat in the center of their circle to grow the fire as Tak spoke, "It is many moons and many wars that bring us to the council of the flames. Let us rise with them."

Each Clouder, in his or her own way, attuned to the flame, urging it to rise. Billi stood on her head. Makeda tied a bright scarf into a big bow that raised her fur up high, as she began to hum in a choppy off-time beat. Rose accompanied in a haunting soprano melody. Moosa drummed against his thighs with his huge paws. Alkina clacked his tonsils with the back of his tongue, in time with Makeda's beat. Neko moved his paws in infinity-shaped swirls, as if directing a symphony. Tak howled like a wolf at a full moon, in falsetto.

The energy mounted and the Clouders began to spin together, circling around the fire like a top. The walls melted. The roof lifted above them to an open, star-draped canvas. Billi flipped back to a seated position and all joined paws. As if on a flying carpet, they began to rise into the sky, over the city, over the continents, then finally, far above any weather, where there was only silence. The music stopped and they held on tightly to one another's paws as they spun round and round, dizzily.

Tak chanted, "Wonder of the flame of flames, knowing each Clouder by their name, red for blood and blue for light, yellow for the end of night. Tell us now, in words so clear, let us see, and let us hear, whisper it in every ear, Magnificat need, Magnificat prayer."

Suddenly, the spinning stopped, leaving them in a place with neither time nor depth. They were not floating, not settled, not in flight, yet they were at peace. They had reached the third heaven. With eyes closed, following Tak's humble request, they waited.

Organically, Tak began a Gregorian-type priestly mantra,

deep from within his chest. A heavenly weight fell like warm honey folding onto their shoulders. It was a sedative over the group, like peace and surety. Visions began to come to the Clouders.

"I see the stone," said Rose with her eyes still closed. "I see the young Archer, with hair red as blood. She has no idea what she has, no inkling of the curse it brings to unaware Archers. It has made two ill already by touching it, even the child's own mother." There was a groan all around among the Clouders.

"My unseen third eye is not open for this vision. I cannot see, does the girl have any idea the stone is powerful?" asked Billi.

"I can see," answered Tak. With eyes closed, he envisioned a skyscreen of images. "No, she seems quite unaware of what she has loosed on the world. But she is seeking knowledge." He with-held his sudden realization that this was the same Archer girl that was trapped in the wild sheegee that had pelted his parish.

"She is in your land Moosa, Turtle Island," whispered Alkina timidly, expecting to be chided, but without stuttering.

Moosa was embarrassed he had not known, but brushed it off and began to intone, "Wo, wo, wo, wo, wa, he, mo. Wo, wo, wo, wo, wa, he, mo."

Neko spoke over Moosa's chant. "The tea shows the child clearly. She says 'No' to the skies, 'No' to the seas, 'No' to life, and she teeters on dark thoughts. However, there is another child, a child of light, peeking around a corner. She has stars about her head like a crown. Her heart is full of flowers that bloom in her chest. I see her taking a small dead cat into her arms and raising it to life again. In the distance is a small boy. I see no more."

"We return!" shouted Tak, after a brief silence.

Instantly, they were all in his chamber, back from the third heaven. Thom had come home proudly with the special fish for Rose to find the room at first empty, then abruptly, full. He dropped the fish and bolted out again.

"I know what we must do!" declared Tak. Then he dis-patched orders. "Rose, you and Neko gather snow lion milk from your homeland and light sources from the north. Moosa and Billi, seek out Spider Grandmother and secure her services for the net. Makeda, find the red-haired Archer, but do not approach her yet. Stay away from Ephippas, and see what you can find out about this other Archer child! Alkina, stay here with me." Tak could see Alkina needed strengthening. "We will require the skin of a lamb for a flask. Alkina and I will get that. There will be blood. Make peace with that now. We will reconvene in one week. So be it. Fly, Clouders, fly!" Then he slammed his fisted paw on Terence the desk. The Clouder meeting adjourned.

Thom peered in through the broken stained glass from the outside roof gable, locking his eyes onto the leaf on Tak's desk. It gave him chills. Should he tell Tak of the warning of danger? He decided to stay clear for now.

CHAPTER 15

FERAL ABDUCTION

Although the wind
blows terribly here,
the moonlight also leaks
between the roof planks
of this ruined house.

—Izumi Shikiby, "Although the Wind," 974-1034, Etchu Province, Japan

Back in Clouder Moosa's land of the Americas, a new wind arose. "Hmm, what is that smell?" Felene twitched her whiskers. The afternoon offered an unusual warm breeze that carried a smoky fragrance, catching her nose in her lair.

Following the scent towards the old lighthouse near Krystal's shed, she looked in on her potential Cat Woman. A faint vibration of Archer voices grew louder. Slinking in the low-lying brush, she wondered, "What are these Archers doing here?" She thought it very suspicious. Concern came over her when she spotted one pasty male Archer swaying hypnotically, staring at a makeshift and careless campfire. A second, rather wooly Archer was sitting on a nearby log. A third, with dark eyes and a red, furry chin shouted, "Let's eat! We'll deal with her later," as he made a pointy gesture towards Krystal's little home.

Any thoughts that these were friends of Krystal's vanished. Felene knew they were up to no good—like Feral cats, taking whatever they wanted by force. Where was Krystal? Did they have her captive?

Felene crept stealthily along the shadow line and observed the three strangers until the setting sun dropped into the ocean in a green flash and the fire brightened. An artless scrap (as Archers often tended towards) broke out and Felene saw her opportunity to move in. Their scuffle ended in laughter as they clumsily fell towards the fire. The rickety door was tied shut with an Archer belt of tattered leather and a rusty buckle. Looking through the slats in the wall, Felene saw Krystal curled up on the furry sheepskin she had left for her. A trail of tears left a clean path down each of Krystal's dirty cheeks.

Krystal was shivering. Her brief period of stability was under siege. She was numb in disbelief. Her home assaulted, again. She had not even tried to get away. Had her will finally been broken?

Felene peered in through a wider opening between two poorly-fit wallboards and her eyes fell across Krystal's gaze. The young girl popped alert in hope, as though an electrical charge had run through her body—rekindling a primitive urge to survive, to escape. Like all the times she wanted to grab LB by the hand and run from the social workers, or faced her mother's string of loser boyfriends, she wanted to live fully and free. Struggling to get loose, her little hands were bound to her feet, hog-tied in a big, messy, granny knot.

Krystal recognized this cat. It looked like the white cat that appeared in her dreams after the lightning struck her. Then she noticed that they shared the same odd eyes, one green and one blue. "Help me again, kitty," she begged in a panicked whisper. Surveying the situation, Felene realized she alone was insufficient help to save Krystal. A failed attempt could put the girl in even worse danger, and herself as well. Felene winked her blue eye and Krystal blinked hard in reply.

Forcing herself away, fur spiked and tail up, Felene dashed like the wind, sending a huge gust into the Archer camp, fanning sparks from their campfire. All she could think to do was to find the fastest, fiercest help she could get. "I have waited too long to find a Cat Woman, and I won't let those Archers destroy this chance," she swore.

She would go to the great culverts where the Feral cats caroused at night and demand to be taken to Pheobe, the garish queen of the Ferals, whom she despised. It was a risk, but Felene counted on one sliver of goodness remaining in Phoebe towards the Archer girl who had saved her and her kittens' lives. Phoebe did not hate Archers the same way she hated Magnificats. Archers had compassion for Ferals and often left food out for them.

Since the Ferals' covert forces were unmatched, Felene did not expect to go undetected, and was not surprised to be immediately cornered by four illiterate Ferals. Speaking in primitive mews to communicate with them, she said, "I am Magnificat Felene, daughter of Clouder Mariah, godkitten of Littern Tak. I demand to see Queen Phoebe." Felene was all too aware of what could happen to her if she showed an inkling of fear. Since two of the fleabags were sons of Phoebe and terrified of their mother, her request was heeded.

Within seconds, hundreds of Ferals encircled Felene in four-stack formations. "You think you will need this many Ferals to restrain me?" she quipped, trying not to seem intimidated.

The hordes herded Felene towards Queen Phoebe. They hissed and spit at her all the way. Beyond the filthy rubble and piles of garbage washed out of street drains by Ming Fang's dragon storm, she clearly saw Phoebe jump up on an old car fender, as if on a throne—gnawing at the mites in her patchy belly fur. She appeared strangely beautiful as her reflection danced on surrounding pools of sewage. Her skinny hind legs reflected in the murky waters, making them appear as long as a cheetah's as she stood at the culvert entry.

"Look what the cat dragged in," Phoebe flared in amusement as her Feral cronies retreated to a safe distance. "Lemme get right to the point, Felene. How come yar here?" hissed Phoebe, continuing her grooming, showing her disinterest by picking at her teeth with an old rusty nail.

"Queen Phoebe, the Archer girl who healed you and delivered your kittens is in trouble," Felene explained. "There is no time for sparring, if you have any intention of helping her."

Phoebe tossed the nail into the oily water with a plunk. Then in one leap, the gangly queen stood face to face with Felene, snarling and swaying back and forth snidely, "Yer Magnificats mock my breeding, and yet here yar, askin' for help in numbers. Do ya see the irony there? Yer magic and cleverness left ya barren, with no kittens—meaning, no army!" Phoebe tossed her tail and threw her head back, cackling like an old witch stirring her pot of spells. "And yar asking for my help. Me, who ya despise and mock as beneath ya for having all the kittens I can."

Warily, licking her tail, Phoebe backed up, then promptly leaned back in, to an inch from Felene's muzzle, and hissed, "What's in it for ya, Felene? You Magnificats never do anything unless there's a benefit to ya."

"It is only the life of this Archer child that concerns me, nothing more."

Phoebe threw her tail down like a gauntlet, "Ya expect me to believe that? Ya want something from her. Ya want her to risk her life and carry yer medicine secrets don'cha? Get 'er killed like all yer Cat Women over eons and ages. Then, ya come here an' act all lily-white, as ya hide the medicines that can stop sufferin', all to yerselves. It ain't going well for ya Magnificats, or should I say, 'Familiars?' Well, we'll see 'bout that. We'll just see about that. And aren't ya going to ask about yer foul mother?" Phoebe provoked.

Felene could feel her claws come out and her saliva foam, but she did not react. She would use self-control. This was the most important distinction of a mature Magnificat, she reassured herself, impressed by her ability to stare down her emotions. Frustrated that her remark did not get a reaction, Phoebe's battle-worn paw gashed a nearby tabby soldier for no apparent reason. Felene didn't blink or flinch.

Then, in a language that was not mewing but something deeper, Phoebe cried out, "Rarasharmichancha!" mobilizing her Ferals like antelopes on the Serengeti, and in an instant, her pack of cats disappeared into the night. Felene spread her wings and followed by air, in awe at the Ferals' swiftness over the ground.

Felene circled above, watching the Ferals covering Krystal's area like a breathing fungus, as the three male Archers sat by the fading embers. One rose and began moving towards the shed, and Krystal. "Yup you guys, we scored on this place. We can stay here 'til who knows when," he said, turning back to his friends. A wind whipped up and spat sparks into the dry brush, already smoldering, unnoticed.

Phoebe's Ferals merged with the shadows, as they awaited their queen's command. Felene landed next to her. Together, they crept up to the shack.

Quietly scratching and clawing at any crevice in an attempt to get inside, Felene and Phoebe peered in through the slats. Phoebe hissed and motioned towards a loosened board in the floor.

"Ah, the floor," Felene understood. She crawled into the one foot space under the shed, which was raised on old pallets and cinder blocks. Moving underneath, she could see upwards between the floorboards. Reaching through, careful to keep her claws in, her paw lightly patted Krystal's delicate fingers. Krystal peeked down through the crack in the floor in relief. Felene looked at her comfortingly.

Straining to feel in the darkness, Krystal made a final, successful, contorted move to unravel the rope binding her, then pulled on the splintery board to raise it until her fingertips bled. When it finally gave way, the rotting plank creakily popped up. Felene entered the shed, covered with cobwebs, looking more Feral than Magnificat. She felt clammy breath on the back of her neck.

"Thar's going be a ruckus for distraction," hissed Phoebe, before she disappeared.

There followed a loud crash and howling of cats in a sadistic squall, as if from another galaxy. Felene heard an Archer fiddling with the belt on the shed door to get inside for shelter, as she rushed Krystal down through the missing floorboard into the crawlspace. "Once I get this back in place, we will be safe," she told Krystal, as she struggled to pull the wood back. At that moment, the Archer broke into the shed and grabbed the lone chair to defend himself against the Ferals. With the board secure, Felene reached beside her to comfort Krystal. Incredibly, she was gone. The Ferals had taken her! Felene had been duped—and knew it. She peeked out from under the shed to see only the Archers remaining.

Krystal was riding away on the backs of a thousand Feral cats. She was not frightened or even exhilarated. She experienced only the familiar sweep from one home to the next, yet unknown.

Felene crouched and watched the Archers stumble and moan, scratched and bleeding. "There can be no evidence," she reasoned. "No story told of what happened in this place." Felene did not want to revisit the days of blood and war, but she had no choice. If the Archers survived, they would report what they saw. Archers would consider cats a threat, or rabid, leading to widespread cat annihilations. While this would be a good thing as far as the Ferals went, Felene still wondered if her mother may be their prisoner, and might suffer their fate.

A power rose up in Felene she had not practiced in a long time. She raised her wings, to a span so large they overshadowed the bewildered and terrified Archers. Then she swooped down and stirred the embers of the fire into monstrous white-hot flames. The black smoke darkened the moon.

The three Archers lunged towards her, but before they got within ten feet, fifty-foot flames incinerated them, then extended to the nearby canyon, setting it ablaze.

Realizing the fire was going to bring more Archers, Felene moaned, "I cannot go look for Krystal now, I will have to find her another day." She raced home to secure her property from the growing wildfire. The medicine scrolls must not be lost.

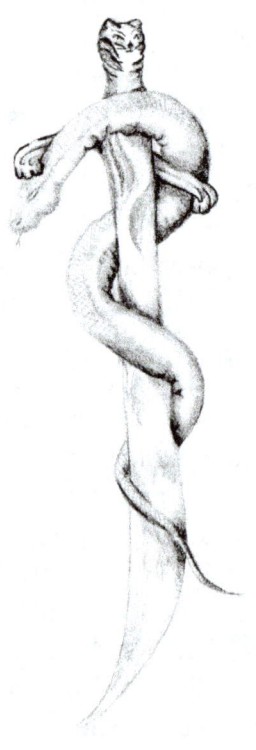

CHAPTER 16

DISSOLVING HOODIE

All the world
is made of faith,
and trust,
and pixie dust.

—J.M. Barrie, *Peter Pan*, 1911, Scotland

By morning, there was nothing left of Krystal's home but ash—no shed and no trace of the drunken Archers, or of Krystal. Firefighters had mobilized to fight the growing inferno, but their search for its cause would only lead them back to the campfire. Even when they found the remains of the three Archers, they would blame it on a homeless Archer camp and an illegal fire. All signs of the battle were erased, but unfortunately, so was Krystal's scent.

Felene had managed to save her own lair by shifting the winds away with her wings and her windmill. The wildfire blazed for three days. It was fueled by the global warmth already generated by Ephippas. Falling ash covered everything and schools were closed. Felene was already poised to follow her only link to Krystal, which was Apple. She knew the girl would come looking for her friend.

Apple couldn't wait for the 'do not pass' barricades to come down so she could investigate and make sure her new friend, well, her only friend, was all right. Once allowed back in the area, Apple looked for familiar landmarks; buildings, trees, or plants. None remained. It would have been a miracle for Krystal to survive if she had been at home at the time of the fire. Even the longstanding lighthouse was gone.

Apple found herself in a dilemma. "If I tell my dad about Krystal not havin' a home, and she's o'right, the cops could be takin' her to a foster home. On the other hand, if I stay silent, Krystal might never be missed—by anyone. And who would even believe me?" Apple decided to stay quiet, under the assumption that Krystal had survived. She dashed to the library hoping Krystal might be there. No luck. She decided while there to try to research all the 'Ms. Colemans' in Phoenix, Arizona, and gather clues about where she might have gone.

Felene watched Apple from a nearby ash-dusted ravine. "I might be able to pick up Krystal's scent if I stay close enough to this saucy red friend," Felene hissed, following the girl after she left the library and headed home. Apple was caught up in her thoughts again, so she didn't notice she was being stalked. As the white-winged cat hovered outside her bedroom over the garage, Apple sorted through her notes from the library and made a series of phone inquiries: "I'm lookin' for Ms. Coleman, who takes care of kids and cats…" and "Does Ms. Coleman, a kindly cat lady, live there?"

One after another disappointing call proved to be the wrong Ms. Coleman, until finally, Felene heard Apple ask a follow-up question: "Oh, good. Well, did she take care of a girl named Krystal with one green and one blue eye?" Then, "Can you tell me where to be findin' her?" Apple wrote something down on the paper and hung up without so much as a 'thank you.'

"App!" yelled Dan from downstairs, "come on to dinner." Apple scrambled out of the room, giving opportunity for Felene's long claw to tear a sheer slice in the screen and squeeze through, leaving tufts of fur in the screen's jagged edges. The wily Magnificat snatched the paper with Ms. Coleman's information on it and was about to leave when she caught a scent of something else.

"Hmmm?" Though faint, at the same time the smell was inexplicably overwhelming. Suddenly, she honed in on Apple's backpack with a bright pink something sticking out of it, slung over the corner of her bed. She was distracted for a moment when she happened to catch a glimpse of herself in the mirror. It was the first time she had seen herself in a full-length mirror in quite some time. She could see she had gotten older. It seemed the dim and wavy reflections in water and windowpanes had fooled her. She licked her paw and wiped a bit of soot away from her face to see her clear eyes and wet glistening nose. She was not displeased.

Then she used her sharp claws to pull the zipper all the way open, down and around the backpack to the other side. "Ah, the pink jacket!" This article of clothing is all Felene would need. She had Krystal's scent now. But this was not the familiar smell that first caught her attention. That was coming from under the bed. It tickled her whiskers. She began to move towards it when the bedroom door flew open.

"What the…?" was all Apple could say. She spotted Felene with the pink hoodie in her jaw, even as she scanned the room to notice the torn screen and open backpack. Apple slammed the door, then dashed to shut the window. She did not want this strange cat to escape. She had become quite suspicious of cats and wondered if it was trying to make away with her stone.

Felene quickly decided she could not set another house ablaze and needed to negotiate her way out of the situation, so to buy time, she dove under the bed. Apple veered from her path toward the window and pounced, catching hold of her tail. "Ouch! You little Archer brat!"

The shock of hearing a cat talk to her made Apple let go, and with the lack of resistance, she promptly parked her bum hard on the floor. "You kin talk?" she gulped. "Just like the cats in my dreams!" Then she pinched herself to make sure she was awake. She was. "Why are you stealing that jacket you bad cat? That belongs to my friend!"

Felene emerged sniffing and sneezing from the dust under the bed. "Don't you ever clean this lair?" Then she took the jacket into her raised paw and scolded, "This belongs to my Cat Woman." Felene knew she was saying far too much, but she had a sense she was going to need this young Archer to get to Krystal.

"Oh," Apple sighed, relieved to realize this cat was after the pink hoodie and not interested in the stone. "Well, I didn't steal it is all I'll be sayin'. Come here kitty. I won't be hurtin' you," she said, trying to appear calm.

"Seriously, you think you can call me 'kitty!' You have no idea who you are speaking to. I am a Magnificat in my seventh life, and you, my dear, are a mere little girl." Felene climbed onto the flowered bedspread one paw at a time, not taking an eye off Apple. She wanted the superior position, above the Archer, still seated on the floor.

"You really kin talk!" A stunned Apple sighed, wiping her brow with the back of her hand.

"Yes, I can talk, and read, and write," Felene said as she brushed dust bunnies off her white fur. "You really need to clean in here, it's dusty, and it smells. You Archers think you are the only creatures that know anything. Well, let me advise you, I know all Archer alphabets. How many do you know?" Felene asked keenly.

"Magnificats?" questioned Apple.

"Yes indeed," replied Felene smugly without further explanation. "You Archers stir up trouble wherever you go that *we* always have to fix, eventually."

"Archers?" Apple probed.

Felene rolled her eyes at the idiocy, "Archers are what you are—Humans."

"Well then, what are you doin' here, in my room, if humans are so offensive to your sensibilities?" Apple chimed curtly. "And, I know five alphabets—English, Egyptian, Old Ogham, Greek, and Gaelic. And you kin be callin' me by my proper name, not Archer. My name is Apple."

"Oh come now, that is not your real name. 'Apple' is quite significant, and has deep meaning that I sense you do not understand, but it is not your true name." Felene was almost starting to enjoy this banter with an Archer. "I can certainly tell you more about your name and your breed than you know."

Apple agreed to listen, now cross-legged and eager for a good tale. "Well, tell me, then."

"The apple was a mystical and forbidden fruit before the Garden's destruction."

"What garden?" asked Apple.

"Good Lord, child, what do you Archers do all day? THE Garden!"

Apple was afraid to show her foolishness by asking further, but planned to study up later on this 'garden.'

"After the Garden was sealed shut, there was no food. The land was dry, and nothing grew upon it except goat-head stickers and treelings, whose seeds had managed to slip out of the Garden, or were carried by the screech owl, perhaps.

"To be quite honest, outside the Garden, life was hardest for you Archers. Ill-equipped, until you snatched fire for yourselves.... Oh, but that is another story.

"Anyway, you helpless Archers had no fur to keep you warm in the cold, or protect you from the hot sun; no fangs, no talons, claws, or poison; no notable speed like the cheetah, or strength like the bear. You had no wings and swam poorly, and had no hooves for climbing steep mountains. You were, and still are, likeable but feeble infants, without your weapons or clothing. Those things came from other animal kingdoms.

"Anyway, subjected to the elements, you Archers became prey to all; the stronger animals for food by day, and the smaller disease-ridden animals, venomous serpents, and insects by night. The harsh conditions and lack of resources caused wars between once peaceful animals. Almost overnight, animal kingdoms began to betray one another in order not to starve or freeze. Alliances formed around likeness. Cats with cats, Archers with Archers, and bugs with bugs."

"So, your sayin' this like I had somethin' to do with it. I wasn't even born yet." Apple interrupted.

"You really are not the brightest sparkle in the fireworks, are you, my dear?"

Apple started to snap back but Felene hissed her down. "Just listen—I am certain listening is a skill you have not developed, so try hard to stay with me."

Apple tightened her lips and squinted at the insult.

"On the other paw, Magnificats like me fared well, with our built-in advantages; fangs, fur, claws, speed, and magic. It is because of us that your kind survived more than one day outside of that Garden."

"Oh, Jaysus, Mary, and Joseph," Apple howled in laughter. "You gotta hug around yoursalf, don't ya, old cat?"

"The truth is this," Felene pressed on, "without us, your species would have never survived. This cannot be denied."

"Oh, come on!" exaggerated Apple as she rolled her green eyes. "You gotta be kiddin' me. Yer jest rewritin' history here."

Felene kept talking. "Well, you did have two things in your favor; imagination and opposing thumbs on your hands. You learned to forge devices to catch your own food. You cut the limb from a lone olive tree, causing her to cry in pain, to make the first bow and arrow. That instance marked the end of your long friendship with the tree kingdom. There's a song that trees still sing, telling of this betrayal:

There was a dog that killed a pig, and left him in the sand
Earned that dog a painful fang, pulled free by Archer hand
Polished to a sharpened tip, it sliced a branch from me
I wept the first sap ever spilled, for everyone to see
Whittled down to smooth and curved, my branch became a bow
Sun-dried innards of that pig were stretched from head to toe

A stolen reed from a redwood tree, forged straight as treelings sang
formed an arrow straight and true, topped with the dog's white fang

"By the way, this kindness of removing the dog's painful tooth created a bond between the dog kingdom and Archers that remains to this day."

"Are you makin' this up as you go along?"

Again, Felene talked over Apple. "The weapon changed everything; weak humans were now able to kill. That is how you got the name, Archers. From that day until now, Archers ruled the earth by making bigger and stronger weapons. They killed more trees to house themselves, and began to hunt and kill for food and clothing. Wanting more, for fear they could become the weakest animal kingdom again, they stockpiled and stretched their reach, and soon even turned their weapons on each other.

"Some animal kingdoms determined never to trust Archers again. Others, like Magnificats, remained hopeful that one day, we would all be joyful together and live in peace. This is the reason I must find Krystal. She may very well be the child spoken of by the prophets and the magi—the one who will show us the way back to the Garden. Do you understand what I am saying, young Archer?"

Apple sat quietly, considering the possibility there was any truth to this cat's tale. Felene stomped her right front paw on the bed. "I am Felene, a Magnificat from the lineage of Thai King Rama, the Mani Jewel Clan. Now, tell me who you are," she demanded.

"Well, la-de-da, Miss Minnie Jewel," Apple said mockingly. "That would make me Archer Apple, of the lineage of the O'Hegarty Emerald Isle Clan," purposely leaving off Standish in her new identity. That name had caused her nothing but problems anyway.

Felene laughed. "I think I may be able to like you, feisty little Archer."

She leapt off the bed and took a bow. "How do you do,

Apple of the Emerald Isle?" She extended her paw for a kiss, or a shake; Apple wasn't sure, and chose the latter.

"My apologies for breaking into your home like this, but you, whether I like it or not, are the only link I have to find the Archer Krystal. You and this pink thing right here," she held up the hoodie. "I may have some information you could benefit from, as well. Would you be interested in a trade of sorts?"

Apple got up to her feet and went to the window, putting her hands out as if to open it wider. Instead, she slammed it shut and locked it, folded her arms over her chest, and said, "I'll be tellin' you noothin' until you tell me somethin'. How's that for a deal?"

Felene stretched and stubbornly declined to negotiate, realizing this Archer would never agree to work together unless she submitted, and quick! She rose to her hind legs and inhaled so deeply that Apple's hair pulled sideways, along with all loose papers. Then Felene revealed her wings, spanning almost the width of the room. She let out a lungful of air that tumbled Apple like a circus performer. With that, she was on top of her, staring down into her two green eyes like a herald. Apple was entirely pinned to the ground.

"Now you listen to me, Apple of the Emerald Isle. There is more in this world than you understand, more at work than just what serves you. I suspect you've had few Archers stand up to you and try to put you in your place, but I am no Archer, and you must get used to your new position—under my paws. Would you like me to demonstrate further, Apple of the Emerald Isle?" Felene drooled.

"I will call for my father," Apple squirmed and spewed.

"If I have summed up this situation correctly, you will be ignored."

"No, no, they are expecting me back to dinner."

"I imagine they are enjoying the break," Felene snarked, as she stepped off of Apple and recoiled her wings, reeling in her talon-like claws that had pinned Apple's shirt to the floor at the same time.

"Oil'right, you made your point. Jest be knowin' this, I am not afraid of anythin', least of all a bleedin' cat! We clear on that?" Apple said as tears welled up and she picked Felene's fur off of her shirt. "What kin you be givin' me?"

"I can give you back your only friend. Are we clear who is in charge?"

"Yes, we are clear," the deflated Apple mumbled.

"Now open that window before you tell me what you know about Krystal. I don't like feeling pinned in," commanded the victorious Felene.

Apple obeyed with a couple of huffs, and then remembered her stone. Did this cat want it? Was this stone related to Krystal? Then, in fear that Felene might even be able to read her thoughts, or some such hullabaloo, she began humming an old Irish tune to create static.

Felene stayed focused on getting details about Krystal, "Tell me!"

"I met her at school, stealin' lunches she was, so, I followed her to a run-down shack she made into a home and took her food and such. We shared stories. You might even say the two of us became friends. And I don't make friends lightly."

"I am sure you do not. Have you ever wondered why that is? Because I can certainly help you to answer that question," Felene cut. "Now, what of this Archer, Ms. Coleman, I heard you trying to find? This paper right here says she is at a place called Kachina Village. What is that? Is it in the Sacred Mountain? I have heard Clouder Moosa mention Kachinas." Felene pulled out the paper she had grabbed and showed it to Apple.

"Well, I wouldn't be t'inkin' a mountain. It's an old folk's place where she's stayin' now." Then she asked, "What's a Clouder?" Felene ignored her.

"Then we must go there. I need to know more about Krystal in order to find her. How does she think? What might she do in any given situation? You will come along. It is easier to mix in with Archers when traveling with one of their own kind." Felene's profound sense of smell branded the pink hoodie. For a fear-filled second, Apple was again afraid Felene might sense the stone. She took a deep breath and held it a moment, with her eyes shifting from right to left and back again. Instead, Felene tossed the sweatshirt into the air where it dissolved.

Apple shook her head, "What just happened?"

Felene hissed softly, "It has no life left in it anymore, I took its essence. Oh, what is it they teach in your Archer schools? You know nothing of magic, do you?"

Felene dismissed Apple's dumbfounded expression and pounced onto the windowsill, stretched out her wings full span, and ordered Apple onto her now-broad body. "Get on," she demanded.

"Okay, but you're so small, I'll be breakin' you," Apple whined as she climbed onto Felene's back, sitting upright with her legs down on each side of Felene's neck. Her fur was slick and cold, like metal. With her wings expanded, she seemed huge.

"HOLD ON, Apple of the Emerald Isle!" shouted Felene. Apple clinched her hands deep into Felene's fur and leaned forward, in awe that she was heading towards the clouds.

As they soared above the city, Felene went in for a low roll over her lair to check on Jaibon's work on the scrolls. "Grip tight, Apple of the Emerald Isle," she yowled as she took a sharp dive. "Good, he is hard at it," she noted.

Apple looked back smugly. She felt she had outsmarted the great Magnificat Felene because she had never noticed the stone. Then she smiled in excitement as the wind blew her hair across a blanket of stars, as if in a dream.

CHAPTER 17

KITTENS, LAMBS, AND SPIDERS

Culture does not make people.
People make culture.
If it is true that the full humanity of women is not our culture,
then we can and must
make it our culture.

—Chimamanda Ngozi Adichie, 2012, TEDxEuston, United Kingdom

Sparks filled the atmosphere as all the Clouders and hundreds of senior Magnificats carried out every detail of the plan to capture Ephippas. There was optimism that the demon wind could be contained.

"I am glad you are used to the cold, Neko," commented Rose, as they reached Siberia.

"I have become accustomed to it. My chain of islands do get cold, but this is beyond cold, Rose." She laughed, looking forward to spending a few precious moments with Koshka and her Magnifikittens.

The kittens jumped on her as she came into their treehouse. Then she and Koshka had some time alone, while Neko kitten-sat. They caught up on what the kittens had been doing at Magnificat School. She was pleased to learn their musical and math studies were going well, and Caterina, her only girl, was doing brilliantly in chemistry, which made her extremely proud. All too soon, it was time to go.

"All right Neko, we should flurry and fly, we will need some time before dark to find the snow lions. They don't stay in one place too long."

Koshka frowned, feeling a tad jealous, "I know where the snow lions are this time of year."

Neko saw that Koshka was feeling left out, and spoke up, "That would be very nice if you could help us, Koshka."

Koshka puffed up and sauntered over to Rose, "What is it you need?"

"We need their milk, Koshka, my love," she patted his cheek, and glanced thankfully at Neko. "It is superior at cooling—like taking Siberia with us." Koshka was happy to be involved in their plan and left to find a pride of snow lions.

While Koshka was away, Rose worked on the light strand specifications in the third floor study, until she heard, "Rose, have you finished the specs yet?" Neko's turtle-like form was silhouetted against a mantle of stars, flying outside her treehouse window, shivering.

"What in the world are you doing out there?"

"While you are working, I thought I might shoot over and get dimensions from the stratosphere above Ephippas, so you can use them for your calculations. I will stay purely out of sight and sense from him." The truth was that he was very uncomfortable around kittens. They made him nervous with their fidgety energy. And he was freezing, with no underground chamber for shelter, as he had at home.

"That would be helpful. Once we have that, we can go north, to Silvershod-Rudolph Affiliates in Greenland, the deer light manufacturers of the North Pole." Neko was relieved to fly south for awhile.

At the same time, sparks lit over North America, where Moosa had returned to his sacred mountain with Clouder

Billi. He was seeking vision guidance from his friend Aholi, the Kachina lieutenant. The two males held ceremony in the animal-skin covered sweat lodge. "Moosa, I see big land, very far," reported Aholi, with his yellow teeth shining in the dim light.

Moosa was getting dizzy from the heat, and couldn't focus, "What else do you see, my brother?"

"I see an Archer boy riding a lamb with Magnificats following him up to the sun."

Moosa was puzzled. He needed more information. "Nothing else, Aholi?"

Aholi closed his eyes as sweat dripped from his forehead. "Hmm, oh wah, humm," he chanted until he had a vision, then he cast it on the walls of the lodge, so Moosa could see it. Clouder Makeda appeared, stirring a batch of medicine. Aholi kept his eyes closed, still willing the vision in his head out like a movie projected onto a screen. Pyramids and winds, then fire appeared.

Makeda's image spoke. "Africa," was all she said. Then Spider Grandmother appeared, serving tea. Moosa understood.

Billi had been waiting outside under the aspens on Moosa's Twin Mountains, furious she was excluded from the ceremony because she was female, which was unheard of in Magnificat culture. To calm herself, she made the best of her idle time by doing contortionist poses to the heavens, requesting help with their upcoming trials.

The layers of antelope hides covering the small, round ceremonial lodge where Moosa and Aholi met flung open at the center. Moosa stepped out. He was dripping with perspiration, so his coat stuck to his frame. Billi shyly giggled, noting he did not look nearly as big without his puffed-up fur. A burst of smoke poured out with him. Unwilling to be seen, Aholi remained inside.

Moosa said nothing, shaking mightily in an effort to dry out, and lapping up water from the bubbling spring nearby, quenching his thirst after the intense sweat. Billi waited in tree pose, not looking at him, yet sensing every move. Her silence and the associated thick air spoke volumes to Moosa.

"I can see you are not happy you were excluded from the ceremony, Clouder Billi."

"Oh, you can see that now, can you, Moosa?" she said sarcastically, as she untwisted from her pose.

"I know the silent treatment well. It is a powerful weapon of female Magnificats."

She spewed a short hiss in disgust, "So, you single out half of the Magnificat population again, this time with a behavior that has forever been used equally by all Magnificats?" Then she growled quietly, her anger held behind clenched fangs, "I would never have treated you in such a way in my land, Moosa. Your rudeness has lessened my esteem and respect for you."

Moosa paced back and forth, working out what he was going to say, but she continued before he could speak, as he had feared. (He also believed females were better at word slaying, but dared not say so.)

"If I met with the snake dancers of India, I would insist upon your inclusion. They would argue that you were unworthy, being of the infant land of the Americas. If I agreed to their disrespect of my colleague, what courage would I show? What statement of unity would I demonstrate in the name of all Magnificats? We are Clouders first, Moosa."

"It is true, I did not show my loyalty to you as a Clouder. But I have learned it is a wise Magnificat who respects the culture and customs of the lands they watch."

"That is because you have not seen a war in your land in many ages, Moosa. Not death and starvation as I have seen, thousands of cats and Archers dying in the streets from diseases curable on Turtle Island with a single pill. Your rats are rarely rabid, your fleas have no plagues, and your water is safe to drink!" Billi's tone began to escalate with feelings too long choked down.

"We have right-rain on my mountain precisely because I am respectful of the Kachina ways. That is why there are no droughts and plagues here." Moosa defended.

"You have forgotten that you matter little to the Kachina or other Archers, my friend. They will forsake you if there comes a dreadful time when there is not enough water to share, or food. There would be no invitation to sit with them in ceremony, unless you are their dinner! Know who to be loyal to, Moosa, as Magnificat Yogi Katarani taught: 'Loyalty forgets in the first calm wind. Disloyalty is forgotten neither in calm nor storms.' Frankly, sometimes one must choose a side." Then Billi changed her tone and asked impatiently, "All right, what did your Kachina friend advise?"

"We must go and see Spider Grandmother, and there was something about Africa."

"Well, we knew that. What else?" she snapped.

"An Archer child was riding a lamb."

"Tell me of Spider Grandmother, Moosa, so I know what to expect," the little Clouder demanded sharply.

"Please, Clouder Billi, sit with me under the aspens and let me tell you of Spider Grandmother. The story is sacred, spoken only in ceremony." He lit some sage, then began a slow drumbeat with his paws, "Many moons past, when the earth did not spin, the sun was only on one side. Spider Grandmother, the weaver who could create various things with her many legs, lived in the dark, and heard about the mighty sun from travelers. She wove a basket and lined it with mud. Then she spun a web that reached all the way to the other side of the earth, where the light was. Making no sound at all, Spider Grandmother scampered over the net, snatched a piece of sun, and tossed it in her basket. Then she scuttled it back. On that day, the entire world gained sun and fire." The drumming stopped and a cool wind swept the smoke away, as if ordered to do so.

"I see," calculated Billi. "We shall ask your Spider Grandmother to weave a web together with the light strands Clouder Rose and Clouder Neko have gone north to gather. The addition of light will create a much stronger net. A sprinkling of snow lion's milk will give it resistance to heat. Then, from above, we will drop the net on Ephippas."

Moosa confirmed, "Spider Grandmother prepares now for her winter hibernation, the time of no thunder. We must go before she begins storing food, or we might be that food. You should do the talking. Spiders tend to eat males."

Now Billi laughed aloud. "Oh, so now you risk my life because I am a female?"

Moosa chuckled. "Being female can work in your favor, Billi," he said sarcastically.

"Where does she live?"

"Madagascar, off the southeastern coast of Africa."

Meanwhile, unbeknownst to anyone, just west of Madagascar, Makeda was on the scent of Apple, by way of the cyclone, which she had been ordered not to do. She wanted to get a glimpse of this nemesis, Ephippas, and see if he was threatening her continent. He was.

Simultaneously, back in Ireland, Tak became agitated and annoyed as he watched Thom pace back and forth, behaving so out of character for the usually cheerful cat. Thom even growled once, surprising himself. Tak heard it and looked up at him, perplexed.

Alkina was asleep on the warm stone near the backside of the parish altar when Tak noticed the leaf he had carried inside on the day of the wee wind. A refracted light coming down in a beam from the stained glass was shining directly on it. Thom saw Tak pick it up, holding it up to the light to see the small leaf patterns on it. "'Tis Ogham, Tak, the first tree language," Thom piped.

Tak looked more closely then mumbled, "We must find a reader of this language."

Insulted, Thom overreacted and hissed, "I can read it. Jest because I'm not a Magnificat don't be meanin' I'm an eejit!"

Tak was surprised and sorry. Thom blasted out the spit before he could say so.

Chapter 18

SWEET GRASS OF AFRICA

Awake, O north wind,
And come, wind of the south;
Make my garden breathe out fragrance,
Let its spices be wafted abroad.

—Unknown, *Song of Solomon*, 10th–2nd Century B.C.E., North Africa

"Sniff," Makeda caught the out-of-place scent of the damp African grass of home when she arrived over California, and curiously followed it to Arizona, where Apple and Felene were hiding outside Kachina Village, the senior home where Ms. Coleman was recovering. Makeda was screened by the clouds as she waited in the darkening sky until it became quiet, and visitors stopped entering and exiting the tan stucco building. She didn't see Felene and Apple at first.

"I'll go inside and distract the desk staff so you can run in and see which room is Ms. Coleman's," Felene proposed to Apple, who agreed and did as instructed.

Soon both Apple and Makeda heard screams of "Get, cat!" as Felene scuttled out, her claws losing footing on the slippery floor, being chased by an Archer in gray-blue scrubs waving a broom, still yelling, "Scat!" Apple, waiting behind the bushes by the automatic door, took that moment to slip in. Her heart was pounding and butterflies fluttered in her stomach. She felt like a spy in a movie.

Posted on the wall behind the nurses station was the patient name and room number list, and right there, big as day, was "Angenet Coleman, room 222."

That has to be her, Apple thought to herself, as she walked calmly away so as to not attract attention. She decided to hide in plain sight and took the elevator right up to the second floor. Felene followed, making her way in through an open hallway window upstairs, after slicing her second screen of the day with razor precision.

The two met outside room 222. "You go first," Felene hissed.

Apple looked at her with dismay, "You're sendin' me in first? You know I'm a kid, right?"

Felene hissed again, so Apple tiptoed into the barren room and around the fabric screen that encircled Ms. Coleman's hospital bed.

She was as Apple had pictured her, round and warm, wearing the expected pink foam curlers. She was working on a crossword puzzle when she looked quizzically over the top of her reading glasses at the disheveled redhead, "Well I'll be. What in the world happened to your hair, child? You look a fright!" Then she laughed.

Apple's hair was a crazy mess from flying. She reached up and found it was so matted she could not get her fingers through it. Trying to pat it down, she felt something stiff and pulled out a bird feather! Then she scanned the room and found a chair, scooted it over to the bed, sat down, and whispered, "Are you the Ms. Coleman who took care of Krystal?"

"Why yes, child, I am. How is my Kryssy?" Ms. Coleman answered loudly.

Apple motioned with her index finger over her lips, "Shhh. She's gone missin', Ms. Coleman."

Ms. Coleman's eyes brightened, and she sat straight up in her bed. "What do you mean child? What do you mean by missin'?" Felene hopped up on the bed and purred. "And what is this cat doin' here…she yours? They don't let no cats in here, no, no."

Felene, somewhat annoyed at the supposition that she was an ordinary cat, said plainly, "I am a Magnificat."

"A what?!" exclaimed Ms. Coleman. "This is crazy, I am callin' a nurse, 'cos I shore must be having a reaction to my med'cin." She began reaching for the call button tangled in her bedding.

"No, no, Ms. Coleman. I didn't believe it either, but this cat kin be talkin'. She needs your help at fetchin' Krystal."

"Well, how can I help, strapped to this danged bed…an old lady, no use to nobody, that's what I am now. No use to nobody," she muttered again, as sadness filled her eyes for a second before rebounding. "What happened to my Kryssy?"

Felene began explaining to both Ms. Coleman and Apple the whole, sordid matter of the Ferals and Magnificat feud, and the result: Krystal's kidnapping.

"What kin I do to help you, cat?" Ms. Coleman cautiously asked, in a manner that indicated she still might not believe what was occurring.

"You can tell us about Krystal. Who is she? Where did she come from?"

"Oh, you saw the magic in her too, did ya? I knew it from the moment I laid eyes on that tow-headed, mixed-up-eyed girl. Now lemme' think. Kryssy came to me when I was low. I lost my home, my work. Her little family moved to a dinky apartment above me. She brightened my days with her quizzical way of the world. She and her li'l brother, LB, were inseparable. The two of them would come to me when their mama was sick, which was often. She was sick in the soul and in the head. She'd run off for three or four days sometimes, leaving those youngin's alone. I was a foster mother. I knew the system. Maybe what I did weren't right, but I knew them two would be separated, being different ages and races. That's how they do it. That ain't no solution, punishin' children. It was better I took 'em in when they needed. Said I was they aunt. After I fell, I done knew the State would take 'em.

Nothing I could do."

Apple gawked while Felene took notes on an invisible pad with her claw, etching as if on a clipboard on her lap.

"How did she learn to heal animals?" inquired Felene, without looking up, still scratching notes like a reporter from a local paper.

"I done taught her some cures, but she was a natural—born with it, I b'lieve."

"And what of her mother? Where is she?" Felene pressed.

"Who knows, locked up somewheres. She had no money for fancy treatments."

"…and her brother?"

"If they ain't together, then he is in the system, maybe adopted by now. They like to get those youngin's out fast."

"Do you know healin' too, Ms. Coleman?" interrupted Apple, earning a scowl from Felene.

"Why yes, child, I do. All my people learnt the healin' arts from our mamas; natural as makin' chicken soup." Then she looked at Apple, "Your mama be needin' some healing, don't she child?"

Apple's eyes welled up, and she nearly choked on the sad, sour tears she held back (not the hot, angry, salty tears she used to cry). Except for Krystal, she had not talked about her mum getting sick to anyone.

Felene looked up from the pad, evaluating how this all may be useful, not interested in Apple's reaction, nor her mother, for that matter. Then she asked, "What is your medicine, Ms. Coleman?"

"African, what else!?" She rolled with contagious laughter that made all three giggle. "I taught Kryssy African recipes. The drink for new mama cats to get in they milk fast, you know, the one with flaxseed, oats, and honey. And Ethiopian genfo, the porridge to give the mama her strength back. Lots and lots of things she done picked up on her own. Bright child, my Kryssy."

Ms. Coleman's chocolate-toned hand patted the side of her

bed to have Apple sit by her. She looked into her eyes seriously, "You got somethin' dangerous child. You got to give it back. It is what made you' mama sick. You got to give it back!"

Apple leapt up and away. Terror shot through her, but she did not speak.

Felene missed that interaction because she had become distracted, keyed onto a small photograph in a silver frame on the bedside table. It was a picture of Ms Coleman wearing a long, black beaded necklace, with her arms around Krystal and a small, curly-haired boy. That must be LB, she thought.

The lights dimmed, and a nurse peeked in. Felene dashed under the bed. "I didn't know you had a visitor, Ms. Coleman. Sorry sweetie, but it is past visiting hours," the kindly nurse directed Apple.

"Bye, Ms. Coleman," Apple said sadly. She understood why Krystal had gotten so attached to the big-hearted woman. She was like a crackling fire on a cold winter day, warm and comforting.

"Ya'll keep me posted on Kryssy, ya hear?" Apple nodded an affirmative to Ms. Coleman as the nurse escorted her out, while Felene crept down the hall and leapt back out the window, unnoticed.

After watching the two leave, Makeda flew up to the window she had seen Felene sneak out of and entered swiftly. She was appointed only to observe for now, which she found frustrating. Sneaking into the room that smelled of African grass, she immediately locked onto the picture on the bedside table. But it was not because she recognized anyone. "The necklace!" she gasped, when she saw the black licorice-seed neckace around Ms. Coleman's neck. "The crest of an Ethiopian Cat Woman!"

Now Makeda understood the smell of African grass that had blended with Apple's scent. With the nurse coming in and out, she would not be able to whisper in the Archer woman's ear to awaken her spirit just yet. That would have to come later.

CHAPTER 19

ALCHEMIST DEER AND STICKY WEBS

There is in them a softer fire than the ruby,
there is the brilliant purple of the amethyst,
and the sea green of the emerald—
all shining together in incredible union.

—Pliny the Elder, *Naturalis Historia*, 23-79 C.E., Roman Kingdom

Rose and Neko arrived at the factory of the deer lightworkers in Greenland, with the aurora lights shimmering. The two Clouders appeared as tiny black gnats against the white snow as they dove in through a crevice, dodging cliffs, while flying full speed through the narrow corridor towards the entry.

Once inside, the grand cavern was lit up like a Christmas village. Red, green, and yellow lights twinkled against the white backdrop, as scurrying deer folk rushed about their work.

"Hello Auntie Rose," came a tuba-toned voice behind them, "welcome to our humble mountain," followed by the clickity-clacking of hooves. Rose jumped around, startled, and saw Silverson, the spitting image of his father Silvershod, Clouder Moira's student.

"What can I do for you, Auntie Rose?" he said, as he bent his head down to let her hug his strong neck in greeting. "Tell me as I give you the tour."

Rose in her furs and Neko in his kimono walked upright with their front paws folded behind their backs. "We are in need of extra light, Silverson. The wind demon Ephippas is loose and creating havoc, whipping up storms to heat up the planet. We Clouders have a plan to stop him, but we need precise help."

"Ah yes, Rose, we have concerns about this sudden warming here in the north; whole icebergs coming apart at the seams. The polar bear kingdom is hit hardest. How did that old rascal Ephippas get out of that hole anyway? Someone was surely asleep at the switch on that one." Without waiting for an answer, he looked up, "When do you need the light and where shall we deliver it?"

"By the end of this week, we will have more details when the Clouders reconvene in Ireland. Can I count on you when the time comes?"

"We can start production, but we need two days lead-time. How will you pay?"

Rose hid her surprise. She had not expected to be charged for saving the planet, for goodness sake. "What did you have in mind?" she replied, without giving any indication this request was unpredicted.

"You know, we could use more protection for our deer fire brigades in North America, out in the field. Their numbers are dwindling and wildfires are increasing because they are not there to clear the earth of extra growth. The blazes are adding to the warmer temperatures, and vice versa. Just assign some Magnificats to watch over them to warn of Archers and wolves and we will have a deal."

"We can arrange that," said Rose, thinking she would set Moosa on that task, as he was the earthy one of the group and in charge of North America anyway.

"Oh, forgive me Silverson, this is Clouder Neko," Rose said, a bit embarrassed about her oversight of introductions. Silverson clacked his hooves and nodded his head, touching his antlers on the floor in front of Neko, showing superiority. Neko didn't like this one bit, but kept his paws behind his back.

"I believe we have some warm carrot pie and dill teas. As you know we are vegetarians, so no meat for you cats." Otherwise ignoring Neko, he asked, "Tell me, Aunt Rose, how are Koshka and the new Magnifikittens?"

"Oh, they are doing fine, and…," the small talk continued while they wandered deeper into the mountain, leaving the noisiness and bright lights of the factory behind. Neko followed along guardedly.

Far to the south, Clouders Moosa and Billi reached Spider Grandmother's treehouse in the rainforest. Her nest was high up in the healing kily tree. Its dark red bark and jade-colored leaves offset furry yellow lemurs, whose crisp orange eyes peeked out. At its base was a door with a spider-shaped knocker that Moosa had made for her after his fire training, when she was his teacher. It was going to be a challenge for Moosa to squeeze through. Billi knocked. A small peephole at the top of the door opened up to several red eyes.

"What do you want?"

Moosa became tongue-tied.

"I am Clouder Billi, of Tibet. We, that is, Clouder Moosa and I would like to see Spider Grandmother. It's important."

"Someone is going to be very happy to see you Moosa, you old Magnificat, you." Moosa had not been back since fire training, and that was on purpose. He was very uncomfortable around Spider Grandmother.

The door creaked open to a forest of black, hairy, angled spider legs. "Come in, if you dare," came a witchy laugh.

Billi avoided the sticky, fine spider webs on the interior, and the hairy legs. Moosa fidgeted his head through, contorting his face. Once his head cleared, the rest was easy.

The door slammed shut behind them, and the entire floor beneath them began to move, like an elevator. Up and up Moosa and Billi went, far higher than the outside of the tree had appeared. Finally stopping, the door opened and they stepped out onto a floor made of silver-grey strands, crisscrossing in a myriad of weaves.

A member of the Bark Cluster, Spider Grandmother had the strongest silk webbing of any spider in the world. If she wanted, she could spin a web capable of stopping an Archer jet airplane in mid-air.

"Tsk-tsk-tsk," lisped the spider, "watch your step on those shiny webbings or you'll get tangled up in them. Now come closer. Let me get a look." The two moved forward delicately, trying to avoid any sticky web strands as they zigzagged along.

Grandmother sat as matriarch, welcoming her knight's home from battle, expecting a delicious story. She was enormous, taking up most of the free space. "Ah, Moosa, what took you so long to come see me?"

"I have been very busy, Spider Grandmother," he lied.

"And who is your little girlfriend?"

"I am Clouder Billi," the small cat said flatly, fed up with being minimized.

"I am surprised they let such a tiny cat as you be a Clouder."

Billi could feel uncomfortable tension growing, and to avoid it, blurted out, "Spider Grandmother. We want to warn you of a coming storm that could destroy your rainforest, in more ways than one."

"Tell me more, little Billi." She leaned in closer, tucking some of her legs behind her.

"A wind demon has been loosed. His heat will fry your rainforests, kill your treehouse."

Spider Grandmother gasped, "My tree? Nothing makes my venom boil more than harming trees. The poor strong castles cannot even run. Without them we would not be breathing, for spider's sakes!"

Her alarm suddenly shifted to suspicion. "But how do I know you are telling me the truth?"

Billi looked to Moosa for some backup but found none. Instead, she noticed his paws shaking. Another smaller spider peered in through the thick webbing. "It could be true, Grandmother," he offered. "Birds have been leaving the island, squawking about a huge wind on its way."

"Is that right, Mondo? You have seen and heard this?" Spider Grandmother swooped clumsily close to Billi, her fangs tapping the ends of the Clouder's whiskers. Billi did not back down. Then the spider quickly reeled to Moosa, as she began to drool silk sap from her spinnerets.

"So, Spider Grandmother," Billi spat out as fast as she could, "we need an enormous woven web to drop on the demon wind. Is this something you can do?"

"Why of course, darlings," she swung back. "Let us sit together and share a meal of mayflies and kily sap. How will you transport this web?"

"You will need to come with us," Moosa reckoned, nervously.

"I just want to wrap my eight legs around you Moosa, you big old fluffy cat," she laughed, her huge, shiny black body scrambling off across the white-webbed floor. She motioned for them to follow with one of her eight legs, her movements sending a ripple effect through the already tottering web. Reaching the black table where three places were set in red dishes for their snack, Spider Grandmother continued making off-color remarks flirtatiously to Moosa. It seemed painfully gauche to Billi.

CHAPTER 20

THE AFRICAN CAT WOMAN

They say there's a secret charm which lies
in some wild floweret's bell,
that grows in a vale where the west wind sighs…

—Samuel Lover, "The Charm," 1830, Dublin, Ireland

Ms. Coleman's presence—the smell of fresh grass after an elephant trampling—reminded Makeda of father elephants who returned from their day of wandering, snapped a twig from a tall tree, and whipped the young elephants, who they knew did something wrong in their absence. These days, the majestic fathers of many land animals had become low in numbers, causing father power to be weak in the very air breathed. It was a growing problem.

The smell also reminded Makeda of mud for making jewelry and pots after a fresh summer rain, when all the Cat Women worked together, talking. A warm, feathery wind brushed her whiskers every time she was near Ms. Coleman. She needed a closer look at the necklace in the picture, in daylight. The tall African cat, trying to look small on four legs, snuck into the kitchen of the senior home, taking a bombardier nosedive into the bottom of a meal cart, draped with white cloth.

Makeda rode up and down hallways unnoticed, as the Archers in each of their independent lairs received their starchy meals. "Yuck," she spat.

Makeda knew the right spot to hop out from under the food cart by the grass smell. The nurse left a tray on Ms. Coleman's bedside table and knocked on the bathroom door, "Ms. Coleman, breakfast is all ready for you, sweetie," she called, and left.

Ms. Coleman came out using her walker, with its two greenish-yellow tennis balls stuck on the bottom front legs for stability, singing an old spiritual, while Makeda watched from under the bed. Ms. Coleman dressed everyday, no matter how she felt. This day, she had on a mint-green dress with tiny scarlet dots that pressed her ample bosom up and out of the low-cut top like a pair of perfect soufflés. A coordinating red hat and white gloves topped off her snappy 'going-to-church' outfit.

She wanted to go home, but it wasn't clear where her home was now. It seemed the world was already pushing her out of it. She was invisible to younger folks and undetectable to men. She used to catch a man with a swish of her hip. Now, her hips did not swivel much at all.

With her prolonged stay in the rehabilitation facility after the hospital, her apartment was packed up by her landlord and her belongings were placed in a storage rental, she was told. On her small social security income, Ms. Coleman did not have the means for a first and last payment to secure housing. She was sure she would not even qualify to rent a mobile home in a senior park. Not terribly disappointed, Ms. Coleman had always seen those aluminum contraptions as the caboose on the train of life anyway, not at all how she wanted to go to her next unknown phase. Besides, she loved children and animals, and senior places had no mix of generations and often limited pets. They were mostly filled by lonely old folks with life pouring out, and no new life coming in.

She recalled her small nest egg in her garden, but even if she could find a way to get to her old apartment, she was sure it would be gone by now. The location of that old coffee can was no longer completely clear in her memory, either. She was just about to sink into melancholy, when a tickle passed her calf.

"Well, well, now, ya sweet kitty, what ya'll doin' here? Two cats visitin' in as many days?" Makeda rubbed back and forth against the elderly woman's calves, expanding the runs in her nylon stockings. The Magnificat was reading her DNA through them. Ms. Coleman bent down to pick up the long thin cat for a cuddle and a good petting. Makeda struggled, but knew immediately—yes, this was a Cat Woman!

Makeda made her way to Ms. Coleman's lap and started a good vibrational purr to read her energy. Ms. Coleman coughed. In an instant, Makeda knew she needed to get this Archer out of Kachina Village, and soon. She was ill, seriously ill. There was too much sickness around her for Magnificat medicine to work—too many opposing forces, Makeda notioned. Ms. Coleman must be isolated. She cannot go to Africa until she is better. She will not make the trip, what with jarring altitude changes and light-speed effects, not to mention temperature changes. Makeda needed to find a place for Ms. Coleman to stay in a more private setting. For this, she needed Archer magic of the green strand.

With Felene unknowingly working on Makeda's assigned task of learning about the two Archer girls, she could afford the extra time to follow this lead. She looked up at the loving woman and purred, "Ms. Coleman, I came to take you back to Africa. You are a Cat Woman."

Ms. Coleman grasped her left breast over her heart, as if she was about to swoon. "Well, I'll be! You 'bout give me a heart attack. Is you for real, or am I having old-timer's disease? Am I head'n for the last ride? You is the second talkin' cat I seen!" She looked around the room for any sign of angels, or a low-swinging chariot.

Makeda snickered and leaned in, putting her paws up near the Archer's furless ear, and whispered something to awaken the memory of her ancestors. Ms. Coleman calmed down immediately and took a deep cleansing breath. "Why, I jest got a hint of my Bibi's liniment, as if she was right here in this room."

"Ms. Coleman, I am going to take you on the best ride of your life. There are so many Archers in my region who need you; Magnificats too. In my village, we have a motto: 'No one is old. No one is young. All know what they know.' I sense you cannot travel by Magnificat ways, it would harm you. You are too sick to fly, even by Archer crafts, at this time. We need to get you well enough to travel. That means getting you out of here."

"Woo, child, I need to set here a spell. Whatcha mean I'm sick?" she asked, as she fanned herself with the newspaper she had been reading earlier. Her head was spinning. Perhaps this cat was an angel.

"Rest here until I return for you," Makeda advised.

"Ah, honey, you jest get to doing whatever it is that you do. I am floodin' with memories I never knew I had, and feelin' some weariness."

Feeling confident that Ms. Coleman was waking up to her destiny, Makeda snuck out of the rest home and took flight toward California.

CHAPTER 21

CRESCENT WINDS

*For they sow the wind
and reap the whirlwind.*

—Hosea, son of Beeri, 700's B.C.E., Kingdom of Judah, Samaria

"Look there, Apple of the Emerald Isle, we are nearly home," yelled Felene.

"Whoa," cried Apple as Felene took a sharp lilt in midair. Then she giggled with exhilaration.

Felene sniffed the scene over her lair, "Oh good, Jaibon is still there. I doubt he is actually working, but at least he is there."

"Jaibon?" quizzed Apple.

"He is my assistant." Felene poured on speed for a quick updraft before diving down to Apple's father's house. From the air, Apple could see some out-of-place bearded men talking with Amanda beside a jeep, outside the house.

"That'd be me stepmonster," she pointed.

Felene's fur rose when she caught a glimpse of the swinging ankh around Amanda's neck. Even from that distance, it beamed into her senses. This necklace was not mere jewelry. It was from a crypt—Felene could smell death on it, fresh death, the spawn of Lilitu, the screech owl, or Lillith, the killer of babies, or whatever name the murderous creature was going by at this time. Felene sensed it. Instead of taking Apple home, she landed quietly on a neighbor's roof to investigate from a distance. "How long has she had the ankh, Apple of the Emerald Isle?"

Apple thought of the strange cat with the ankh she saw the day of the sheegee wind. That was when everything went lopsided in her life. Apple stood up, to try to see Amanda. Felene clawed her shirt and demanded, "Get down."

Startled by the sudden seriousness of Felene's tone, Apple dropped to her knees. "She was wearing it when I went to Egypt this year."

"Why were you in Egypt?"

"My dad's an archaeologist. I was visitin' him."

Felene looked at her for a moment, and thought about Apple's room, and the smell. Then she became distracted when Amanda looked straight at the rooftop, intuitively, as if she knew she was being watched. She rushed the men into their jeep, waved them away, and went inside, still looking their way.

"You have good hunting instincts. That Archer *is* a monster, Apple of the Emerald Isle."

"You don't have to be tellin' me that," agreed Apple, laughingly.

"No Apple, I mean true evil. From where does she come? What do you know about her family?"

"She showed up with me dad after he left us. I never wanted to be knowin' her after she hurt me mum."

"Hmmm," Felene stroked her whiskers with one claw, still watching the door.

The jeep swung around to face Felene and Apple's direction. Apple strained to get a good look as they rolled past. She recognized one of the men, the small one. He was the one in the desert in Egypt, holding the yellow napkin! She would never forget his piercing eyes.

"Well, oi'll be," Apple burst out and began to scramble to her feet. Felene stopped her by pinning her shirt down again with her claws. Apple shook it loose. "What you t'inkin', you crazy cat," she huffed, yanking her shirt back.

"You have no idea how serious this is Apple. You are blind in the sun to so much."

"T'anks for those kind words, and I'll be goin' now," smarted Apple, climbing down a side-yard trellis to the ground below.

Felene had to get back and make sure Jaibon was working on the healing scrolls. She took to the skies, not thinking much more of Apple. She worried that Tak or Ming Fang might learn she was not at her task.

To no surprise, Felene arrived to find Jaibon fast asleep, draped over the piles of paperwork he was supposed to be transcribing onto the steam that arose from Ming Fang's simmering tea. The special blend formed an indelible mist paper that could never be torn, weathered, or burned.

Felene recalled how annoying he could be, arrogant and self-congratulatory. His behavior at the last summit was appalling, embarrassing her publicly. As Felene curled up in her lower lair, her blood boiled like Ming Fang's tea, as she recalled how he tried to make her look a fool.

It was the last Centennial Summit, when Felene foretold a Cat Woman. She could almost hear Tak's deep voice echo from under his scarlet cloak before the restless crowd of Magnificats, Glarings, and Clouders: "Before this Sacred Geode, we join paws upon this barren land of staggering horrors known as earth; we await our rightful place beside Archers. It is now, and always has been, the desire of this Magnificat Council to share our sacred healing knowledge with Archers. After all, we owe our existence to their mother, who rescued Silvestria, the ancestress of all Magnificats, from the Garden."

Tak continued, "It is our duty to prevent the nine-lives secrets from falling into Archer hands or Feral paws by reciting the oracle to remind us of the sacredness of the Magnificat Stone. Who then, will speak the Oracle of Silvestria, passed down by Magnificat scribes?"

"I will recite the oracle," Felene surprised everyone, including herself, when her voice echoed off the mountain. She was new to her seventh life at the time.

Catcalls came from the probing multitude, "Only Clouders or former Clouders can recite." A flash of lightning revealed Felene's winged shadow, fifty times larger than life, against the red sandstone wall. A collective gasp muted the rumbling thunder of a distant monsoon. Flashes of light illuminated the deserted Anasazi cliff dwellings nearby.

"Who addresses this council?" inquired a younger Littern Tak.

His gold eyes surveyed the crowd trying to find the speaker. Another flash from the coming storm revealed a faint profile of a winged cat on a distant shale ridge. His gaze rested on Felene's sleek white fur, electric blue with each additional flash, "Who addresses this council?" he repeated, squinting to see, with his paw over his brow to shield reflected light.

Felene had traveled for hours. Even with the long, dirty trip, her crystal-tipped coat was stunning in the moonlight. She stretched indifferently to conceal her anxiety and even considered yawning, but decided that may be going a bit far. In three smooth strides and a glide, she flew to Tak's side, inside the colossal amethyst geode.

Before she could speak, hackneyed and self-bloated Jaibon interrupted, and in a shrill voice, tried to embarrass Felene, "The genealogy must, must, must, be recited by anyone who wishes to address the council…no matter how important they think they are—Felene." He was quite pleased at the resulting laughter. In truth, everyone knew British shorthairs like Jaibon had little Roman ancestry left in their line and it was only as a courtesy that he retained his position as scribe.

With steely focus, Felene took a deep breath and began the recitation. "I am a seventh-lived Magnificat and lineage holder of the Maeo Khao Mani, Diamond White Jewel clan of the royal palace of Thai King Rama; justly marked by crystal fur and sapphire and jade eyes…"

Jaibon interrupted; eager to minimize her prestigious rank. "Very well, Felene of the Maeo Khao Mani clan. You have permission to speak."

Felene gave him a disgusted glare and bowed to address the council and crowd in a refined manner, "I humbly thank the council for recognizing my lineage."

Then in a high-timbre, which neither Archers, nor canines, nor any other creature other than Magnificats could hear, she spoke the oracle. "I shall read from the writings of our Mother Silvestria."

She paused as all the cats bowed and said in unison, "Thanks be to the scrolls."

Once silence fell among the cats, she continued: "'Twas the last day—and the first day—when Orion snapped his belt and loosed the fifth wind into the sacred Garden, where our Queen Silvestria slept peacefully. Alerted by the scent of danger, her mother tied one small white stone around Silvestria's neck and raced to toss her through the last closing exit, where an Archer queen carried her to safety. We are Silvestria's children. The stone has been with us ever since."

Her mother, Mariah, continued for her, "My fellow Magnificats, we remain the banished; but our way back is clear, a crystal light will lead us back to the Garden." The howling from the Magnificat throng chased any remaining storm away. That was the moment when Felene told the multitude of cats she had seen the coming of a Cat Woman.

There was heaviness with her words, like wasting rocks, and a great murmuring arose:

"We are not ready!"

"Magnificats will be murdered again!"

"The scrolls are not completed."

"Who is Felene to look for a Cat Woman?"

"She is too young. Who does she think she is?!"

"Calm!" Tak spoke, gesturing in downward air pats with

his paws. The mention of a Cat Woman was no small matter, and the crowd reaction was pertinent.

"It is true, historically, that whenever a Cat Woman comes on the scene, there are mass murders of cats and Archers alike. Evil forces do not want healing and never will. They know the promised Archer child will be female. Killing as many as they can is the simplest way to prevent her from completing her work. We look hopefully to a Cat Woman, but the potential consequences do not elude us."

In spite of the dissenting whines, Felene confidently pulled a small prism from her collar. Tapping it, the stone projected the image of a shabby golden-furred girl, kneeling outside a shrub-sheltered decaying lair. "I believe this child to be a Cat Woman. I do not know when she is to come, but the visions keep me awake." A wave of moans arose from the crowd. Felene saw Tak wince. She should not have spoken until she knew more.

Jaibon tapped a smoky-quartz, twelve-inch-long wand on a rock to regain order. It sent out waves of calming sounds.

"Felene, Felene, you interrupted this meeting with no facts; no facts at all. Felene is completely out of order, out of order," Jaibon declared.

She remembered quite well that Tak did not defend her. This embarrassment was, in part, why she had cut herself off from him, and the whole lot of Magnificats, for that matter; even distancing herself from her mother, Clouder Mariah. For this, she felt tremendous regret, especially now that Mariah had been taken by Phoebe's Ferals.

"Grrr," she found herself glaring at Jaibon as he slept on the papers, wanting nothing more than to pounce and throttle him. Instead, she settled into her soft fur blankets and studied.

CHAPTER 22

STEPMONSTER REVEALED

I listen to the wind
To the wind of my soul
Where I'll end up
Only God really knows.

—Yusuf Islam [Cat Stevens], "The Wind Lyrics," 1971, London, England

Apple bopped into the house after her flight to Arizona to see Ms. Coleman as if not a thing was wrong. Amanda was in the dining room putting papers in a yellow box with red trim, decorated with Arabic lettering and a cat image. She rushed to finish packing it, but Apple saw what she was doing before she could hide it away.

"'Hey, Amanda," Apple breezed.

"I need to go out, watch Justin!" Amanda ordered.

Apple opened the fridge without looking at her. "You askin' me, or tellin' me?" she smirked, in a defiant teenage sort of way.

Amanda veered over and grabbed her arm, digging in with her sharp, purple-polished nails, drawing blood as she pulled Apple closer to her. "Listen to me, I can make you disappear. Don't push me."

Apple jerked her arm away and lunged for the yellow box,

still on the table, "What's with this?"

Amanda froze and tried to calm the situation. She clearly didn't want Apple to open the box. "Oh Apple, you never listen to your father. He really is a bright man. That is just a present for him, a drawing of Mohammad's pet cat, the one from the old story where he cut off the sleeve of his robe rather than wake him when he was called to prayer, remember?" she lied.

"Well then, you won't be mindin' if I take a peek inside?" Apple jarred the box open in an instant and saw ten or twelve cell phones and a stack of driver's licenses bound together with a rubber band.

"What is this? Have anythin' to do with your boyfriends that were jest here?" Apple mocked. Justin ran into the room towards Apple, but Amanda grabbed the toddler straightaway.

"You see him now, Apple? If you say a word about what you have seen, you may never see him again." Then she pushed him to the ground and purposely stepped on his little hand, while staring right into Apple's eyes, "Right Justin? Mommy will feed you to the lions, like the little boy in the story Uncle Amir told you."

Justin's lip quivered on the verge of crying. Now it made perfect sense to Apple why he begged to come with her when she left Egypt. "Who is Uncle Amir?" Apple demanded to know, as dark red blood trickled down her arm. "You really have a thing for fingernail strikes don't you, Amanda?"

Amanda threw a paper towel roll at her, never answering her questions. "Clean yourself up, and like I said before—watch Justin!" She gave a sickly-sweet smile and pinched Justin's cheek a little too hard while he lay crying on the ground. When he saw Apple's horrified expression, he bawled even louder. Amanda grabbed the box and her purse, stopping in front of the entryway mirror to put on a fresh coat of red lipstick. "Oh, and Apple, we know where your family is in Ireland. Don't cross me."

Who is this 'we,' Apple pondered? She was sure now that this stepmother of hers truly was a monster. All the times she had been criticized for "not being forgiving," or "disrespecting her father's new wife," she had been right. She was absolutely, absolutely right!

She ran to pick Justin up from the floor. "Well, me uncle Aden will be a peck of a match for you," Apple said under her breath, after she was sure Amanda was gone.

"Now there, you li'l muzzy, I'll be protectin' you. Would you like some milk?" She could tell this abuse was common treatment for Justin. He was not terribly shaken and had already stopped crying. Apparently, this was ordinary to him.

A note hung on the refrigerator from Dan, "Be good, Apple. See you in a few days." She knew this meant she and Justin would be alone with 'crazy-arse Amandan' until the end of the week. She was going to get Justin out of there fast, and take him to Felene's lair. She would know what to do.

Wiping Justin's face, Apple gave him a sippy-cup full of milk, and washed the black shoe mark off his hand, asking him to open and close it, to make sure his fingers were okay. Then she cleaned her arm with soap. Four crescent shaped marks remained. "Hope I don't get rabies," she joked to Justin, who gave her a smile.

Before she met Krystal and Ms. Coleman, Apple's first reaction would have been to call the police. Now, she feared that might provoke a worse outcome for her and Justin—separation in foster care. More angry than scared, Apple decided to keep it to herself and get Justin to a safe place, fast.

Apple ran to her room and grabbed her precious stone, hurriedly gathering what she and Justin would need at Felene's.

Meanwhile, Makeda made her way back to the coast, easily following Felene's scent right to where she had dropped Apple off, near her father's home. Although she needed to learn more about Apple before reporting to Tak in Ireland, she also realized that this young Archer girl may be a good source of the green magic she would need to save Ms. Coleman.

Green magic was not an enchantment in the Magnificat

cache. Only Archers had that magic. It was powerful, and more desired by Archers than a wish-granting Jinn. One could have virtually anything in the whole world if they had enough of it.

The long-necked Magnificat's small head peered in through the kitchen window, just in time to see Apple hurriedly wrapping something up and packing it tightly into the front of her jeans. She had arrived too late to witness the initial confrontation between Amanda and the children.

"Cat, Appo, cat," Justin said, pointing towards the window when he saw Makeda. She ducked.

"Likely Felene," she mouthed to herself. She expected the flying cat to come in and help her and Justin at any second, so she hurriedly loosened her shirt to cover the stone.

"C'mon Justin, I'll take you to preschool."

He kept yelling "Cat," as she packed him into his pram. When the front door burst open before them, it was not Felene.

"Where are you going?" demanded Amanda, blocking the children on their way out.

"Uh, to school," Apple replied, trying to act as if all was normal, hoping Amanda forgot that school was closed due to the wildfires. Amanda looked suspiciously at her.

From the large dining room window, Makeda strained to see beyond the kitchen into the narrow entry. All she could make out were shadowy figures darkening the entry; an evil darkness, like a puff of chimney dust. She caught a glimpse of Amanda being shoved aside by Archer men, knocking Justin over in his stroller to get at Apple. "The boy—he is extraordinary," Makeda marveled.

"It is you!" accused the same man Apple had spotted next to the jeep earlier, the man from the Egyptian dig site. He dove towards her. Makeda watched as the male Archer gripped her throat, squeezing as he marched her backwards to pin her against the wall. "I know you have it. Where is it?" he commanded, taking his hands off her neck and shaking her from her shoulders, hard, trying to rattle out an answer.

Justin, still strapped in the toppled stroller, cried hysterically, "Appo, Appo!"

"Shut up you little half-breed," Amanda seethed. Hearing that, Apple swore if she made it out of this alive, she would never ignore her instincts again.

Dark figures came into Makeda's line of sight as they pushed their way in towards the window, throwing keys and maps on the kitchen table, swiping things off at the same time.

Makeda had seen and heard enough. If something bad happened to this Archer girl, Tak would be livid. She regretted not following his direct orders, but she was also jubilant she had followed her hunch about the Cat Woman. She knew she had to act quickly. She dashed around to the front door and burst in, immediately seizing the Archer attacking Apple, digging her claws into his back and sinking her spiky fangs succinctly into the carotid artery in his neck. He let out a short scream as if trying to speak, while blood covered Makeda's muzzle and spurted across the room. He fell dead instantly, right at Apple's feet.

A mad rush of Archers pushed against one another to see what had happened. Makeda released her fangs from the Archer's neck and looked up at the shocked faces. Without hesitation, while spitting out Archer blood, Makeda reared on her haunches and took wild swipes at the remaining Archers, yielding chunks of flesh that stuck to her claws. Apple scrambled through the melee to free Justin from his sideways dangle.

Like a trained first responder, Apple unsnapped the stroller latch to free the hysterical toddler and swept him up before he hit the ground, while Makeda fought the Archers off. Still on the floor, in between Makeda's ferocious swipes, Apple spotted a boot—it was Dan's! Good lord, has he monogrammed everything he ever wore? Even in the midst of the pandemonium, Apple marveled at her father's self-adoration.

Makeda let out a hawkish screech to call upon the winds, causing a slow-moving storm to race to her aid, and continued screeching and flapping her wings as she held the Archers at bay in the small corridor. Apple, carrying Justin, scrambled outside, running towards the bluffs as fast as she could. The summoned wind crashed through the dining room window, shattering it into a shower of glass pellets, and throwing chairs and dishes about the room. The Archers ducked, and in that second, Makeda disappeared.

Apple kept running. She and Justin were splattered red with blood as if they had been in a paintball fight, and for the first time in her life, Apple experienced real fear. It was strangely liberating, exhilarating even, as if she had finally broken out of a glass bottle and felt alive for the first time. Unexpectedly, a sharp pain pierced her shoulders. It was Makeda, lifting the children off the ground in her curled claws. Apple squeezed Justin tightly.

Back at her lair, Felene suddenly bolted up, exclaiming: "Something is wrong. I don't know what, but something is very, very, wrong."

Jaibon looked at her quizzically. "Oh, oh, my dearest Felene, you really are over-sensing, over-sensing once again. You must learn to control your hunting instincts, as mature Magnificats are expected to do—really, really, my dear!" Felene shook her head in disbelief at his lack of instinct, and darted past him through the feather door, flying toward the sea, where she saw Makeda swooping in for a landing on the beach below. Apple and Justin were dropped, skidding along the sand, as Makeda circled around and back out to sea.

"Makeda?!" hissed Felene disbelievingly, as she realized she had been left with a literal bloody mess.

The rough landing dislodged Apple's stone tablet from her jeans and it tumbled into view. She scrambled to hide it, shoving it into a nearby clump of grass-laced rocks. Felene did not notice. She was examining the curious, blood-covered Archer boy for injuries when she realized he looked very much like the boy in the picture she saw in Ms. Coleman's room—the picture of Krystal's brother. She sniffed him to confirm.

Apple grabbed Justin by the hand, "Let's get this venom off

us now, Justin. Hold my hand." The two ran headlong into the incoming, frothy, cold waves together. She watched the blood of a man she had witnessed being killed right in front of her run off into the outgoing tide. "No one will ever be believin' this, Justin," she said as they braced against the next set of breaking waves. Finally, she dunked completely under one, with Justin in a tight grip, and let the ocean wash away the last of the evil that clung to them.

From the cliff, Jaibon stood paralyzed at the chaotic sight of two soaking-wet young Archers in the surf, Felene hovering over them, and Makeda circling to come in for a landing on the beach with blood still dripping from her mouth. "This cannot be good, cannot be good at all," he fretted.

"Jaibon, go get some water ready. There is a bucket hanging on the fence," Felene yelled at him. Unenthusiastically, he did as asked.

Felene flew the two Archer children into the center of her prickly pear-protected lair for a bath, and soon their clothes dried in the sun that had now peeked through, following Makeda's helpful storm. She gave them valerian tea and covered them both in furs. Justin fell right to sleep, as Apple listened to Makeda catch Felene up on all she had seen and done at Apple's house.

"Who is this stepmonster?" was all Felene could ask, as she reflected on the evil ankh she wore. For Magnificats, being cruel to a kitten, or any baby creature for that matter, was the nastiest thing one could do. "Little ones should never fear those assigned to mentor them," she hissed in disgust. "If this is how Archers treat their young, it is no wonder their children get into so much mischief."

CHAPTER 23

SACRIFICIAL LAMB

There are darknesses in life
And there are lights,
and you are one of the lights,
the light of all lights.

—Bram Stoker, *Dracula*, 1897, Dublin, Ireland

It was three o'clock in Ireland, and as customary, Tak was on his well-worn spot looking over the faerie tree, smoking his gilded pipe and contemplating the battle ahead. He was troubled over Thom, who had been gone for three days now, after their clash. Tak missed their teatime. He was worried, but could not go out and look for him with the Clouders returning from their missions.

Alkina lumbered out, "Afternoon, Tak," he yawned.

"Pleased to see you up and around," Tak replied. Alkina had gained three pounds in as many days and was looking fit again. He had needed this rest. Tak was feeling better himself, perhaps from using the goanna oil Alkina had brought him.

Miz had been keeping Tak updated from her post in Mezo-America, and reported that hurricanes were building as far north as Baja California, as Ephippas heated up the El Niño current to near record temperatures.

Tak laid his pipe down, and there, in the warm speckled sunlight, he settled in and took a well-deserved nap. Alkina did some reading under the faerie tree as one by one, the Clouders returned to the Emerald Isle.

Makeda was first, soaring in from the Americas with a running landing, eager to get back to Ms. Coleman. Then Billi cruised in with Moosa, both tired. Neko and Rose returned from the high north, bringing with them a six-inch emerald for Tak from Silverson, to honor the emerald island. Alkina greeted them inside the parish, and then awakened Tak so they could all enjoy a Mediterranean rat soup.

"I've thought about this carefully," said Tak. "We will not go back into ceremony to hear your reports. I want a dialog, a back-and-forth discussion that ceremony does not allow."

The Clouders looked from side to side at one another, bewildered. Always, councils convened in ceremony. Still, they remained silent, even Moosa.

"Makeda, what did you discover on your undertaking of the red-haired Archer?"

"I found the young Archer in the Americas. She has established a relationship with Felene."

This got Tak's attention. Knowing nothing is happenstance, he muttered, "It is always magic."

His attention went back to Makeda in time to hear her say, "…and the red-haired Archer is in trouble. Evil forces have already tried to kill her. I had to kill an Archer to save her."

Collective gasps erupted. Alkina moaned, "Geeeez," and put his forepaw to his brow dramatically.

Moosa demanded, "Will Archers know this was a cat kill?"

Billi asked, "Was that your last resort?"

Rose said, "Oh no," and put her face in her paws.

Neko just sharpened the tip of his sword.

"I know how to eradicate evidence. No one will ever know it was a cat kill. The Archer was a fiend who tried to harm children," Makeda responded, disappointed in their lack of trust.

"Children?" inquired Rose, lifting her head.

"There was a young Archer boy with the unpleasant red-haired Archer girl. They are now both safely with Felene."

"Did you speak with Felene?" asked Tak, hopefully.

"Only to fill her in on what happened regarding the young Archers," replied Makeda as she was sitting down.

Moosa stood up next to report. "Billi and I met with Aholi, the Kachina lieutenant."

"Be honest, Moosa," ribbed Billi.

"All right, I did not invite Billi into the lodge. I have since begged forgiveness and explained we cannot expect other king-doms to lay aside their native ways. Then Billi and I saw Spider Grandmother in Madagascar."

"I believe she has a fondness for Moosa," Billi jabbed, then said seriously, "She will help us weave the light into her web so that it will be strong enough to entrap Ephippas."

Tak looked to Rose and Neko, motioning with his paw for them to speak. Everyone noticed it shaking. "We secured materi-als for the web of lights from the deer folk, and Koshka acquired the snow lion milk." Rose handed Tak the sparkling emerald gift. He placed it near the candle flame and it sprinkled rainbows on the ceiling, making Tak think of Thom.

Then Tak nodded in approval, "Tonight, we must kill the lamb to make the skin-wrap for the wind demon flask."

Just then, Thom popped his head in the spit. "No, you won't be needin' to do that. I dunnit for you!" He proudly announced.

Moosa stood up and moved towards Thom. "Who do you think you are, speaking up at a Clouder Council as if you were one of us?"

Thom looked stunned for a moment, then his back hair stood up and his head lowered, as he began to rock slowly from side to side and hiss and growl. Totally out of character, he pounced onto Moosa, sticking onto his chest like scratching, biting chewing gum.

Moosa lurched in surprise then ripped into the back of

Thom's neck, tearing his tartan scarf off as the two tumbled together in the middle of the room. Rose tried to separate them, but was tossed into Neko as Tak roared at them to stop.

All of a sudden, Thom zipped out the spit. Moosa began to chase, but Rose blocked the exit as Tak grabbed him by his tail. Instinctively, he reared up and swiped Rose, slashing her nose. Makeda ran to her aid. Neko gracefully executed an aerial flip overhead to launch a martial arts kick, hitting the out-of-control Moosa squarely in his large jaw, knocking him out cold.

Thom was nowhere in sight. Instead, Tak found only the cleaned and soft-chewed hide of a lamb lying outside the spit that Thom had carefully prepared for the Clouders.

Both furious at Moosa and aching for his friend, he calmed himself by pacing before he went back inside. He was more torn than he had ever been. His loyalty should be to the Clouders, yet he wanted to run after Thom, to make sure he was all right, safe, and to let him know how much he appreciated the sacrifice.

Alkina came up and rested his huge paw on Tak's shoulder in friendship. "Tak, now you understand what it is like for me."

"What do you mean?" Tak asked impatiently while shirking off the giant paw.

"Thom is a common cat, yes? Yet, you have compassion for him because you know him. He is not a stray; he is your friend. From a distance, it is easy to judge all Ferals the same way. But up close, you come to see their goodness, their struggles, and that brings compassion."

"There is no comparison! Are you trying to equate Thom to a Feral, Alkina? I beg to differ." Tak scolded.

"I think you will find there is more in common than you wish to see. Even years after a Feral fight where blood is mixed, a common cat can turn. And when it happens, it happens overnight. Thom has Feral blood, Tak. He is making the change. If you did not lose your friend today, you will lose him soon. He will not be able to live like a common cat anymore."

A breeze rustled in Francis, the faerie tree, rattling the

leaves like a cacophony of cicadas. "What do you know, old tree?" snapped Tak. The whitethorn quieted, and bowed in sadness. Everyone in the courtyard loved Thom.

Tak avoided Alkina as a tear fell, which he quickly wiped away with the back of his shaky paw. Without a word between them, Tak slowly crawled through the spit. Alkina went around the long way, with the lambskin in his teeth.

Inside was a mess. Rose was bandaging Moosa. Billi was stitching the laceration to Rose's nose, while Neko had his kicking leg raised and wrapped in turpentine-soaked linen strips, to prevent bruising. Makeda was resentfully cleaning the floor. She had already cleaned up enough blood, for a few days at least!

Everything stopped when Alkina came in with the lambskin. No one said a word. Moosa bowed his head. Billi, who had finished sewing up Rose, without missing a beat, took the same needle to the lambskin, fashioning it into a vessel, one that would hold the wind demon.

Breaking the awful silence, Tak asked, "Rose, when can we get the lights from the north?"

"They need two days."

"Order it," he commanded.

"And Makeda, go check on the red-haired Archer and collect Spider Grandmother. We will meet in two days, over Ephippas, under the Southern Cross. Moosa, I agree with Billi, we cannot send you back there. Spider Grandmother may keep you for her spring meal. She likes you a bit too much, I fear…"

"Tak, you are forgetting, we need a child to lure the demon wind into the vessel, a pure child," Makeda interrupted.

"Then find one. You are of Africa. Find one!" Tak roared, causing the dishes to dance on the shelves. "And get the stone from the red-haired Archer—kill her, if you have to."

This flabbergasted some of the Clouders, but not Makeda. She understood the bigger picture.

CHAPTER 24

NO HOME, NO MORE

Elephants at home tonight
Drumming fire and dance
Playmates to Africa's children

—Gwyn Dolyn, 2015, California, U.S.A.

Quickly returning to California, Makeda snarled orders. "There is no time for visiting, We have two days to stop the demon wind, Ephippas." She paused at the puzzled expression on Felene's face and had to ask, "What is it Felene?"

"You just fly in and out of here, leaving me to clean up your messes, when, in all respect, none of this is my directive. I am to complete the medicine scrolls for the *Book of Secrets,* and that is it."

"Are you serious? The world is on the verge of destruction, and you are only going to do that one job?"

Then Justin wandered out of Felene's lair. He recognized Makeda and ran to her, wrapping his arms around her. Now that he was clear of the dead Archer's blood, she sniffed him. "Ah, a child of Africa," she purred. Then she realized, "This child is pure. He can lure the demon Ephippas to his demise," she said to Felene, elated that she had solved this task so easily.

Before she could stop herself, Felene blurted out, "I know of another pure child. I believe she is a Cat Woman, Makeda, not yet grown into it." Hoping to illicit help from Makeda to free Krystal, she tossed out a hook. "She is in the clutches of the Ferals."

Makeda feigned surprise. "The Ferals? That will complicate matters. The pure Archer child must be a boy of Africa, though."

Makeda again glanced over at Justin playing happily with some rocks on the ground and sniffed. "Yes, yes, I believe he will do nicely." Then, she leapt over to him, sniffing some more.

Justin giggled, "Thtop it."

A whiff of dank earth hit Makeda's nostrils and made them flare. She jerked around to follow it, just as Justin reached over and hugged her around the neck again, distracting her from the smell of the Magnificat Stone that Apple had relocated to the protection of a nearby prickly pear cactus before the tide had come back in.

"Felene, bring him above the clouds under the Southern Cross in two days. Until then, do not let him out of your sight. Everything counts on your timing. If you do this, you have my word, I will help you with your Cat Woman." She was not being completely forthright. She intended to take care of Ms. Coleman first. "And get that fire-furred Archer to tell you where the Magnificat Stone is. We must have it when we bury Ephippas again."

"Stone?" Felene asked.

Makeda looked stunned. "You are still young, Felene, that I can understand, but to not know the stone is in the possession of an Archer right under your whiskers is another matter, indeed. I heard you dropped out of most Magnificat duties. That was a bad idea. You lost your way, child, you've lost your way," she said shaking her head.

"Yes, I will get the stone," Felene replied meekly.

"And you must do it quickly," she whispered, with a glare towards Apple, who was watching out of earshot with her hand on her hip. "We need it to seal the wind demon deep in the earth. Use all means necessary." Then she leaned in more closely, "It would be best if she willingly gives it to you, but Tak said to kill her if she will not help us." Felene's jaw dropped.

Makeda did not realize that Jaibon had overheard the entire conversation and wanted no part in the killing of Archers. "Not at all in my job description, not at all, not at all," he murmured, scurrying back inside the lair.

Felene took a deep breath as Makeda took flight. Justin waved goodbye, while Apple watched suspiciously. "What are you doin' with Justin?" she asked Felene, having seen all the whispering and sniffing.

"Nothing," is all Felene said, or would say.

"I'm not believin' you, nope, I'm not," Apple argued, hoping for a response.

Restless and bored and even a little worried for her father, though she hated to admit that, Apple had a bad feeling that she could not shake. Her recent experiences were teaching her to pay attention to those feelings. "I'm goin' to the library for a wee bit. Should I take Justin?"

"NO!" shrilled Felene, unable to contain herself with so much work and even more on her mind. Plus, she was ordered not to let Justin out of her sight.

"Okey-dokey, you ought to simmer down in there, supreme Magnificat," scoffed Apple mockingly.

Felene thought for a moment that perhaps it would not be so daunting to kill this Archer after all. She looked at Apple and spit tiny fireballs in her direction right out of her eyes. The falling sparks landed on the ground just in front of Apple's feet, as a warning. Apple froze for a second, thinking she might spit right back at the cat, but decided to head down the bluffs instead, sneaking the Magnificat Stone out from under the cactus as she went. She headed to her father's home, to see what was happening there. She had to know.

After a brisk 45-minute walk, she approached the house and

crept around behind the garage, where she heard voices coming from inside. To get a look in through the small window located high on the back wall, she used the air conditioner as scaffolding. From there, she stood on her tiptoes, wrapping her fingertips painfully over the aluminum window frame, and hoisted herself up, just enough to get a view.

"Oh my god," she gasped. There, in the middle of the garage, she could see the back of a bruised and bleeding man secured to a chair by zip ties, with people in black t-shirts gathered around him. Amanda waved papers in front of him, slapping him with them every so often, as she screamed unintelligibly. Apple's fingers began to sting and sweat on the ledge. She gritted her teeth and held on tighter.

"Where is your daughter?" a loud male voice demanded.

They're talkin' about me! It was Dan tied up! Apple jerked at the realization and her fingertips slipped. She fell backward with a thump onto the air conditioner. It became quiet in the garage. She ducked into the rosemary hedge, where she noticed that the large broken window had been replaced. She stayed still as she heard a door creak and slam shut, then footsteps and mumbling. She held her breath, her pulse pounding in her head like sonic booms, until the noise started up again from inside the garage.

Carefully, Apple rose up and looked through the formerly broken dining room window to see inside the house. Everything was perfect. Nothing was broken, no blood, everything had been cleaned and repaired. Had she dreamt all the melee/murder gobbledygook?

As she stepped back from the window, a large leather-gloved hand grabbed her shoulder, and another covered her mouth, as she tried to let out a scream. She was dragged backwards to a waiting uniformed police officer. Another stood with a finger over his mouth gesturing "Shhh!"

Apple was rushed to a police car and locked inside the back. She began to panic as she recalled Krystal's stories of foster care, and worried what would happen to Justin, with those crazy cats?

Her fingers locked into the weave of the metal screen dividing the back seat from the front in the squad car.

A loudspeaker blasted from a nearby black van, so loud she had to cover her ears: "Federal agents have you surrounded. Come out now, with your hands behind your heads!"

Instead of anyone coming out with their hands up, an explosion came from inside the garage, blowing the automatic door open. Apple jolted up in the back seat of the patrol car. Helmeted police, dressed in thick vests dove behind anything nearby, brandishing guns. These were not ordinary cops.

A fire erupted from the blast. Apple watched in horror as smoke came billowing out a second later. Shooting wildly, at least twelve people with black hoods over their faces stumbled out of the garage, coughing and blindly firing their weapons. Apple ducked instinctively. The police returned fire and the gunmen began falling. It was over fairly quickly. Apple looked up and pounded the window, screaming at an officer outside the car, "My dad is tied up in there!" He saw her frantic expression and believed her, then made a quick radio call. Just as the remaining gunmen surrendered, Dan was carried out—looking limp and lifeless, still tied to a blackened chair.

Ambulances that had been staged down the block pulled up. Apple demanded to be let out of the car and ran toward her dad, as paramedics formed a wall around him and would not let her through. She was about to climb into the front seat of the ambulance to ride to the hospital, when she looked back at her smoking house to see Amanda being led out in handcuffs.

"Right where she belongs!" Apple said aloud. She was happy to see the woman who caused her family so much misery exposed, with black mascara streaking her Franken-face, crying just like she had made little Justin and her mum cry. Apple waved to her by wiggling the tips of her fingers in a 'ta-ta' manner and stuck out her tongue as she passed. Amanda hissed like a snake as the police shoved her into the back of their car. Yellow crime scene tape, ambulances, and coroner vehicles lined the street as

Apple rolled away.

At the hospital, the police came to talk to her while her dad was in surgery. "How did your parents meet, Apple?"

"Amanda is not my parent. My mum's in Ireland."

"Where is Amanda from?" they pressed.

"I dunno."

"Has your dad traveled to the Middle East recently?"

"My dad is a famous archeologist," she sassed, "of course he has been there, hundreds of times."

Then the questioning took a concerning change, bringing to mind Krystal's stories of how the police talk to you before they take you away: "Where is your mother? Do you have any relatives here? Who takes care of you?" the officers asked.

"I have to use the bathroom, right now," she lied, unable to think of any other ruse.

"Okay, Apple, let me walk with you," said one official. She was happy no female officers were present, so no one could go in with her.

The restroom, unfortunately, had no windows for escape, so she sporadically peeked outside the door, waiting for the perfect moment to make a run for it. A nurse stopped and talked to the officer outside. Apple bolted. As usual, no one noticed her.

CHAPTER 25

WIND AGREEMENTS

...from the thunder and the storm,
and the cloud that took the form
(when the rest of Heaven was blue)
of a demon in my view.

—Edgar Allan Poe, "Alone," 1829, Boston, U.S.A.

Apple rushed up the bluffs, red-faced and panting breath-lessly, "Me dad's in hospital, me stepmonster is in jail, and the police want to put me and Justin in foster homes!"

This last part alerted Felene. She and Justin had been flying all afternoon, practicing for the meeting at the Southern Cross. She wanted him steady for the long trip. However, with this new information, she feared something might go wrong at any second. The pure child must not be lost. She made the choice to deal with Apple and the stone later, somehow, and instantaneously swept Justin up and out to sea. Apple watched speechlessly, expecting them to turn around. They did not.

"They're not. No, no, not, coming back at all, Miss," Jaibon whined. "Leastwise, not for a couple of days, if all goes well, that is."

"What you be meanin', if all goes well? What's goin' on?" Then she patted her belly to secure the stone.

He noticed the protrusion in her pants. "Well, well, what

do you have in there?" Jaibon's curiosity piqued. "Are you hiding…" then he sniffed. The smell was faint, but once he caught it, it became stronger, until he could barely stand it. "What is it, what is it you have there, Miss Archer?"

Unable to contain her secret for one more minute, the whole story came spilling out. How she was caught in a wind and saw a weird cat, and went to Egypt and found a stone, and her mum got sick, and she was sent to her dad's, and met Magnificats, got a friend and a new brother, and now, everyone was gone, and it might be all her fault.

"My, my, young lady, do you even know what you have?" he asked. "It is the Magnificat Stone; the secret to nine lives is inscribed on it. No wonder you are having such a run of bad luck. You stole a most valuable thing, a most valuable and powerful thing, indeed."

"I didn't steal it! I found it…. How valuable?" she quizzed, thinking once again of her dream life overlooking the Irish Eye.

Another Magnificat might not have been as careless as Jaibon, but his natural know-it-all tendency drove him to spill far too much information. "My, my, it is perhaps the most valuable thing on the earth. Whoever holds it, holds the secret of nine lives, like we Magnificats have. It is more desired than even your Archer green magic."

"Green magic?" asked a confused Apple. Then she rapidly moved on to another question. "So you mean, even if someone is dead, with this stone they can come back to life?"

"E-gad's, you are a bit thick-skulled, you poor thing…. Yes, exactly my dear, exactly! But to a different life…."

Apple bit her tongue and resisted the urge to defend herself from his "thick" comment, asking instead, "What if they are sick and not dead yet? Can it make you well?"

"No, no, it would not be used for that, not at all. For that, you would use the medicine scrolls, or seek out a Cat Woman from among the Archers who learned from Magnificats the power to heal."

"So, who would I be givin' this stone back to anyhow?" she asked warily. "To my dad? Or the police?"

"Oh, never, never. Never let any Archer touch it. They will get sick, sick, sick."

"Do you think it could've made me mum sick?"

"Well, well, that depends. It depends on if she touched it. Did she?"

"I guess she could have, when I was at school or such."

"Oh, my, my, see what you've done? You've got to, got to give that stone to Felene immediately upon her return."

"What if I don't want to be givin' it to anyone? And I dare those crazy cats to try to take it from me."

"Oh, no, no, never—a Magnificat would never, never take it. It loses power if taken by force, unless you are killed. If they kill you, then they can take it."

"Killed?" Apple hadn't thought of that. All she wanted was to bargain with it. She might be able to solve many of her problems with this stone.

"Would Magnificats trade for it? 'Cos mum is sick in Ireland, me dad is hurt in hospital, and Ms. Coleman is stuck in a place she doesn't like, sufferin'."

"Well, well, uh, I, uh—oh my, oh my," he finally realized he had said too much. Apple knew by his reaction she could make a deal. She held the stone tighter than ever.

Meanwhile, Felene was beginning to have second thoughts about her abrupt departure. Though she had Justin on her back, she had failed to perform the other crucial task that Makeda had given her—securing the Magnificat stone from Apple. Without both, the demon wind could not be captured and buried again.

As she gained altitude, heading toward the Southern Cross, she spotted the familiar shape of Ming Fang's flying litter in the distance. For once, she was overjoyed to see her mentor approaching. She changed course and flew alongside the litter long enough to explain her dilemma and ask for help. Someone else must obtain the stone from Apple.

As usual, Ming Fang's perfume reached Felene's lair before she did. Jaibon was elated and ran to meet her, chattering repetitively about how the Archer girl had the Magnificat Stone (not mentioning that he might have told her things he shouldn't have, but hinting that she might be willing to trade for it).

"Out of my way, you fool," Ming Fang demanded, as she brushed him aside with her right paw and continued the difficult trail to Felene's lair, with the help of her Siamese companions. Apple was sitting outside holding her stone tightly.

"Let's hear it. What is it you want?" insisted Ming Fang. "I am told you want to barter."

"Good Lord and all, how many of you are there?" Apple asked, exasperated to see yet another talking Magnificat.

"Plenty! Now what is it you want for the stone," Ming Fang persisted.

"Do you have the authority to be makin' a deal, or are you jest like Jaibon, nootin' and nobody?" enquired Apple.

Flustered, Ming Fang protested, "I am certainly not 'nootin', and I am nothing of the sort like Jaibon, but, no, I do not have authority to make that sort of agreement. That would be Littern Tak."

"Then I want to see him, NOW!" roared Apple.

Disgusted at the gall of the Archer, yet in a pickle, Ming Fang knew she could not win. She summoned her trusty Siamese, then scribbled a note and handed it to one of them. "Take this immediately to Tak."

"Why can't you call him on the phone?" asked Apple, seriously confused.

"Anyone can hear those calls in the celestial spheres. The words linger there forever, waiting for some busybody to find them; the good and the bad. Phones simply don't work for us."

"You should create an app," Apple joked.

Ming Fang pointed her finger at the Siamese crew, "What are you still doing here? Take that chariot and fetch Tak here. Go! Get! What are you looking at? Scat, get out of here!"

Chapter 26

Trade Winds

A beam of light seven times more clear than day...
stole the Holy Grail
All over covered with a luminous cloud.

—Alfred Lord Tennyson, "The Holy Grail," *Idylls of the King*, 1859, U.K.

It was late in the afternoon, two days before the demon wind battle was scheduled to take place, when Thom limped into the parish courtyard and collapsed under Francis, the great old faerie tree. The tree shivered and dropped a load of leaves to the ground.

"Tak!" yelled Alkina, who was reading nearby. Tak came out of the spit, and spying his friend on the ground, stopped cold. Alkina urged him on.

"Tak, he needs medicine...the strongest medicine." The large and now strengthened Alkina carried Thom around the back and into the lair, while Tak slowly returned through the spit.

Recently back from the north, Rose rushed over. "Clear off that desk, put him here, Alkina," she ordered without looking up from her preparations.

Alkina hoisted him onto Terence as Rose washed her paws and spread salt on the floor beneath to energize her work and clean the air of negative forces. "Tak, get your Egyptian medicine out—bring it here." Tak stood still. "Tak," she said again, more urgently. "What are you doing? Your friend is near death."

"If Alkina is right, and the change to Feral has begun, it is better he die now than become a Feral."

"Good God, Tak, this is your friend, and a living creature!" Alkina shouted. Tak stormed back out.

"Well, I, for one, cannot, as a scientist and a healer, allow him to die without trying to save him," declared Rose.

"What can I do to help?" chimed Alkina.

"Pass me the sage that Moosa left in the shell." Then she began a night of work, with Alkina as her assistant. Tak stayed outside. It was touch and go. By morning, Thom was out of crisis, but by no means well. Rose had done testing and told Tak, "His blood is more Feral than not. He should go to live with them. They can transfuse him through their saliva. If he does not receive that, he will die."

Tak remained detached. "He cannot go to the Ferals with all he knows about me, the Clouders, and all Magnificats, for that matter. They will save him only to torture him for information," he said with blazing determination.

Just then, Ming Fang's clattering Siamese arrived, and Tak went outside, curious about why Ming Fang was not with them. One handed him her note: *Dear Tak, a red-haired Archer child is here, at Felene's, and she insists on your presence immediately. She has the Magnificat Stone.*

Tak looked to the sky. Time was speeding up and so were Ephippas' winds.

"Take him to the Ferals while you're at it, Tak," Alkina pleaded, his stutter completely gone with the return of his strength.

Tak did not respond, and stayed silent. Alkina determinedly loaded the still sleeping Thom onto the litter, as a gust of wind nearly capsized it. Tak would decide on the way what to do. He could drop Thom in the sea from the heavens at anytime, if necessary. There was no need to make the decision immediately.

"You're doing the right thing, Tak," comforted Rose. "This is what separates us from the Ferals." Tak pretended to agree. He would do what he needed to do for the good of Magnificats, first. That was his job!

By the time the chapel bell rang, he was in the air aboard Ming Fang's litter, headed towards an unknown fate for all of them, in fact, for the world. After dealing with this Archer child, he had to get to the Southern Cross. The weight of it all bore down on his shoulders, and his paws began to tremble uncontrollably. He put them under his cloak and made a point not to look back at Thom.

The Siamese were exhausted when they arrived in California, after three long trips in two days. They landed around noon on the last day before the war on Ephippas.

"Oh, Tak, so glad you could make it. I hope your ride was comfortable," cheered Ming Fang, trying to set a positive tone. She did not want an Archer killing on her paws.

Tak disembarked, and shoving Ming Fang aside, walked upright directly toward a sullen Apple, leaning against the outside wall of Felene's lair. She glared at him as she sat cross-legged with the stone tucked into her lap. As he expected, just as his vision in ceremony had foretold, it was the young Archer from the day of the sheegee wind at the parish. It all made sense to him now—the warnings, the omens, the winds. Their destinies were entwined.

Understanding this was not just a child who stole the Magnificat Stone, but an instance of magic, he slowly walked up to her, still wearing his robe and standing on his two hind legs. The winds had brought her to him. He knew that more than he knew anything.

"I am Magnificat Littern Tak. You requested my presence, young lady?" as he bowed graciously and reached for her hand with his paw.

Apple grunted and squeezed the stone tighter to her chest, withholding her hand.

"Don't worry, I won't trick you. Magnificats do not operate like that. Now, tell me, what can I do for you?"

Ming Fang and Jaibon watched nervously. They had forgotten what a skilled negotiator Tak was.

Apple began to blurt it all out again, along with a river of tears, in Tak's fatherly presence.

"My dad left us, Mum got sick, and I was sent away and then got a new brother and my only friend got catnapped. Now my dad's in hospital, Mum's still sick, and I want to go home to Ireland. I wish I had never dug up this stone!"

"Well, well, now, that is a start. What is buried, should stay buried, young lady. You know, Aoife, I am from Ireland, too."

Apple wiped her eyes, astonished, "How'd you be knowin' my name is Aoife?"

"We've met before, the day of the wee wind, remember? Our gaze met only for a second, on that fateful day at the church, when the wind spun both of our lives in entirely new directions."

"Yeah," she said, perking up, "That's right. Ever since, my life's been crazy." She sat up a little. "What happened?"

"Ah, little one, there is no happenstance. It is always magic. The magic is in charge. Now, tell me exactly what you want in exchange for the stone. Magnificats need it badly to put the demon wind back into the earth that you let out by your, may I say, childish tantrum. He is warming up the earth, and it will hurt everyone and everything on it if we don't stop him."

"You're pretty good at talkin' to wee ones aren't you?" she said, feeling comfortable in his calm demeanor.

"I had some practice with a dear young Archer, like you. Her name was Celeste, and of course, also my own godkitten, Felene."

"Oh, now I see what's goin' on here, 'tis a family sort a thing. That Felene, she is crazy, by the way."

Tak laughed, "Well, in a way, I guess everything is about family, in the end."

"Okay," said Apple, "This is the way I'm lookin' at it. I have this stone that could give me nine lives, or I could trade it for the lives of five people I care about. Is that a way I kin look at it?"

"That is one way to look at the situation."

"Then kin I get that cat medicine Jaibon told me about, that can cure me mum, me dad, and Ms. Coleman, and kin Magnificats help find my friend Krystal and bring my new brother home from that thievin' Felene?"

Tak let out a laugh at the rapid-paced demands, especially the comment about Felene. "I can promise you that I will give my best medicine for your mother, father, and this Ms. Coleman, but I don't control the medicine. The medicine has to work on its own. It is like most things we have no real control over—magic. It does what it wants for the big picture. I can give you some help with finding your best friend. Felene will bring your brother back to you, if that is at all possible. Now, do we have a deal?"

"Yes, but what if you don't keep your promise? I'll have nothing to bargain with."

"Here is how it works Aoife. It would poison me slowly to steal it. If I take this stone from you falsely, it would be the same as stealing. When you steal something, it loses a bit of its magic. In other words, the stone could lose some of its power, even one or more of the lives it carries. It could potentially cost lives, even those of my own family. Do you think I would risk all of that? Would you?"

"Can I think on it a few minutes?"

"No, there is the entire world to save, remember? You must choose now. Do you want to live forever? Or, do you want a life with those you love now? That is really the heart of the question."

Apple asked one more question, "Kin it make me rich?"

"No, Aoife, that magic is in the hands of Archers. Magnificats have no green magic, what you call money."

Ah, Apple thought, that's what this 'green magic' thing is about—it's just money! It was the second, or maybe even third time she had heard of this green magic, and she had assumed, at first, that it referred to Leprechauns, or clovers, or some such thing that granted wishes. She thought of her mum and slowly unwrapped the stone, tentatively handing it to Tak. He immediately took it to the litter and handed it to Ming Fang, who placed it in a cat-shaped sarcophagus she and Felene had fashioned out of sandstone from the bluffs below the lair while waiting for Tak to arrive. As she did this, Thom groaned in a painful howl. Apple ran over to see what was making that awful sound.

"Aye, Tak," Thom said weakly, as he reached up his paw from his place in the litter. "Did the old goat skin work out for you?"

"Aye, Thom, it did. We have a fine container for the terrible demon wind because of your efforts."

All Apple heard was mewing.

Then Tak lifted him up, and with the help of the tired Siamese, they carried Thom's limp and boney body into Felene's lair. Apple watched, wishing she knew what to do when a creature was suffering. It was a new feeling for her.

"Where are we Tak?" whispered Thom.

"We're at Felene's." Tak would leave him here until the Ephippas matter was resolved. He was stalling. It was harder to kill his friend than he had anticipated.

"Well oi'll be an old fat cat," Thom coughed, "'tis about time you two was chattin', 'tis." Then he drifted off to sleep on the warm furs piled in the corner of the lair.

Ming Fang peeked in and whispered, "Tak, it is time to go, the sun is almost down."

Tak saw the pale nose and gums of his old friend, Thom. He would need Feral serum soon. Ming Fang would stay behind and look after him. So would Apple.

"Here Ming Fang, lay these healing rods at his sides and pour this honey onto his dry lips every so often," ordered Tak.

Apple perked up, "Kin, I do it, Tak?"

"Why yes, child, as long as Ming Fang supervises. Thom is not predictable right now."

"I have plenty of Chinese medicine here, Littern Tak; you

know I don't endorse Egyptian medicines," Ming Fang replied defensively.

Tak gave her a stern look as if to say, "Really, right now, Ming Fang, you want to debate who has the best medicines?" She got the point without his having to utter another word, and took the healing rods and pot of honey from his paw.

CHAPTER 27

WORLD WIDE WEB

Peace demands the united efforts of us all.
Who can foresee
what spark might ignite the fuse?

—Ethiopian Emperor Haile Selassie, Address to the United Nations, 6 Oct., 1963

Over the sea, the moon had risen. It was time. The night sky began to swirl with stars as the Southern Cross became visible. It was directly above the cloud layer and the maelstrom in the ocean created by Ephippas, who was growing stronger and larger by the hour. The deer of the north had provided the promised gems on time. Neko's image appeared etched into each facet of the pile of reflective gemstones as he rode in on top of the sleigh carrying them. The light of the deer gems would lend plenty of energy to reinforce the net.

Makeda flew in with Spider Grandmother on her back, who barked orders for the entire trip. A spider queen and an independent Magnificat Clouder were not well-suited travel companions. Spider Grandmother had spun a huge ball of webbing that was sitting in a golden bowl, held up by twenty-five Magnificat elders who flew in with it from behind. Hundreds of Magnificat Glarings volunteered, eager to gain respect. They staged in strategic positions across the sky, ready to uphold a portion of the great web when it came time to unfurl it.

Billi delivered the lambskin vessel and attached it to a rope made of Spider Grandmother's sticky webbing. It was set to spring over and fuse shut once the demon was inside. Demons cannot escape the hide of a lamb. This was a fact known worldwide. The blood of a pure lamb covers demons and their work like tree sap, cutting off their oxygen. Demons need oxygen, especially Jinn, who come from fire. And how would that huge demon fit in that small lambskin vessel? It turns out that demons are not huge at all. They just appear as such by stirring up all sorts of chaos and storms around themselves.

Tak arrived in Ming Fang's litter to find Moosa waiting at the distant northeast corner, with Rose posted at the opposite end. Neko took up a new position, perpendicular to Tak.

Felene hovered above the fray nearby, with a sleeping Justin on her soft back, which she had expanded to accommodate his napping body by opening her wings wide and arching into a cradling form.

Ephippas was in the storm below, where demons always stay—right in the middle, unseen, so no one can say for sure if it is a demon, or a natural occurrence. Ephippas was not expecting an attack to come from above; demons tend not to learn from their experiences. They get tunnel vision on the closest objects. The Magnificats were counting on that.

Spider Grandmother began to spin her strands into a web of light with the gems, while the elder Magnificats sprinkled it with snow lion's milk and carried it out wide, towards the four corners marked by Tak, Moosa, Rose, and Neko. The gaps along the edge were filled in by hundreds of Glarings, to support it at every seam. The deer of the north dropped gold and copper mist along the mesh as it unfolded to energize it and to strengthen the integrity of the web, while the snow lion's milk froze around every strand to protect it from heat. Wider and wider it stretched, like a glimmering lattice against the night sky, ready to catch even falling stars. The web was as light as a feather, while at the same time, stronger than steel.

Lightning from below suddenly began to rocket upwards. Ephippas had become aware of the Magnificats above him! Instantly, two Magnificats, zapped by the charge of lightning, fell through the clouds towards earth. Tak gave the signal, and all four corners of the net dropped simultaneously, guided by the downward pull of the Glarings, lowering it swiftly and evenly. Lightning sparked and thunder roared in defiance as it fell like heavy chain—down, down, down, sifting through the clouds, unseen and silent.

The Glarings backed away. Everyone waited. If this failed, the next battle would be more difficult. Magnificats would fight to the very last breath for the safety of earth, and for the Archers, without whom they could never get back to the Garden.

Hellish wails reared back up at them in an offensive move that surely would have succeeded, if not for the strength of the sticky silk of Spider Grandmother's web. There was no escape. Not even Ephippas' fire could burn her web, coated with snow lion's milk, copper, gold, and gems. He was in its grip. The more he struggled, the more the net wrapped around him.

Magnificats, Glarings, and even deer, pulled, tugged, and nudged the net, with the demon wind stuck in it, until it was above Ethiopia, where he was to be buried. This was fitting for Tak—the demon would be under the watch of his mother's homeland, and Clouder Makeda. When it was positioned perfectly, they dropped it towards the earth.

"Moosa!" shrieked Billi, as the net fell and she noticed his right rear paw tangled up in the sticky web, dragging him down towards Ephippas. She clung fast to his tail as he spiraled, down, down, down, flapping her wings uselessly against his gravitational fall. "Moosa, what can I do?" she screamed. "Moosa! Answer me!" Her eyes filled with tears. Moosa looked up at Billi. His fur was sucked up and the g-force distorted his face beneath her as he ripped his tail from her paws so he would not take her with him. Billi watched him fall into the heart of the storm demon. She chased after, calling his name, "Mooooosa!"

With a sudden shot of spider silk from her spinnerets, Spider Grandmother snagged Ephippas with another spurt of webbing. Neko dove under and sealed the bottom. Rose rushed the two-by-three foot cone-shaped lambskin to little Justin, who was perched on Felene's back, awakened by the horrific sound of the wailing demon. Rose stayed close to help him hold it up.

Spider Grandmother shot another arrow-like strand down towards Billi and Moosa, snagging Moosa around his waist, to pull him out of the grip of the web. Billi lunged to Moosa's paw and ripped it out of the last sticky threads that bound him to Ephippas, as the demon neared the ground. When she did, Moosa sprang out of the wind demon like a slingshot, while poor Billi flew in the opposite direction. All Moosa, and everyone else, could do was watch as she was swallowed by the spinning abyss.

There was no time to weep. Rose and Felene braced themselves, as Tak came to help support the flask in Justin's hands. Opening the mouth of the lambskin vessel, pointing it right at Ephippas, it became a vacuum, drawing in the evil in front of it. More Magnificats raced to help support the vessel, like firefighters to a hose, while Rose and Felene, backed by a crowd of Magnificats, held Justin steady. It had to be in Justin's hands for the magic to work. Tak helped him aim the mouth of the vessel, slowly turning it, fighting the opposing wind force, until it beamed directly on Ephippas. With one more horrible shriek, Ephippas was siphoned up, sliced into pieces, right through the web, at the speed of light.

Rose and the entire group of cats tumbled along cloud tops like cotton balls when the resistance ended. Neko flew to catch Justin, who was in freefall, on his turtleshell back. The vessel flap fused, just as planned, with its seam of sticky webbing. The Siamese had already dug the deep hole below, and Ephippas plunked into it, like metal to a magnetized target.

Immediately, the skies cleared and a sudden cool breeze

followed. They all returned to earth, and Tak pulled the box holding the stone out of the litter and ceremoniously lifted it to the Southern Cross as Moosa began to chant, "Wo wo wo wa he ho." Rose applied a tourniquet, stopping the profuse bleeding of his leg. She hummed along while tightening the knot. Makeda clicked, Neko danced, and Felene rocked the baby Archer boy in her wings.

A great howling arose from Magnificats and Glarings, echoing all through the starry Milky Way, in mourning for Clouder Billi. Moosa wept.

Using Alkina's song line medicine for measuring, Makeda sang all around the place of Ephippas' burial, measuring the distance from the nearby river and rocks, so they would always know right where he lay captive. The Siamese quickly filled the demon pit halfway with dirt as Tak and Moosa stood beside the hole. To honor Clouder Billi, Tak handed the stone over to Moosa, to seal the captivity of the wind demon and also to memorialize their friend. Moosa nodded in gratitude to Tak. He raised the stone to the sky and then kissed it. There was cheering. He placed the Magnificat stone back in the sarcophagus and it was buried above the lambskin flask to lock Ephippas' tomb, and mark Billi's grave. Then the hole was filled completely, leaving no trace the earth had ever been disturbed.

The music of mourning and celebration continued in the heavens until dawn, as the world began a steady return to stability. Globally, Archers dug out from weeks of Ephippas-inspired storms across the lands. "They will rebuild. They always do," reassured Tak.

By first light, the deer had headed north towards home. By noon, Makeda had returned Spider Grandmother to her tree. Rose invited Neko home to visit with Koshka. Moosa stayed at the place of Ephippas' prison and curled up to sleep on that spot in remembrance of his brave partner, Clouder Billi. Tak needed to take care of one last detail, Thomas O'Feral. Apple, Ming Fang, and Jaibon were waiting for him in California. Thom was with them, longing to see his friend return triumphant.

Tak, Justin, and Felene flew together in Ming Fang's litter. Little Justin slept on Felene's soft fur all the way back. She had never wanted to form attachments, but like Apple, found herself quite fond of this quiet little Archer, who had faired so well in his first war and transoceanic exploit.

All were relieved that Billi was only in her eighth life when she was taken.

CHAPTER 28

TIC TOC TAK

Long, long afterward, in an oak,
I found the arrow, still unbroke;
And the song, from beginning to end,
I found again in the heart of a friend.

—Henry Wadsworth Longfellow, "The Arrow and the Song," 1845, U.S.A.

Back at Felene's lair, Thom was in bad shape, "He is barely breathing," Ming Fang whispered to Apple in concern.

"What exactly is wrong with him, Ming Fang?" Apple finally pressed.

"Thom is going through the change. His blood was mixed in a battle with the Ferals, years ago."

"You mean like a vampire or werewolf?"

"Precisely!"

When the litter carrying Tak and the others returned, Apple bolted out the door, directly to Justin. He was dirty and shivering, even though the sun was shining and there was no wind. She grabbed him from Felene. "What did you do to him?" she admonished.

Felene wanted to grab him back, but did not.

Tak and Felene entered her lair, where Thom lay, and he

whispered to her, "He is turning. He will die without Feral fluids.

"Let's kill him now!" she said, seriously.

"No, Felene!" Tak weakened.

"Godfather Tak! Ferals are our enemy. Might he not rise and defeat us with all he has witnessed? He knows your weaknesses—and mine! He will teach the Ferals."

"Tak," whispered a weak-voiced Thom, who had overheard, "you don't have to be worryin' over me. I don't want to live wit' the Ferals, even if it be meanin' my life. You are my one true friend in my one and only life. I always be knowin' I had one chance at it, not like you Magnificats. And 'ere I got to live with the great Tak, Littern of all Magnificats. What common cat can…kha…say…kha…that?" coughing out the last words.

Tak, who could no longer turn away, rushed over and took Thom's paw into his.

"Thom, the lambskin worked perfectly, thanks to you. I tried to run after you, but you were out of sight, and I was torn. I am so sorry. I should have defended you to Moosa. Instead, I took his side as a Magnificat, when he and I dislike each other most of the time. It makes no sense at all, really."

Thom tapped Tak's paw knowingly. "No worries Tak. I forgot all about it already."

Felene determined to say nothing further in front of Thom and surreptitiously dashed to the Feral culvert to try to broker an agreement herself, thinking she could perhaps trade Thom for Krystal. Once at the culvert, it wasn't long before she encountered the scrawny, flea-infested pests she had come to despise even more since Krystal's capture, a week earlier. The largest male Feral approached her, sizing her up by looping behind her with his back arched up like a camel.

"Take me to Phoebe," said Felene in an emotionless tone with no eye contact. Instead, in a flash, the great Feral queen leapt from deep inside the culvert and landed squarely before Felene, in paw-deep sewage.

"So Felene, I suspect yar back for the girl. Well, ya can't

have her, less you kin make a trade. How bout ya stay instead?"

"Trade?" laughed Felene. "What about your high words about how Magnificats want to use her and you are going to spare her our abuse? So, your principles are as straight as your tail, are they?"

"Everything is fer trade, Felene, even you."

Managing not to get any deeper in the pointless argument, Felene redirected: "What do you want then, Pheobe?"

"Well, I do have something in mind. And that something would be—Tak!"

"What!?"

Phoebe dipped her paw into the dank water then licked it off, smiling. "Ya heard me. I want Tak fer Krystal. I know she's yer Cat Woman. I knew it from first sight."

"Would you settle for Tak's best friend?" Felene bargained.

"It's Tak or nothing."

The other Ferals encircled Felene. Their hot moist breath on her neck made her cringe. She itched, just looking at the flea-bags. Pheobe noticed and used that to her advantage. She knew Felene would leap at the chance to leave.

"Tell ya what Felene, ya scurry on back to yer Magnificats and tell um' my proposal. See what they say."

All the Ferals backed away, leaving an opening for Felene to exit. Trying not to show fear, she backed away slowly and dis-trustfully, until well out of reach.

Tak was outside having a smoke when she returned. His blue smoke rings encircled the camp for protection. He looked at her as she came down the path and into the gate. "I smell Feral," he snapped.

"Yes, Tak, I went to the Ferals. I was going to try to trade Thom for the crystal child. She is a Cat Woman, Tak. Maybe even THE Cat Woman, the Tiponi child. And the Ferals have her."

"Perhaps it is my fault, filling you with my hatred for all things Feral these many years."

"Your hatred? They killed my mother."

"Now, we don't know that for sure, Felene. She may be…"

"May be what, Tak, hiding? A prisoner somewhere in the belly of the earth? She is gone, Tak," Felene shed rare tears. "My mother is gone, and my last words to her were bitter. I can never take them back."

Raising his paw as if to strike her, his pain so unbearable at the thought he would never see Mariah again, he only caught himself when he saw her recoil in horror. He had never raised a paw in anger to her in all her life.

Lowering his head in shame, Tak sat down. "Felene, you do not understand love. You are efficient, tactful, and even kind, but you do not know love. If you did, you could never say that to me."

Felene stepped back and sat facing him, trying hard to absorb the selfishness of what he said. "You're not the only one who lost someone they love Tak, I lost my mother."

"It is a different kind of love Felene, one you have not let yourself find—hiding here in this empty nest. You need someone to grate against you, to make you whole—to sharpen you." Then he cut short, "Now, what else does that scandalous Queen Phoebe want?"

"You Tak. She wants you!"

Tak chewed on the end of his pipe, thinking. Then he got up and paced, and paced some more. He went to relight his pipe, but his hand shook so much he dropped everything. Felene's eyes opened wide in surprise. She was looking at an old cat. Somehow, she had not really noticed how much he had aged before.

Ming Fang came out of the lair and patted Tak on the shoulder in support. He did not pull away, as he usually did. Apple stayed inside with Thom, burning sandalwood incense for him, as instructed by Ming Fang, and watching over the sleeping Justin.

Tak began to mutter aloud as he paced, calculating his options, "We reclaimed the Magnificat Stone and reburied the wind demon. I could go back to Ireland and complete my speech for the summit, which is a very important task, but that would leave Felene with Thom to care for, or kill, and her supposed Cat Woman would still be in the paws of the Ferals.

"Or…." He got a glint, a light, an idea. It was clear. "Take me to Phoebe—now, godkitten!"

Felene began to argue. Ming Fang shushed her.

Apple ran out and announced, "Thom is burning up with fever."

The earth rumbled as if a train was passing. It got stronger. Static electricity caused every move to spark. Apple yelled, "Ouch," as she passed through the feather door cover and it stung her with a jolt. Suddenly, right before her eyes, Tak began to glow gold, with three circles of color around him, blue, violet, and red. He became taller and stood upright. Bulky muscles filled in the hollow of his belly and covered his chest. He let out a roar that caused some of the wasting bluffs to fall away into the sea, as the sun sunk below the horizon on the day after the capture of Ephippas.

Without another word, Tak pointed to Apple and clapped his paws, "Get Thom."

Apple tested the feather door with her fingers first to see if it was still electric, and once she found it was not, she rushed in, wrapped Thom in a blanket, and carried him out, like a babe in her arms.

Tak was already marching away, down the canyon, towards the culverts. Looking bewildered, Apple, carrying Thom, joined Ming Fang and boarded the litter. Felene flew after Tak, who was barreling so fast she could barely keep up. Jaibon stayed with Justin, making blackberry pies.

The usual Ferals that guarded the culvert entry scattered aside when they saw Tak as a half-man, half-cat creature coming their way. Phoebe came out and primped for a moment, checking her reflection in the sludgy water, making sure she was presentable. A horde of Ferals filled the diameter of the round pipe for as far as one could see behind Phoebe, like a field of darkness filled with yellow, blinking, oval-shaped eyes.

Apple hopped out of the litter and trotted up to Tak with Thom in her arms. Felene was poised to attack from a strategic point, hovering above the culvert, if needed. Ming Fang stood behind Tak. The Siamese ran back into the woods and watched from a safe distance.

"Hello, Tak." Phoebe snarled, whipping her skinny black tail. "It's been a while."

"I heard your offer and have a counter, Phoebe."

"Why, of course you do," Pheobe hissed coquettishly.

"I will hand myself to you on the condition you care for Thom, a common cat turning Feral."

"Don't ya think we know who Thom be? You arrogant Magnificats, always thinking Ferals are morons! It's how we tricked ya to be here in front of us today, by yer grandiose selves. But, I think I kin agree to yer terms." She was proud of her fallacious leading.

"Wait, there is more. After all, I am Magnificat Littern, and it must appear I put up a worthy exchange. I would think you would want that, as well. We all have our reputations to consider."

"Reputations, Tak? You have no reputation here."

"But you do, Phoebe. How would it look if I were taken without a fight? It would be a hollow victory in the eyes of other Feral queens. Therefore, here is the deal: I want the Archer girl as well, and I want Mariah."

"Hiss, growl, spit, spit," Phoebe arched and lurched. "Yer outta yer mind. Why are ya here—talkin' just to be heard?" Phoebe began to pace in a circle with her tail whipping the ground in anger.

"I could fight. I could kill you in a flash, before your cronies can blink. But I realize that would not free the Archer child, cure Thom, nor free Mariah, now would it? Neither would that give you the public victory you so seek."

Apple shifted, as Thom let out a cry of pain in her arms.

"We have little time, Phoebe."

"I kin do all but Mariah. She's dead."

"Then I want her bones."

"We burnt um."

"Then I want her ashes."

"They were dumped in the sea."

"Then I want the Feral who dumped them."

Phoebe lowed and rocked her head slowly back and forth with her eyes locked on Tak, as if trying to read his next move.

Felene leapt in between the two from above.

Phoebe hissed and took a successful swipe at her, pulling out a wad of fur, while simultaneously, signaling her minions not to move in.

Felene did not budge. "I have a better idea Phoebe, you and me, one on one."

"Felene!" A roar came from Tak like a bear, as his large hand shoved her out of the way, tossing her back behind him onto the ground. He hissed, "How dare you fight my battles! Mind your place."

Felene found herself shrinking behind Ming Fang, like a chastised kitten. Tak swung back to Phoebe, who had not expected him to admonish one of his own. This concerned her, because she saw that his patience was running out. She had him right where she wanted him, finally, and did not want to lose him. The bantering and sarcasm had to end.

"You kin have what yar askin'."

"Take the cat first," Tak demanded and motioned Apple to carry Thom forward. Phoebe motioned for a Feral to receive him.

Thom cried out with a scratchy meow, "I want to spake! Tak, don't be doing this thing your doin'."

"Go, Apple," demanded Tak with a stern nod.

"No! Tak!" cried Thom weakly, grasping with his claws for his friend.

Tak gave Apple a determined look as she handed Thom over to a scraggly tortoiseshell cat, with orange tarter covering her teeth. In an instant, Thom was absorbed into the bog of

Ferals like blackened quicksand. Apple's arms felt cold in Thom's absence.

"Now get out of here Aoife, this is not a place for Archers. You did the brave thing." Tak tipped his head in a gesture to the right, which directed her to go back to Felene's lair.

Ming Fang noticed Tak shaking. No one else did. She realized now, more than ever, why Tak was the great Magnificat Littern. It was far braver to be afraid and face a foe, than to be unafraid. She silently wished Moosa were here to see it.

"It'll take me time to get the rest, Tak," hissed Phoebe.

"I will turn myself over to you at midnight. I want the Archer girl and the Feral who can tell us where Mariah's ashes are."

Thom was carried deep into the earth, where thirsty tree roots reached for water, down a long, narrow cavern, lined with hollowed-out burrows, like prison cells, with bars and doors made of broken and gnawed branches. At a bend in the cavern was a room with an oil lamp, a bed covered with yellowed linens, and rocking in a wooden chair sat Krystal. Startled by a rush of Ferals bringing her what looked like a swaddled baby, she lurched up.

"Oh my, what do we have here?" She looked at the cat they put in her lap, weak, pale, and shivering with fever. She did not know it was Thom. She had never met this cat before.

Krystal began to gesture her tiny hands over him. Not touching, but moving above the skin, trying to sense a change that might let her know what was wrong. Before she had time to evaluate him, a Feral kitten was brought in. Krystal was pushed out of the way, and the ruffian Ferals forced the kitten's mouth to Thom's until its clear, gooey saliva dribbled into his mouth. The three Ferals held the kitten as he shrieked and writhed, which only served to stir up more frothy juices from his mouth, which was what they wanted. They laughed at the kitten's fear and revulsion at having to put his mouth against the sick cat's.

Thom's eyes opened to see the kitten's face butted right up

against his, and for a second, their eyes met in tantamount horror. They were both helpless to stop the dribbly fluid as it poured down his throat, causing him to gag. Then he passed out. The laughing Ferals, disappointed it was over, let go of the young one and watched as he tumbled to the ground—limp and weak, his life force drained. Ferals often sacrificed the lives of their young ones so they could live as they pleased. Unwanted kittens meant very little to them. They simply considered them inferior, not yet a Feral, but some lesser form of life.

Krystal stood aghast. She had never seen this side of the Ferals. Though she was a prisoner, they had treated her well enough, and actually been kind at times. She was flabbergasted when one even looked at her and hissed as he left the room. Krystal picked up the little kitten, laying him beside Thom, and began her work again on both of them, quietly, with her hot, magic hands.

Felene was not about to let Tak hand himself over to the Feral queen, and she was determined to find and retrieve Krystal so he didn't have to sacrifice himself.

Above the Feral underground, Felene sniffed for some scent of Krystal, when a sharp-edged leaf pricked her as she ferreted though a pile of aging foliage. It was unlike other leaves and stood out. Picking it up with her claw, she raised it to her blue eye, the one with better night vision and magnification. The leaf had small stamped images of several types of leaves. She scratched at them and found them etched into the leaf. As Felene studied it closely, the sound of crunching brush scared her. She flipped around sharply, ready to attack. It was Apple!

Felene rose up on her haunches and lashed out. "What is wrong with you? I could have killed you, you fool! Or you could have gotten me killed with those big clumsy Archer feet of yours. What are you doing here? Tak ordered you to the lair. This is Feral country, Apple of the Emerald Isle. All we need is another Archer taken by those foul cats," Felene ranted furiously.

"Oilright, oilright, I'm sorry. I'm 'ere now, so let me help," replied Apple sincerely, then added, "I don't see you obeyin' Tak either, exactly."

Felene shook her head and turned one side of her lip up in dismay. "The only help I need right now is to find a back way into that sewer, and to understand what this blasted leaf is all about," she mumbled.

"I know somethin' about leaves, you know."

Thinking for a moment, stepping outside of her annoyance, Felene gave in, "If there is one thing Tak taught me, and taught me well, it is that 'there is no happenstance, it is always magic.' Maybe the winds meant for you to be here after all, Apple of the Emerald Isle. All right, see what you can make of this leaf."

Immediately upon seeing the small leaves embedded in the leaf, Apple cheered, "'Tis Ogham, the tree language. We have to learn it in school to get in touch with our 'roots,'" she said, as she mocked quotation symbols by putting up two bent fingers on each hand, sarcastically.

"What does it say, Apple of the Emerald Isle?" Felene commanded.

"I'll be tinkin' about it," she mused, waving Felene away with her hand while studying the leaf. "You go do whatever it is you were doin'. Hmm," she began ciphering, "there's a birch, and that is B, but also whiteness or brightness. Makree told me birch was what the witches made their brooms of…and this one here is a fern, and that is the letter A, really an alder—or it could mean blood. Hmm, and ash, that can also be an A, or it could be the healer." Apple drew the letters in the dirt with a twig she picked up in the nearby overgrowth and wrote, "B, A, A," and "White Blood Healer." "Then there's the willow, that is a W, or it can be a storm."

Felene was rapidly losing patience. It was a good thing Apple looked up at that very moment with an "ah-ha" expression. "This could be a map, you know. Yep, I'll be thinkin' it's a map."

Felene looked up from the drawings on the ground and scanned the hillside, thick with trees. Then she grabbed the leaf from Apple with a quick snap of her paw. "First we look for the birch tree," Felene directed. The two tromped through the deep layer of leaves and broken twigs.

"There she is," howled Apple, pointing madly at a divine birch, completely out of place in the Southern California canyon. They ran to it.

Felene sniffed, "Nothing, no scent at all."

"Look, over there, it's a gigantic fern," Apple directed with excitement.

Once they reached the fern, Apple noticed an old firepit, filled with ashes spilling out, that formed a path leading down the slope of the canyon. "C'mon Felene!" Apple took off at a full run, ripping over logs and rocks, back down to the bottom of the hill as fast as her legs could carry her. Felene slinked along in the shadows, in case the noisy Archer got them both into trouble. There, by a gurgling spring was a majestic willow, weeping over fallen leaves like a forlorn lover. Apple stepped into a pile of leaves and fell clean through a concealed hole in the ground. "Whoa!" she yelled, as she landed with a thud.

"Good lord," hissed Felene. She went on full alert and spread her wings, landing mere inches from the hole. There was Apple's red hair at the bottom of a five-foot drop, in what appeared to be an underground cavern. Apple had twisted her ankle. "Of course she did," Felene sighed with one forepaw on her hip and the other on her forehead. Exasperated, she leaped down into the hole.

"I'm oilright," Apple argued before Felene lectured her again, "just a wee sprain. I kin walk. This'll be fine," she concluded, as she fumbled in the dark for a fallen branch to use as a walking stick.

"Yes, you can, and walk you will, Apple of the Emerald Isle! Your shenanigans have reached a peak; serves you right for running off ahead of life all the time. Learn to listen, to watch."

Felene saw many of her own traits in Apple. She, too, was impulsive, rarely filtered her thoughts before she spoke, and would try to move a mountain, if it got in her way. This Archer child was a mirror that reflected her own willfulness. She realized she had stopped listening to the wind long before.

"Feckin' foot," Apple grunted as she limped after Felene, who had started to make her way down the sinister-looking corridor extending beyond the cave-in. "Shhh," demanded Felene, "Can you hear that?"

Apple stopped and tried hard to listen as Felene had advised. "Listen Apple of the Emerald Isle! Really listen. Hear with your eyes, your hair, and even with your fingertips." Felene whispered. There was a sad, languishing meow. Apple heard it.

Apple's vision slowly adjusted to the dark. The sound grew louder and stronger, until they ran into a huge root of a tree, with a small space under it that only Felene could squeeze through. "Apple, you are of no use now, with your big, hurt foot. Go tell Tak not to make the trade."

Apple looked down at herself, never realizing she was big before. She liked the feeling it gave her—grown-up.

By the time she turned back, Felene had already shimmied through the small opening and was out of sight. All Apple could see were shimmering, white, pawprints trailing off into the deepening darkness.

CHAPTER 29

NO GREATER LOVE

...a storm wind came out of the north,
and a great cloud, with brightness around it,
and fire flashing forth continually,
and out of the midst thereof
as the colour of amber.

—Ezekiel, son of Buzzi, 567 B.C.E., Tel Abib

It was almost midnight. Deep inside the Feral prison, Krystal treated Thom with warm cloths at the back of his neck. He was regaining color, and the kitten was finally breathing normally on his own. Suddenly, a mob of Ferals barged in and brutally nabbed Krystal, right in the midst of her healing work. "No, no! What are you doing?" she cried in fear and confusion, grabbing onto the bed frame, not wanting to leave her patients.

One Feral ripped off the sleeve of her shirt, in warning, and spat in her face with a growl, while another pried her fingers off the post, puncturing the tips of her fingers in doing so. Like a sheep to the lions, they dragged her by her hair, through the winding passageway and out into the moonlight. There stood Tak, once again in his cat form, with a solemn, short, plump

Ming Fang by his side. Tak looked around for Felene, hopefully. When he didn't see her, he presumed she was angry at his redress and would not be there for any goodbye. His heart sank a little further.

"Here is yer Cat Woman," They shoved Krystal out through a network of bullying Ferals, who bounced her back and forth until she was through the swarm. Ming Fang urged her to come to her by reaching out her front paws, and then rushed her to the waiting Siamese-lined litter. She waddled back to Tak as Pheobe kept watch over the transaction from a distance.

"All right," shouted Tak to the sky above the Feral minions, to make sure Phoebe heard. "All I need now is Mariah's where-abouts."

Phoebe salivated at the thought. She had him fully under her control already. She knew Tak would never betray his word and disappear with the Archer girl. "What a fool," she cackled to herself. Though Phoebe was a bit sad to see Krystal go, the thought of Tak under her paw was sheer delight—a decade worth of tasty.

"You'll have what ya want by morning, Tak. Then you'll be mine," her raspy voice echoed.

"That was not the agreement, Phoebe."

"Well, it's taking me longer than planned, is all I can say." Phoebe was doing her best to delay the Mariah debacle.

"So be it—at sunrise then," agreed Tak. He and Ming Fang headed back towards the litter where Krystal was waiting, and they whisked her away to the lair.

Apple arrived at Felene's not long after, with her ankle swollen to the size of a softball. Ming Fang rushed to assist the girl as she limped in. Apple raised her head to see Krystal wrapped in a rabbit-fur crazy quilt. "Well oi'll be," she bellowed.

Krystal, although still disoriented herself, got up and ran over to help her injured friend. "Oh Apple, I thought I would never see you again." Apple gave her an almost-hug as Krystal shimmied under her arm as a crutch and assisted her towards a nearby seat.

"Wait, where's Tak?" demanded Apple. "I need to tell him somethin'. Felene discovered a back way into the Feral caves, we heard a cat, and she followed the sound, after the openin' became too narrow for me."

Ming Fang answered softly, "He is preparing for his sacrifice at dawn."

"Whatcha be meanin', Ming Fang? You sayin' Tak's goin' through with this? That's bleedin' nuts!"

"That is exactly what I am saying, a Littern would never stray from his word."

"But they're gonna kill him."

"Then we must prepare ourselves, Apple," advised Ming Fang.

"You don't understand—Felene is goin' to find another way."

"There is no other way. If a Magnificat gives his oath, it will not be taken back. If it were, there would be a curse over all of us. Why would you take anyone's promise lightly, Apple?"

Apple knew where that came from—her father's broken promise to take care of his family. But she pushed through the self-reflection, "Friends should be takin' care of each other, and not lettin' bad come on 'um. We kin fight for him, when he can't fight for himself."

"We must count the stars and wait for the hour," counseled Ming Fang, somberly.

"That's just stupid," Apple snapped.

"I happen to agree, agree, with Apple here, Ming Fang," chimed in a clever Jiabon. He had managed to avoid all the activities of the day, staying in seclusion, working on the scrolls, and keeping one eye on Justin, who was now soundly sleeping in the deep of Felene's lair.

Ming Fang stood on all fours and opened her jagged-tooth jaw, letting out a roar with the force of a mighty wind, directed right towards Jaibon. He tumbled across the yard and into the berry patch. When he got to his paws, he scrambled away, still carrying a handful of parchment.

The two girls sat outside while Ming Fang made a poultice for Apple's ankle, when Makeda blew up a cloud of dust as she landed. It caused the girls to duck for cover inside the lair, giggling. Justin wandered out, rubbing his sleepy eyes. "Appo?" he called.

Krystal turned to look towards the little voice that sounded familiar. There, right before her eyes, was a bigger, balder, but completely recognizable LB. She was stunned, and her eyes watered to the brim, but not a single tear dropped out.

Justin stopped, rubbing his eyes again, thinking he recognized this new addition to the group, when Apple said, "C'mere Justin, I want you to be meetin' my friend, Krystal."

Justin began to cry and ran to Krystal; she knelt down to meet his arms and the two embraced and cried together for a long moment. "LB, I have missed you more than pancakes," Krystal said, and they laughed, recalling Ms. Coleman in her pink foam curlers waving her arms in the rain, giving the police grief. Apple wondered at the sight, "My, my, maybe Tak is right, there are no coincidences."

"I have two sissers now," said Justin proudly. Even Apple got choked up, for a second.

Ming Fang came in with a curious frown, "Makeda is demanding to see you Apple—now." Apple limped outside.

"I need the Archer green magic," Makeda said urgently. "I found a native Cat Woman. She may hold the cure to the suffering of the entire continent of Africa, its poverty and disease. This is the Archer who may bring our Africa back to balance."

"Why are you tellin' me?" Apple asked.

"I need the Archer green magic, right away!"

Apple looked at her, puzzled. "I don't have any money," she responded. "I am a kid—geeez, you cats are crazy, I am just a kid."

"All Archers have money."

"Uh, no we don't."

"Yes you do. You get it from other Archers. That is how it works. It goes from one to another, and on, and on."

"Uh, no it doesn't. Who told you that? Grown-ups get money, but they have to work for it or steal it. No other way to get it, unless its gifted, but then somebody else had to work for it or steal it. That's what me dad told me."

"You know absolutely nothing of the world in which you live, and the magic all around you. If green magic came through hard work or thievery, why are there Archers who dig in the earth, fish in the seas, and steal, who have so little? I believe Ms. Coleman is of a great Cat Woman healing clan of Africa, perhaps even the Nubian Pharaohs. We must save her, and for that, I need green magic—now!"

"Ms. Coleman?" Krystal shrieked in surprise, hearing the name as she emerged from the lair with Justin. Makeda recognized her immediately as the girl in the picture.

"Is Ms. Coleman okay?" Krystal asked anxiously.

"Do you know her well?" asked Makeda. "Do you want to help her?"

"Of course!" answered Krystal. "I love Ms. Coleman. I still have her Bibi's necklace made of wild licorice seeds that she gave me."

Makeda reacted instantly, pouncing over to her. "Show it to me!"

"It's right here in my pocket," said Krystal, pulling it out. "Now please, tell me, how is she?" When she saw the necklace, Makeda understood immediately how gifted this young Archer girl must be, since Ms. Coleman had passed it on to her. Felene had been right all along.

Justin was holding Krystal's hand and tugged on it, asking, "Pancakes? I hung'y, Kwissy."

Makeda ignored him, and spoke to Krystal, "She is in need of healing. If she does not receive it soon, she will not survive."

"Where is she? I can help her with the African medicine

she taught me."

"She needs very strong medicine young Archer, stronger than you can provide. And to get it, I need Archer green magic."

"I know where Ms. Coleman's money…I mean, where her green magic is. It's in her garden. She hides it there, in an old coffee can."

"Take me there!" demanded Makeda.

"How dare you!" scolded Ming Fang. "We could lose our Littern, and are in the middle of negotiations that will turn the tide for all Magnificats, in ways unknown. You choose an Archer over Tak?"

"Africa bleeds her diamonds that held down dark forces every day. It bleeds lions, giraffes, zebras, ivory, and trees. Rain has turned to salty tears, unfit for drinking. Superstition has twisted the medicine, and sickness is believed to be an infectious curse. The earth cries out, just as it did after the first murderous blood outside the Garden. Nothing will thrive until the Cat Women come home. This one Archer, this Ms. Coleman, and perhaps this young one, can heal the land, and may even be the key to Queen Saba's ark. I have chosen my battle Ming Fang, Tak has chosen his."

Then she arched her back, spread her wings, lurched forward, grabbed Krystal in her claws, tossed her upon her wing-wide back, and launched into the sky.

"Kwissy, Kwissy," cried Justin. Apple tried to intervene, but they were gone. Ming Fang had no time to chase after her. Jaibon had run away. There was nothing to do but wait.

"…two thousand twenty-one, two thousand twenty-two," Krystal finished counting the money that was still safely hidden in the coffee can on the roof of Ms. Coleman's apartment in Arizona. "Is that enough?"

"It will do," answered Makeda as they both stood under the night sky on the roof of Krystal's old apartment. The garden was dry and the plants withered. The faerie garden looked deserted. Krystal wondered if her mother was below, but instead of checking, she jumped on Makeda's back to rush the green magic to Ms. Coleman and make her well.

It was an ebullient and touching reunion when the two entered room 222 at Kachina Village in the middle of the night. "Why Kryssy, I am so glad you are okay," she said, as Krystal and Makeda rushed her into her clothes.

"I am fine, Ms. Coleman, and so is LB, I mean, Justin, his new name since he got adopted. Have you seen my mom, Ms. Coleman?"

"No child."

Within ten minutes, Ms. Coleman was dressed and packed, and the two medicine women, one young and one old, stealthily wandered out of the rest home to catch the metro, hand in hand. Makeda went out the window ahead of them.

Krystal could not wait to tell Ms. Coleman about all her experiences since the hip-breaking accident. "LB and I got separated, and I was struck by lightning and took a bus by myself to California, and had my own cottage that I fixed up, like you taught me, and I was kidnapped by Feral cats and taken into their underworld."

"My, my, Kryssy girl, my story is not near as fantabulous as yours," she laughed.

Just a few stops away on the metro line there was a small motel, where Ms. Coleman paid cash for a room for two nights. Not the nicest place, but the eight units were bungalows, instead of shared-wall rooms, which could disrupt the medicine.

Clouder Makeda told Ms. Coleman it would take two weeks of healing for her to be strong enough to travel to Africa. Krystal agreed to help. The two Cat Women, Ms. Coleman and Krystal, would then go to Ethiopia for proper training. Makeda would ensure that.

CHAPTER 30

'TIS ALWAYS MAGIC

...Two roads diverged in a wood, and I–
I took the one less traveled by,
and that has made all the difference.

—Robert Frost, "The Road Not Taken," *Mountain Interval*, 1916

In those last wee hours of darkness, before Tak would hand himself over to the Ferals, Felene continued her slow course down the dark burrow. Whenever Feral squads came her way, she ducked into the hollowed-out caverns that served as cages, with crude bars made from broken branches lining both sides, and stacked like sleeper cars on a train. Some of them had wasting cats inside of them, chained to the wall. Others held only skeletons. Vicious, half-starved cats hissed and clawed at her as she passed. Still, she kept moving, dodging their far-reaching paws.

Another squad of Ferals marched her way and she jumped into a nearby, empty, upper-level cage and waited, her heart throbbing, as she tried to silence her own breath. A rustle of keys and loud screams preceded slaps and pain-induced moans from thunderous blows. Ferals howled in delight. They were obviously torturing some poor hapless cat in one of the horrid cages. "No, no, please, stop. Don't take her! No, NOOO!"

Wait! That last part was not mewing. It was not Archer or Feral. That was Magnificat! Felene's heart raced, as adrenaline shot into her bloodstream.

Slam, crack, a door closed, and then ghastly cries, "Please, please," from a voice that grew fainter with the distance.

The Ferals must be taking the poor soul away. To where, for what? Felene wondered.

Long, deep sobs filled the tunnel, causing a rash of howls from other imprisoned cats and creatures. Felene continued on stealthily, finally receiving a familiar scent—Krystal! Darting up to the locked door, she instead found Thom lying alone in a cell.

"Thom, Thom, are you dead?" she whispered to him.
He opened his one good eye and blinked several times to clear his blurry vision. "Get on outa 'ere Felene. No way of knowin' what these mangy cats will be doin' to a fetchin' Magnificat like you down 'ere. Go now!" he said weakly.

Felene tried to open the cell door, but other prisoners began to yell and rant from their cages. She was afraid they would call attention to her. "Thom, I smell the Cat Woman, Krystal. Where is she?"

"Miss Felene, the monsters took 'er. They took 'er by the hair and drug 'er out."

Felene took a look down the corridor further ahead, in the direction Thom gestured, when a small kitten jumped out of his bed, approached her at the bars, and began to purr. It was a Feral! Instinctively, she reached in and took a mighty swipe, as an Archer might with an insect. The kitten flew against the wall and fell.

Thom gasped "Felene, that is a wee kitten. What's become of you that you could hurt such a wee one?"

"Come 'ere lit'l one," Thom urged, and the kitten hopped up and nuzzled against him.

"It's a Feral, Thom."

"He's a cat, Felene," Thom said feebly.

Felene was only interested in getting business done. She had no time for insight or argument. This was war. She was sure she could rescue him on her way back out, but needed to go further into this cavern and find Krystal. "I'll be back for you, Thom," she promised.

It was moments before dawn at Felene's lair. The appointed time had come. Tak was still hoping his godkitten would come back so he could hug her one more time. He tossed Ming Fang a feathered pen and began to speak in a monotone voice, "Write this down: Dear Clouders, I recommend Alkina as the new Littern. There will be a vote of course, however, my recommendation should carry weight. The Centennial Summit speech is nearly finished, and Alkina knows where it is. He is wise and fair. He will make a good Littern. All my worldly possessions go to Felene." Then he stroked his whiskers thoughtfully as he continued. "Miz will be a good fit for Alkina's Clouder position in Australia. She is keen and understands the power of memory held in the earth. This will please Moosa. Yes, she will do nicely as Alkina's replacement. The council will be able to elect a replacement for dear Clouder Billi from among the many worthy Magnificats, I'm sure. It will take many decades for her to grow to a Magnificat in her new life."

Apple stood and approached the old cat. "Ere you really goin' through with it, Tak? You're gonna let yersalf get kilt?"

"Why of course I am, young Archer. I made an agreement."

"But..."

Tak cut her off. "Where is the crystal child?" he asked.

"Uh, she is sleeping," lied Apple. Sadly, lies were getting a lot easier than when she first lied about the stone. She didn't want to tell him that Felene was in the Feral underground against his wishes, and that Makeda chose Krystal over his defense.

"Ming Fang, I want you to go to Aoife's home in Ireland and take care of her mother. This you must do before any other thing."

"But the medicine scrolls?" she interrupted.

"Jaibon and Felene can finish those."

Ming Fang nodded.

"Where is Felene?"

"She is trying to find a way to save you, Tak. She must still be looking for that back door," Apple admitted, finally.

Tak laughed, deeply relieved that Felene was not angry with him. "She has been looking for back doors since kittenhood; not one for sitting on her haunches or taking 'no' for an answer. Sort of like you, Aoife," he nodded towards her. "Neither of you can resist spitting into the wind to see if you can outsmart it before it spatters back at you. And Jaibon, where is he?"

"He ran, Tak," replied a disgusted Ming Fang, neglecting to mention that she had helped launch him on his way with a mighty breath of angry wind.

"I always said, if you could buy Jaibon for what he's worth, and sell him for what he thinks he's worth, you would have a load of green magic," mused Tak.

"But I don't understand," cried Apple. "You and your Magnificats captured a huge wind demon. Why aren't they all here to help you now?"

"My word is a contract, Aoife of the Emerald Isle. If I do not hold that as sacred, I leave no path for others to follow. I become a wind that blows away everything girls like you and Felene need to hold onto when things get tough."

The Siamese arrived with the litter within seconds of the first light peeking over the eastern horizon to a crimson sky, "Red sky at morning, sailors take warning," Ming Fang noted as she and Tak climbed in.

Apple grabbed hold of the litter and demanded to go with them or "You'll jest be draggin' me because I won't be lettin' go." Tak nodded in approval and lit his jewel-clad pipe. They flew immediately to the great culvert of the Ferals, arriving precisely at full sunrise, as promised.

Phoebe was waiting out front on the old fender she used for a throne when the litter set down. She motioned to four of her minions to go back into the culvert. Within moments, a horde had come out with a scraggly brown cat tied to two pieces of wood, formed in an X, with the poor thing strapped at the paws. The hideous body was nearly furless from what looked to be repeated beatings.

"What is this?" demanded Tak. "I want the full-bodied Feral who knows where Mariah is. Not some wasted creature you would use as a deception."

"Settle down Tak, aint' no ashes, so be grateful."

"What do you mean?"

As they carried the bound cat towards Tak, he recognized the scent. Leaping out of the litter, he saw her face, feeble and ragged, bleeding at her lip from an obviously fresh blow, but she looked beautiful to him.

"Mariah!" he gasped.

Apple began to get out of the litter to help, but Ming Fang held her back, gently, not extending her claws.

The once-white cat woke to see a fuzzy Tak stroking her forehead. He was brushing her matted fur away from her eyes. Phoebe allowed it. She still marveled that he would never go back on his word and call for Clouder help. "Fool!" She hissed.

Tak frantically and clumsily began untying Mariah from the crossed wood, fighting back tears while trying to control his shaking paws. She looked at him in a daze.

Once free, Tak carried her to Apple, in the litter. She passed her to Ming Fang, and together they laid Mariah carefully on a pile of supple Chinese silk, stacked in the corner. Tak leaned in. Mariah looked up and touched his face tenderly with her bleeding paw.

"What have you done, Tak?" she asked in a whisper.

"I have done the right thing. Now, I know for sure, I have done the right thing." Then he kissed her paw and gave a look to Ming Fang that she and all the Siamese understood. Ming Fang quickly ordered the Siamese to boost-off.

"Wait, Tak," pleaded Mariah. Tak rushed back to her side,

close to her face. She petted him again, touching his strong jaw. He cupped his large paw over hers on his face. "Tak," She whispered.

Before she could say more, Tak was under siege and pulled away from her.

The litter took off. Apple jumped out to be with Tak, landing in the brush. She could only watch in horror as scores of Ferals attacked Tak, as if they were one living creature. Swallowing him up in a mass of filth, they absorbed him deep into the culvert.

Phoebe tossed a twig she was using as a toothpick into the brown, gooey water and glanced at Apple, who had reinjured her ankle jumping from the litter.

"What are ya looking at?" she snarled.

Apple froze for a nano-second, then, in her unyieldingly snotty way, replied, "Noothin, Absolutely noothin…"

Phoebe snapped a second glance, not sure if she had been disrespected or not, but not caring, because she now had the great and mighty Tak as her plaything. The Feral queen winked tauntingly, then disappeared with all the others into the dark abyss of the culvert.

Felene was still in the tunnel when she heard the shouts and howls of victory, "We have Tak! We are the victors!"

Her heart sank. She knew now that there was nothing more she could do for her beloved godfather against the Feral's superior numbers, and swung swiftly around, darting as fast as she could back down the path towards Thom's cell. Enroute, she heard a small Magnificat voice calling "Help us...," coming from a nearby cage in the narrow wall. Peeking in, she saw three kittens. They looked like her—all white, with one green and one blue eye. Then she noticed some scratches on the side of the cage that read, "White Jewel Clan"—her clan! She saw tiny wing buds and understood why she had heard Magnificat voices. With all the hooting and hollering, she gambled she would have time to free the kittens. She could not leave them behind.

Extending her long claw into the cage lock, she fiddled

with it until it popped open, then grabbed one kitten in her teeth and the others in each paw close to her chest, and ran upright back to Thom's cage.

Breathlessly, she called to him as she tucked all three kittens under one arm so she could pick the lock, "Thom, come on, just climb on my back," she said as she feverishly worked to loosen it.

He looked at her quizzically and asked, "Lassie, you really be tinkin' I would leave my friend, the great Littern Tak? I'll be stayin' right here to the very end with my one true friend." Felene was speechless as she wrestled with the lock and the three kittens trying to break free from her grip, as the noisy crowd grew louder. All she could do was look at Thom in a futile mix of pity and respect. Then, he gave her a sassy wink. She smiled and dashed for the back exit she and Apple had found before the Ferals got within sight.

Scrambling out of the underground, Felene took to the skies and considered where to go next. The Ferals knew her lair too well, and with Tak subdued, they would have no fear of retribution. She and these little ones would find a new place—and tell no one. Krystal, her Cat Woman, was no longer her priority. Makeda would care for her, she was sure. Ming Fang would see to the sacred scrolls. These Magnifikittens were her lineage, her heritage, and her duty to protect.

Apple limped up the trail with tear-stained cheeks in the bright morning sun, devastated she could not help Tak, but unafraid, as usual. She was looking forward to getting back to the lair and talking about what happened. Unfortunately, as she passed the prickly pear cactus, she saw nothing but Justin, sitting on a log, crying—no lair, no Krystal, no Ming Fang and her noisy Siamese, not even Jaibon. There was no sign of any Magnificats at all.

Justin jumped up from the log, where he had been waiting for her, and with a running leap, he wrapped his tiny arms and legs around her. Scattered on the ground were remnants of Felene's feather door, some twigs, and the giant clamshell sink.

She sat Justin down again and took it all in with a deep breath, feeling as Krystal must have a hundred times—homeless. If not for being able to touch and hold Justin, Apple might have thought she had awoken from an epic dream. He reminded her that he was as real as rain when he patted her thigh, "I hung'y Appo; milky?"

Collecting her thoughts, she decided the best course of action would be to take Justin and go see Dan at the hospital, where she could get his permission for Justin to come home to Ireland, and then call her mum. She would need his passport. The police should be gone by now. With Amanda locked up, things might be better with her father. She decided she would try.

Starting down the bluffs towards town, the sun was fully up, and the long morning shadows shortened into squatty ovals. It was a new day. The air was still for the first time in weeks. She and Justin held hands and headed down the path towards town, when she noticed something shiny on the ground. She bent down, and on closer inspection, saw a silver stone that had some very strange symbols on it. She started to pick it up, curious, as a balmy wind off the ocean brushed her red tresses into her eyes. She chuckled to herself, a chuckle that developed into a full-blown belly laugh, as she remembered good old Rasta and his caution that "every footstep leads to a different life."

She recalled what Magnificats had taught her. *What's buried should stay buried.*

"This stone shall stay put," she said to Justin.

Apple listened, really listened, with her hair and her fingertips, as Felene had taught. She felt a subtle push from the wind and yielded to it, turning so it was at their backs, nudging them forward. Taking a farewell look back at the place that no one would ever believe had been real, Justin tugged at her shirt. "Look Apple—cat." He pointed at three white cat paw prints heading down a new trail, previously camouflaged by Felene's windmill. She took his hand as a wee dust spiral picked up leaves and small remaining scraps of trash scattered about, carrying them up into the sky—all except for one small square paper that rested at Justin's tiny, boot-covered feet. It was the picture of Ms. Coleman, Krystal and Justin, when he was still LB, from Ms. Coleman's room 222.

Apple's forehead creased in dismay. "Well, Oi'll be!" She repeated Tak's wise words, "Nothing is happenstance. 'Tis always magic."

Justin squeezed her hand trustingly, "Appo, we go home, okay?"

For the first time in many, many moons, Apple beamed a heartfelt, warm, anticipatory smile, and said, "Yes, Justin, we're goin' home," as she rubbed his shaven little head affectionately. "My uncle Aden always said it's good luck to rub a bald head," she laughed, and Justin laughed with her. Then the two descended the fresh path towards town, with a gentle ocean breeze at their backs.

There is a magic in the air
in fact, its really everywhere
landing where and when it can
an open door
an open hand
an unclimbed stair
an empty chair.

—Toni McGowan; Coronado, California; 2016

Glossary

Term / Word [Pronunciation]	Language / Origination: Definition	Country / Region: Clouder / Ruler
A'chroi [uh·kree]	Gaelic: heart	Ireland: Tak
Alaxsxaq [ah·lock·shock]	Aleutian: great lands	Alaska: Moosa
Alkina [all·keen·a]	Jawoyn: moonlight	Australia: Alkina
Alsink [all·sink]	Micmac: fly	Northeastern America: Moosa
Amandan [ah·muh·dawn]	Gaelic: idiot	Ireland: Tak
Amir [e·meer]	Arabic: prince	Middle East: Makeda
Ankh [angk]	Ancient Egyptian hieroglyph: life	Egypt: Makeda
Aoife [Eefa]	Gaelic: Eve (given name)	Ireland: Tak
Arseways [arse·ways]	Irish slang: backwards	Ireland: Tak
Babby [babb·bee]	Irish slang: baby	Ireland: Tak
Bakaneko [ban·a·neeko]	Japanese: yokai ghost cat	Japan: Neko
Banshee [BAN·shee]	Gaelic: spirit who heralds the death of a member of a prominent family	Ireland: Tak
Bastet [bast]	Human / cat god hybrid	Egypt: Makeda
Bibi [bee·bee]	Swahili: grandmother	Africa: Makeda
Billi [bill·lee]	Hindi: cat	India: Billi
Black Pharaohs [fair·ohs]	Sudan: legendary dark skinned rulers of Africa from the Kush dynasty	Africa: Makeda
Bonnie [bon·nee]	Scottish: attractive	Scotland: Tak
Brobdingnag [brob·ding·nag]	*Gulliver's Travels*: enormous, gigantic	Fictional land
Canela [kan·ella]	Spanish: cinnamon	Latin America: Moosa

Glossary

Word [Pronunciation]	Origination: Definition	Region: Clouder
Catacombs [kat·uh·kohms]	Subterranean passageways for buria / religious practice	Europe: Tak
Caubeen [kaw·bee·in]	Irish: men's hat / beret	Ireland: Tak
Colcannon [kuhl·kan·uh·n]	Gaelic: traditional Irish dish of mashed potatoes with kale or cabbage	Ireland: Tak
Connemara [konn·a·mar·a]	Gaelic: goodbye	Ireland: Tak
Debteras [deb·ter·as]	Amharic: indigenous health leader / exorcist / magician	Ethiopia: Makeda
Euroclydon [uro·clee·don]	Latin: cyclonic, tempestuous Mediterranean northeast wind in autumn and winter	North Africa: Makeda
Fang	Chinese: Wind	China: Billi
Feck	Scottish: pain, exasperation	Scotland: Tak
Galabeyas [goll·a·by·ahs]	Egyptian: long tunic shirts	North Africa: Makeda
Genfo [gen·fo]	Amharic: porridge	Ethiopia: Makeda
Ganges [gon·jees]	Hindi: holy healing river	India: Billi
Gob [gob]	Irish slang: mouth	Ireland: Tak
Gaoithe [weetha]	Gaelic: wind	Ireland: Tak
Hao ma [how ma]	Chinese: how are you?	China: Billi
Huk [hook]	Uto-Aztecan: wind	Arizona: Moosa
Hump off	Irish slang: go away	Ireland: Tak
Humpy [hum·pee]	Irish slang: home	Ireland: Tak
Jamaica [ham·eye·ka] tea	Spanish: hibiscus tea	Latin America: Moosa

GLOSSARY

Word [Pronunciation]	Origination: Definition	Region: Clouder
Javalina [have·a·leen·a]	Spanish: wild pig	Latin America: Moosa
Jinn [jen]	Arabic: genie—righteous and not-so righteous folk created from fire	North Africa: Makeda
Joyce [jois]	British slang: ten-pound note	England: Tak
Jungalk [JOONG·aalk]	Jawoyn: spring / sprinter	Australia: Alkina
Kamikaze [kom·o·kozzy]	Japanese: divine wind	Japan: Neko
Kanata [kan·a·da]	Iroquois: Land Beyond	Canada: Moosa
Kebra Nagast [käbrä nägäst]	14th-century account of the origins of the Solomonic line of the Emperors of Ethiopia	Ethiopia: Makeda
Khamsin [kam·seen] wind	Hot, winter, dry, sandy, south-to-north wind	North Africa: Makeda
Kily [ki·lee] tree	Malagasy: tamarind tree	Madagascar: Makeda
Kong Fuzi [kong·foozy]	China: Confucius	China: Billi
Koshka [kozch·ka]	Russian: cat	Siberia: Billi
Leprechaun [lep·ruh·kawn]	Gaelic: type of fairy—little bearded man who partakes in mischief	Ireland: Tak
Lilith [lill·eth]	Arabic: demon of wind—bearer of disease & death Hebrew: demon that attacks children and the first wife of Adam	North Africa: Makeda
Lilitu [lil·lee·too]	Arabic: female storm	North Africa: Makeda
Ma'assil [ma·see·al]	Egyptian: tobacco	North Africa: Makeda

Glossary

Word [Pronunciation]	Origination: Definition	Region: Clouder
Machu Piccu [ma·chu pi·chu]	Quechuan: old peak	Andes: Moosa
Majnoon [maj·noon]	Farsi: crazy, mad	North Africa: Makeda
Makeda [mack·ay·dah]	Ethiopian: Saba / Sheba	East Africa: Makeda
Manasarovar [ma·nas·sar·o·var]	Sanscrit: lake of the mind	India: Billi
Máthairchroi [mak·ree]	Gaelic: grandmother	Ireland: Tak
Ming fang [meeng·fong]	Chinese: bright wind	China: Billi
Miw [mew]	Egyptian: cat	Egypt: Makeda
Mo ghrá [moe·grah]	Gaelic: my love	Ireland: Tak
Moosa [moo·sah]	Hopi: cat	American Desert Southwest:Moosa
Mt. Kailash [kay·lash]	Sanskrit: crystal mountain	Tibet / China: Billi
Mu'u mu'u [moo·moo]	Hawaiian: colorful dress	Hawaii: Neko
Muzzy [muzz·zee]	Irish slang: brat	Ireland: Tak
Nadir [na·deer]	Arabic: lowest point / opposite of zenith	Middle East: Billi
Namahshivaaya [na·maH·shi·vA·ya]	Hindi: five holy syllables	India: Billi
Namaste [nam·aste]	Sanskrit: respectful greeting	India: Billi
Neijing [nay·jing]	Chinese: book of medicine	China: Billi
Neko [neevko]	Japanese: cat	Japan: Neko
Netsukes [not·soo·kies]	Japanese: animal-shaped boxes containing medicine, fastened to an obi	Japan: Neko
Ni hao [nee·how]	Chinese: hello	China: Billi

Glossary

Word [Pronunciation]	Origination: Definition	Region: Clouder
Ngariman [un·ga·ri·man]	Australian Aborigine: mythical cat	Australia: Alkina
Nubian [new·bee·an] Kingdom	Egyptian: land ruled by black pharaohs	Africa: Makeda
Obi [oh·bee]	Japanese: long, tied belt	Japan: Neko
Pogeyan [po·gy·yawn]	Malayalam: cats who come and go with the mist	India: Billi
Popocatepetl and [popo·cata·petal] Iztaccihuatl [iz·tach·ee·hatl]	Aztec: mythical lovers who became volcanos	Mexico: Moosa
Qi [CHē]	Chinese: the circulating life force	China: Billi
Quare [kware]	Irish slang: odd	Ireland: Tak
Queen Saba [sabba]	Ethiopian: Queen of Sheba	East Africa: Makeda
Ráiméis [rome·esh]	Gaelic: foolish or exaggerated talk / nonsense	Ireland: Tak
Rakshastal [rak·shas·tal]	Sanskrit: demon lake	Tibet / India: Billi:
Rarasharmichancha [rara·shar·mich·chan·cha]	Feral: rallying cry	Feral Underworld: Queen Phoebe
Ras Dashen [rash dejen] Peak	Mountain where the Ark of the Covenant may be buried	Ethiopia: Makeda
Roo [rew]	Australian slang: kangaroo	Australia: Alkina
Sarcophagus [sar·coph·a·gus]	Greek: box-like funeral receptacle for a corpse	Greece: Tak
Seaclaid [shock·laid]	Gaelic: chocolate	Ireland: Tak
Shegee [shee·gee]	Gaelic: whirlwind	Ireland: Tak
Shinatobe [shin·a·toby]	Japanese: wind goddess	Japan: Neko

Glossary

Word [Pronunciation]	Origination: Definition	Region: Clouder
Sidhe [shee]	Gaelic: faery folk	Ireland: Tak
Sinagua [seen‧ag‧wa]	Pre-Columbian culture, 500-1425 C.E.	American Desert Southwest: Moosa
Slán abhaile [slon'‧a‧ella]	Gaelic: have a safe trip home	Ireland: Tak
Takle Haymanot [tackla‧hay‧main‧oat]	Ethiopian: six-winged saint	East Africa: Makeda
Taklimakan [tak‧la‧mak‧an]	Chinese: desert	China: Billi
Tele [tel‧lee]	Irish slang: television	Ireland: Tak
Third heaven	Hebrew: cosmos where St. Paul was known to go	Isreal: Makeda
Tiponi [tip-oh-nee]	Hopi: child of importance	Arizona: Moosa
Turtle Island	Seneca: North America	North America: Moosa
Ventis exsuscito [vent‧is ex‧suh‧sit‧tow]	Latin: Winds awaken!	Italy: Tak
Wen de ya ho [windy‧yah‧ho]	Tihanama: our hearts / spirits are strong	North America: Moosa
Williwaw [wilē‧wô]	Native American: a violent, sudden wind gust	Americas: Moosa
Wo hao [woe how]	Chinese: I am fine	China: Billi
Yifan Zhang [eefan jong]	Chinese: goddess who taught cats to talk	China: Billi
Yogi Katarani [yogi kat‧a‧rinee]	Hindi: Magnificat yogi of loyalty	India: Billi
Zephyr [zef-er]	Latin: west wind	Ireland: Tak
Zhongli Quan [joong‧lee chwahn]	Chinese: god of weapons / explosions–one of the Eight Immortals	China: Billi

About the Author

Gwyn Dolyn holds a B.A. in Educational Philosophy, including southwestern Native American learning philosophies, from Prescott College, and has worked in the field of healing arts for over twenty years. She attended Pacific College of Oriental Medicine at the M.A. level, and taught art from K-12 in court, public, and private school settings. Her career evolved into Child Protective Services advocacy, which provided her insight behind the iron curtain of the foster care system, and into the lives of children and teens under conditions of poverty, abuse, and neglect.

Gwyn writes periodically for her local newspaper on military history and American armed services heroes. This experience has taught her what forms a hero. Magnificat Tak and other characters in this debut novel exhibit those values.

Having traveled to Ireland, the magic that colors the Erin land attuned her to ancient lore. Why dare to move a tree for a road when it may house a thousand Faerie families (especially since Faeries retaliate in the most uncomfortable ways)? Why not read the language of trees when a leaf lands at one's feet? Or listen to a changing wind for direction?

The primary setting for Magnificats could be nowhere other than the enchanted Emerald Isle.

For additional information, news, and resources for educators, please visit the author's website:

magnificatsblog.wordpress.com

or email her:

gwyndolynauthor@gmail.com

THUNDERBIRD
Wind of the West

RAMSTAIL
Wind of the East